THE Quiche
AND THE Dead

KIRSTEN
WEISS

KENSINGTON PUBLISHING CORP.
http://www.kensingtonbooks.com

KENSINGTON BOOKS are published by

Kensington Publishing Corp.
119 West 40th Street
New York, NY 10018

All Kensington Titles, Imprints, and Distributed Lines are available at special quantity discounts for bulk purchases for sales promotions, premiums, fund-raising, and educational or institutional use. Special book excerpts or customized printings can also be created to fit specific needs. For details, write or phone the office of the Kensington special sales manager: Kensington Publishing Corp., 119 West 40th Street, New York, NY 10018, attn: Special Sales Department, Phone: 1-800-221-2647.

Kensington and the K logo Reg. U.S. Pat & TM Off.

ISBN-13: 978-1-4967-0896-0
ISBN-10: 1-4967-0896-2
First Kensington Mass Market Edition: November 2017

eISBN-13: 978-1-4967-0899-1
eISBN-10: 1-4967-0899-7
First Kensington Electronic Edition: November 2017

10 9 8 7 6 5 4 3 2 1

Printed in the United States of America

To Karen Weiss
With thanks to Adam Smith

Chapter 1

All I could see was the dress. The ghost of weddings past, it swept above the checkered linoleum floor and rooted me in place. My heart twisted, leaving me breathless.

I jolted into motion. The quiche, forgotten, slipped sideways on my oven mitts. I steadied it and gaped through the kitchen window to the pie shop's dining area. No. No, no, no.

Pushing through the swinging door, I intercepted Petronella, my young pie wrangler, before she could reach the cash register.

"Hey, I'll take care of this," I said.

Giving me a long look, Petronella shrugged. "Sure, boss." She slouched toward the kitchen, the *Om* tattoo on her neck peeping beneath her black, pixie-cut hair.

I slid the quiche inside the glass case, nudging aside a potpie and a tray of rectangular hand pies, fruit-stuffed mini-pastries, fresh and flaky and buttery. My reflection wavered, the curved glass broadening my face, fading the blue of my eyes. Slipping off my mitts, I discarded them on top of the counter beside the day-old hand pies, discounted for the morning coffee crowd.

When I'd taken over the lease on the building in

fog-bound San Nicholas, I'd gone retro with 1950s decor. Metal napkin dispensers and spiral menu holders lined up neatly on the pink laminate counter. Frilly white curtains hung in the windows. A dozen or so customers sat on faux-leather bar stools and in booths. Pie was an old-fashioned sort of dessert, and I'd tried to reflect that right down to the neon sign over the window to the kitchen: PIE TOWN! TURN YOUR FROWN UPSIDE DOWN AT PIE TOWN! The words curved inside a swoop of a smile. I gazed at the neon motto now. It never failed to turn my frown upside down, and it didn't disappoint me now, even if my smile was strained.

Fran clacked toward the counter, my ivory-colored wedding dress slung over her slender arm. Its clear, plastic covering rustled across the floor. "Hi, Valentine."

"Hi, Fran." I eyed the dress, hurt and horror knotting my stomach. "How's it going?"

She made a face. "Not too good, I'm afraid. I have to return your wedding dress."

A bead of sweat trickled down my spine. "Oh. Well, that's okay, thanks anyway." I reached for the gown.

She didn't budge, dangling the dress out of my reach. "I tried everything I could think of to sell it, but there were no takers."

Joe, the owner of the comic shop next door, swiveled on his bar stool. Gray head tilted, lips pursed, he regarded the gown, his glasses glinting beneath the overhead lamps.

"Wedding dresses are a tough sell these days," she continued. "And I'm afraid most brides have long ago bought their gowns for the spring weddings."

More customers looked our way.

"Hey, no worries," I said. "You tried." I stretched for the gown, my fingertips brushing the plastic sleeve.

A thick-waisted woman seated at the counter brayed with laughter, and I blinked, feeling wobbly. Why was I being so stupid about this? The woman had probably read something funny in the paper spread open before her. She wasn't laughing at me.

Fran's chin dipped toward her ample chest. "Part of the problem is the nature of selling things online. Especially with a wedding dress, women want to see it, touch it, try it on. . . ." She trailed off, unmoving.

"Er, do I owe you any money?" The only people in Pie Town who weren't staring at us now were some college kids, overflow from Joe's comic shop next door. They played a game involving elves and orcs in the corner booth, their dice rattling across the table.

Joe rose from his stool and slid along the counter to the metal coffee urn. Yawning, he watched us beneath bushy white eyebrows.

"No, I'm commission only, remember?" she asked. "But I did give it my best."

"I know you did," I said, "and I really appreciate it. Here, let me take that off your hands." I made another futile grab for the dress.

"It's such a shame," she said. "It's a beautiful gown, elegant, tasteful. I did explain in the online ads that it was never worn, but people want new for weddings."

Joe sidled closer. He took a sip of the coffee and made a face, his wrinkles deepening. Cripes, was the coffee off now too?

"That's me," I said, "full of good taste. If I can't pay you, can I at least offer you a slice of pie?" I willed Fran to hand me the dress and leave. We could do a hostage exchange, pie for gown.

She patted her sleek stomach. "I couldn't. Not before lunch."

"To go then?" I asked. Let this end, let this end, let this end.

She handed the dress through the counter opening, and my shoulders slumped. At last.

"No, thank you," she said. "And good luck selling that dress. Someone will love it. It's gorgeous." Waggling her fingers at me, she strolled out the door.

I blew out a shaky breath, folding the bulky dress over one arm.

Joe cleared his throat. "You selling breakfast pies now?" He pointed at the quiche.

"What?" I blinked, hugging the dress against my white and pink Pie Town apron. "No. I made that as a welcome gift for our new neighbor, Heidi's Health and Fitness." Pie Town was only five months old, a relative baby. I'd been so intent on starting up my new business that, while I knew most of my customers well enough to exchange a joke or cheerful greeting, I hadn't made any real friends yet. I knew Heidi was roughly my age, twenty-eight, and she was a business owner like me. I didn't think I could go wrong with a quiche in one of Charlene's melt-in-your-mouth crusts as an introduction.

Joe grinned, exposing a missing molar. "She's not going to take it."

"What?" I asked, still reeling from the return of the wedding dress. I could have avoided this carnival of pain if I'd picked the thing up myself. But I'd kept putting it off, hoping the gown would just go away, get sold, and I wouldn't have to think of it and my failed engagement.

It hadn't.

"Our new neighbor," he said. "You met her?"

"Um, no, not yet. But her grand opening is today. I figured I'd head over there when I take my break. Want to come?"

"I beat you to it. And she's not the sort to eat a breakfast pie."

"Technically, it's a quiche, and it's healthy, with spinach, squash, and a bit of goat cheese." I'd even substituted almond milk, and you couldn't taste the difference. Pie was so versatile.

His nose twitched. "Another one of your mother's recipes?"

I smiled. Of Pennsylvania Dutch stock, my mother had not been the quiche and goat cheese type. But many of her pie recipes had been in the family for years, and she'd been my inspiration for Pie Town. "I adapted it from a magazine."

"I'll bet you that pie that Miss Heidi turns her nose up at your offering."

"Why would she? Even if she's not into it, maybe her staff will enjoy it." The gown's plastic wrapping stuck to my forearms, and I peeled myself free. The dress oozed defeat and broken dreams. No wonder no one wanted it.

"I've just got a feeling." He poured himself a cup of coffee from the urn and dropped a dollar into the basket. In the mornings, Pie Town was self-serve, with an urn of coffee on the counter beside a tray of discounted, day-old hand pies. My team and I were in here early, baking, so it made a certain sense to open and let people serve themselves on the honor system. It seemed to be working. I liked to think of Pie Town as a "light service" establishment, but the reality was I couldn't afford wait staff. Yet. I dreamed of the day I could.

"So is that a deal?" he asked.

I shifted my weight, eager to ditch the wedding gown in my office. "You're on. Hey, I saw you making a face at the coffee. Is it okay?"

Looking into his cup, he furrowed his brows. "Coffee's fine, I guess."

"You don't sound too sure."

"I woke up with a weird taste in my mouth this morning.

Everything's off." He wagged a finger at me and headed to the men's room. "Now don't forget our deal."

Ha. This was one bet I'd win. Who was going to turn down a free pie? Hurrying through the swinging door, I passed the kitchen and strode into my office. Part of me wanted to jam the wedding gown into the wastebasket beside my desk. But I'd spent a lot of money on that dress, money I needed. I hooked its hanger on the top of a metal bookshelf. Stepping away, I gazed at its elegant folds, and my rib cage squeezed. I'd have looked good in that dress.

My office door banged open, and Charlene, my piecrust maker, stomped inside. A single, white curl escaped her hairnet. Adjusting her Pie Town apron over her track suit, she pursed her lips. Lines of bright red lipstick vanished into a mass of wrinkles. "I'm short a crust."

"I took one for the quiche." I did a double take. "Wait, you count the crusts?" Granted, we took our crusts seriously. I'd even built a temperature-controlled flour workroom to maintain the temperature of the butter. But tracking inventory was more organization than expected from Charlene.

"Of course I count the crusts. I didn't become the best crust maker in San Nicholas without counting my crusts." Adjusting her glasses, she peered at the wedding gown. "Huh. What's that?"

I pressed one hand to my stomach. "Just a dress. Look, I'm sorry I messed up your count."

Wandering to the dress, she trailed a gnarled hand over its plastic wrapping. "A wedding gown? Ah, I'll never forget where I was the day I heard Princess Di had been murdered."

"Murdered? She died in a car accident."

"That's what they want you to think."

"But the police—"

"Can be bought," she said, her white brows lowering.

I clammed up, having learned the hard way there was no budging my piecrust maker from a juicy conspiracy theory.

"What's this wedding gown doing here?" she asked.

"I'm trying to sell it," I said, attempting to keep my voice light. "Know anyone who's getting married?"

"Why sell it? It's lovely. You should keep it for your next wedding." She glanced sideways at me. "Sorry. I guess in your case it would be your first."

Thudding into the antique swivel chair behind my desk, I peered inside an open envelope that I knew was empty. I couldn't imagine keeping the dress. In the first place, I couldn't see myself ever getting married, not after the Mark Jeffreys fiasco. Second, even if I did get married, marrying one man in a dress that had been meant for another felt wrong. And third, if I didn't need the money so badly, I'd have made a bonfire of the blasted thing.

"I'm sorry, Val. That was insensitive of me." Charlene angled her head down. "I shouldn't have said that after you got dumped and all."

"I wasn't dumped. It was mutual."

"Of course it was." She patted me on the shoulder. "And you're still young." She sighed. "Ah, to be your age and in love. How old are you anyway?"

"Old enough to know better."

"Here." Charlene pulled a phone from her apron pocket and snapped a picture of the dress. "I'll post it to my Twitter followers. Maybe one of them will want to buy it."

Elbows on the desk, I braced my skull in my hands. Great. Spectacular. Let's prolong the agony via the Internet.

In the other room, the front bell rang.

"You'd better get that." Charlene jerked her thumb toward the office door. "Petronella is on her smoke break."

Eager to escape, I bolted out of my chair. It skidded

backward and hit the wall. I didn't hang around to inspect for damage, hustling to the counter.

A blond in a smooth-fitting, green workout suit strode through the dining area. Her ponytail bobbed, her long, lean dancer's muscles moving smoothly, and I had to crane my neck to look up at her. On her jacket, Heidi's Health and Fitness was emblazoned over her heart. She halted in front of the register.

Joe looked up from his bar stool, grinning, but his smile seemed a little pained.

"Hi." Smiling, I laid a hand on the counter. "You must be from the new gym. I'm Val."

"I'm looking for the owner." The corners of her lips quirked, quick, professional, cool.

"That would be me. Welcome to the street. I was about to go to your grand opening."

"I'm Heidi Gladstone."

We shook hands, my knuckles grinding within her grip. Dropping my hand to my side, I flexed my fingers, restoring the circulation. "Thanks for stopping by. I baked a welcome gift for your grand opening," I said, taking the quiche from beneath the counter.

"No thanks." She shook her head. "I don't do dairy."

"I used almond milk."

"Is there any cheese in it?"

"Only goat cheese."

She reared away as if I'd suggested cyanide. "I don't do dairy."

Joe's smile broadened.

I took a deep breath, inhaling the calming scents of baking fruits and sugar. "What can I do for you?"

"You can change your sign." She pointed at the neon above me. "Turn your frown upside down? It encourages emotional eating. Sugar kills, and though it does give a quick emotional high, the satisfaction is fleeting. My customers are trying to rebuild their health. It's not good for them to constantly see that negative reinforcement."

I laughed. She was kidding. Of course. "Right. Good one!"

She frowned, a faint line appearing between her blond brows. "I'm quite serious."

"But . . . it's my slogan. It's on everything—my sign outside, the menus, my business cards." This had to be a joke.

"Exactly," she said. "It's a problem. Do you have any sugar-free pics?"

"My potpies are sugar free. And so is this quiche."

"I advocate a vegan diet. I couldn't eat a potpie or a quiche. Do you sell any sugar-free fruit pies?"

"Um, no." Sugar free? I'd heard of such things, and this was California, where people could be more thoughtful about eating. But a sugar-free pie? That was unnatural and possibly un-American. Besides, fruit was full of natural sugars.

"I'll bring some recipes by tomorrow." She whirled, her ponytail coming within inches of my face, and marched out of the store. The bell over the entrance tinkled in her wake.

Joe wedged himself free of the bar stool and waddled to the counter, arms extended. "I'll take that breakfast pie. And a fork."

Sighing, I handed him the quiche. "All right. You win. Do you want a plate to go with that?"

"No. Why get a plate dirty? I'll eat it from the tin."

"How did you know she wouldn't take it?"

Joe winked. "She kicked off her grand opening this morning with a lecture on the evils of gluten, lactose, and anything that tastes good. I figured at least one of those things would be in that breakfast pie."

I nodded. I had yet to meet a gluten-free piecrust that really sang.

He rubbed his stomach. "And the spread was awful, all twigs and health food."

"It is a gym."

Petronella stomped toward me in her black motorcycle boots, her brows lowered in a slash, a pie in each hand. "Are you working the counter today or am I?"

"You are. Sorry. You can have it back." I edged away.

"Because I need this job, and if you've decided you can do it for me—"

"Nope, you're still chief pie wrangler. Have at it." While I wasn't exactly afraid of Petronella, both she and Charlene were protective of their duties. And since Charlene made the best piecrust in five counties, and Petronella could soothe the most ferocious customer, I'd learned to stay out of their way.

There was a choking sound, and we both snapped our heads toward the counter.

Joe's fork clattered to the linoleum. Bowed over the quiche, he gripped his stomach.

I froze, brows squishing together, coldness piercing my core. Then Petronella and I raced around the counter, bumping into each other as we fought our way through the narrow passage beside the cash register.

Joe fell to the floor, writhing.

I fumbled in my apron pocket for my phone and called 9-1-1.

Petronella clasped one of Joe's hands. "Joe! I'm here. Val's calling an ambulance. What's happening?"

Joe went limp, his eyes rolling back. He didn't answer.

Chapter 2

A uniformed police officer strode through the front entrance, setting the bell above it ringing. His square jaw tightening, he scanned the scene—customers gaping, Petronella and I gripping Joe's arms and shoulders as he thrashed. The officer came to kneel beside us, placing a hand on Joe's chest.

Joe went limp.

Patrons sat unmoving, their coffees and hand pies cooling. Even the gamers stopped rattling their twenty-sided dice across the table.

Charlene placed a floury hand on my shoulder.

"What happened?" The officer pressed two fingers to the side of Joe's neck, checked his breathing.

Petronella choked out a sob.

"He was eating." I motioned to his spot at the counter. "Then he grabbed his stomach and collapsed. He's not choking—we checked."

"Did you notice him behaving oddly before he collapsed?" the officer asked. Below the San Nicholas Police Department badge, his metal name tag read: Carmichael. "Anything unusual? Was he disoriented?"

"No," I said, "but he did look a little tired."

Officer Carmichael loosened Joe's tie. "Okay, the paramedics will be here in a few minutes. They'll need some space."

I nodded.

Charlene tugged on my shoulder, and the two of us backed against the counter.

"Petronella," I said in a low voice.

She squeezed Joe's hand between hers. Rising, she joined us, wiping her hands on her apron. Charlene wrapped an arm around Petronella's waist, comforting.

Paramedics raced inside. A fire truck wailed to a halt out front. More police crowded the dining area.

Officer Carmichael approached me.

"How is he?" I asked.

He glanced over his broad shoulder.

The paramedics shook their heads, folded up their equipment.

"I'm sorry," the officer said. "Did you know him well?"

Petronella hurried into the kitchen. Shooting me a worried look, Charlene followed her.

I scrubbed a hand over my face, feeling rough traces of flour against my cheek. "He owns—owned—the comic shop next door. He liked to come in here for morning coffee." I nodded toward the urn on the counter.

"And the breakfast pie? Was that his?" He nodded toward the partially eaten quiche on the counter.

"He won it from me in a bet this morning."

Officer Carmichael smiled, his jade-colored eyes sympathetic. "You must have been close."

"We joked around, but I can't say I knew him well." My hands fell to my sides. Five months as neighbors, and I knew Joe was a widower who liked morning coffee and pie and baseball. Did he have kids? If he did, they'd likely have been grown by now. "I'm sort of newish in town."

"So am I. What brought you to San Nicholas?"

I looked at him, startled, then realized this wasn't small talk. His pen hovered, poised and ready for action, over a notebook. But I wasn't sure what to tell him. Mark had brought me here, to his hometown, but the words stuck in my throat. "I opened Pie Town five months ago."

A tall, thin man in a brown suit strode to us. Slipping a leather wallet from his breast pocket, he flipped it open, displaying a San Nicholas PD badge. His face was narrow, hawkish, his eyes burning. "I'll take it from here, GC."

Officer Carmichael's expression flickered. He nodded and walked a few steps away, turning and scribbling in his notepad.

"I'm Detective Shaw. You're the owner?" the detective asked.

"Yes. I'm Val Harris."

"You'll have to close up for today. Everyone out, including staff. We'll take your staff's and customers' statements, and once we're done, they can leave." He snapped his fingers. "GC?"

Carmichael turned, silent.

"Did you take Miss Harris's statement?" Shaw asked. He nodded.

"Then you can go, Miss Harris," Shaw said. "Thank you for your cooperation."

I twisted my hands in my apron. Joe. I couldn't believe he was gone. And I couldn't carry on, business as usual, after he had died in Pie Town. But the pie shop was my livelihood. I drew a breath, forcing myself to calm. The detective hadn't asked me to close forever, only for the day.

"Is that a problem?" Detective Shaw asked, his tone careless.

"No," I said. "Can you tell me the normal procedure in a case like this?" Asking how long I'd be closed seemed crass under the circumstances. But I needed to know.

His expression pinched. "This is a possible homicide.

We'll tell you when you can reopen. I take it he was eating here when he collapsed?"

"Yes." A fist tightened around my heart. Homicide? Homicide!

"What, exactly?"

"A quiche." I pointed to the counter.

"Who made it?"

"I did."

"He eat anything else while he was here?"

"No," I said, dizzy. "He had some coffee, but it's self-serve from the same urn everyone else has been drinking out of."

"Self-serve?" His lip curled. "You can go. And we'll be taking the quiche," he bellowed. Walking to the counter, he leaned over the quiche and sniffed it. "GC? Pack this up."

All eyes followed Detective Shaw as he strode out the door. Officer Carmichael snapped on a pair of latex gloves. Grabbing the quiche, he followed.

Numb, I stumbled to my office and gathered my things into my backpack. Homicide. Suspected homicide. But my quiche wasn't responsible for Joe's death. Sure, they had to check, but . . . I'd made that quiche!

Thinking over how I'd prepared the quiche, I thumped into my desk chair. My fists clenched. Second-guessing myself was nuts. It wasn't as if I kept rat poison lying around the kitchen on the off chance I'd like to use it to season a pie. I'd learned at a tender age never to keep anything inedible in my work area after spraying a cookie tin with starch rather than cooking spray. An entire batch of hot-cross buns had gone up in flames.

There was nothing wrong with that quiche.

A vision of Joe's face, contorted with pain, floated before my eyes. Homicide? The detective was just . . . wrong! And how could he have diagnosed poison so quickly? There had been no autopsy. The SNPD was being overly cautious. Sure, someone dies in a restaurant, the authorities have to be careful. They were being smart, taking precautions.

So why had Shaw called it a homicide? Suspected homicide.

My office door bammed open, rustling the plastic on the wedding gown.

Charlene stormed inside, her jowls quivering. "They're closing Pie Town? This is a frame-up!"

"It's only temporary," I said, and hoped it was true.

"And that buffoon of a detective made Petronella cry."

"Is she all right?"

"No, she's not all right. She's gone home. Val, I need to talk to you—"

Officer Carmichael knocked on the door frame and took step inside. "We'll lock up for you," he said. "Have you got a spare set of keys?" He glanced at the wedding dress.

"Um, yeah." I scrabbled in my desk drawer and tossed him a set.

He caught it one handed. "Thanks." He shifted his weight. "I doubt you'll be closed for long."

"We'd better not be," Charlene snapped. "Social security checks only go so far."

"Yes, ma'am." He looked to me. "And I'll need your contact info."

"Oh. Right." I gave him my cell number, and he noted it in his leather-bound book.

"Where do you live?" he asked.

I fiddled with the zipper of my backpack, lying atop my desk. "You can find me at the Seaside Inn."

"That dump?" Charlene asked. "What are you doing there?"

"It's not that bad." At least I hoped it wasn't. I hadn't seen it yet from the inside. "I haven't had much time for apartment hunting." And then I realized where I'd messed up, and my stomach clenched. If they searched Pie Town, they'd see the mattress in my office's storage closet. In my frantic efforts to build the best pie kitchen ever, I'd been pillaging my monthly rent budget. That had left me with only one place to sleep: Pie Town.

My sleeping arrangements had to be a zoning violation, so it was a good thing my budget had finally stopped hemorrhaging a month ago. It was time for me to house hunt.

Carmichael grunted. "That motel's not bad. The area can get a little sketchy late at night though. Be careful."

I grabbed my backpack off the desk. "Well, I guess I'll get out of your hair." I hurried past them, escaping from the room.

My life was not going as planned. But neither, I imagined, had Joe's.

There was a slim chance the police would allow me back into Pie Town tonight, but the idea of staying in a hotel appealed. It had been months since I'd taken a shower outside my gym.

Checking into the Seaside Inn, I got a room overlooking the alley. There was a seaside several blocks away, but the salt air was faint and masked by the rising stench from the alley dumpsters. The room had been painted a murky gray color, darker blots of gray marring the thinning carpet. I doubted its decor had been updated since the 1970s.

What had Joe been doing in the seventies?

Dumping my backpack on the bed, I checked myself in the mirror and pulled my shoulder-length, brown hair loose from its bun. Since I now had the day off, I might as well take care of some personal business.

I'd been sleeping in my office closet ever since my

engagement went kablooey four months ago. Crawling over my mattress to reach the door every morning was getting stale. And then there was the shower issue. Pie Town didn't have one, and it was the only reason I went to the gym these days.

I spread a newspaper on the motel room's cracked desk and circled the cheapest apartments for rent. Some were almost in my price range, and a few had open houses today.

Taking only my wallet from my backpack, I returned to my battered, sky-blue VW Bug and went apartment hunting.

Four hours later, I returned to the motel, beaten by the reality of California prices. Even the apartments I couldn't quite afford had been rundown, seedy. Until Pie Town started turning a profit, I either had to settle for seedy or stay in the closet.

What had I been thinking, moving out to a coastal California town? Oh, right. I'd been thinking the mortgage would be split between me and my new husband. The irony was that my ex-fiancé, Mark, was a realtor. Did I say irony? Tragedy was more like it. I'd passed half a dozen signs with his grinning mug on them in my quest for a new home. Each time one of his signs had flashed past, my chest ached.

It was too early for dinner, but I'd missed lunch, and my stomach rumbled, hollow. Ordering a pizza, I collapsed on the bed, its springs creaking beneath me. Okay, so I hadn't found a place today. Maybe I needed to look further inland. But I couldn't go on sleeping at Pie Town. My eyelids drifted shut.

Someone banged on the door, and I jerked off the bed. Pizza! I checked my watch, marveling at their speed. Grabbing my wallet, I opened the door.

Charlene barreled inside, an odd, white, furry stole draped over her olive-colored, knit coat. "I need your help."

Stiffening, I tugged at the hem of my long-sleeved Pie Town T-shirt. White with pink script, the colors matched our aprons. "Um, what are you doing here?"

"What am I doing here?" she asked, bursting with her usual Sturm und Drang. "My ex-boyfriend was killed in Pie Town, and I'm being framed. That's what I'm doing here."

I stared. "Joe was your boyfriend?" How did I not know this?

"Ex-boyfriend. It was years ago. Before your time. He was a lovely man, but we worked better . . . not together. And now I'm the prime suspect in his death."

"But why would you be a suspect?" I leaned out onto the balcony, hopeful, searching for the pizza guy.

"Haven't you been listening? We once had a relationship! He died after eating one of my pies."

"My quiche."

"But it was my piecrust." She collapsed into the desk chair. "I'll really miss the old coot."

"Charlene, I didn't know—"

"We have a responsibility," Charlene said. "A man I knew was murdered—"

"We don't know he was murdered."

"In our pie shop!"

"My pie shop."

"Adding insult to injury, I'm being framed for the crime. And that really pisses me off."

"You're not . . . No one's being framed."

"It's a frame-up." Her voice quavered. "Just like Oswald."

"Who's Oswald?" I shook my head, trying to rattle my brain-tank into gear.

"Lee Harvey Oswald! The grassy knoll?"

"I know who—"

"The Kennedy assassination? You're too young to remember it, but surely they taught you about that dark day in school."

Her stole writhed, yawned, exposing sharp white teeth.

I jumped backward, banging into the TV stand. "What the . . . What is that?!"

She patted the furry wrap. "This is Frederick. Like so many white cats, he's deaf. And it's a good thing too, because he's very sensitive, and I don't think he'd care for your attitude, missy. On a happier topic, I have good news for you. Your wedding dress is getting lots of retweets."

"What?"

"On Twitter. Some are saying the dress is cursed since you were . . . Well, you know."

"I was what?"

She gave me a look.

"I wasn't dumped." I dropped onto the bed.

"Don't worry, not everyone believes in curses. The important thing is, lots of retweets."

Someone knocked at the door.

"Hold on," I said.

I opened the door to the pizza delivery girl, transacted vital business, and returned to the room. "Look, I wouldn't worry about it." Joe's death had shaken us all, but Charlene loved drama. We didn't know how Joe had died, and certainly not that it was a murder. "There hasn't even been an autopsy. If you ask me, Detective Shaw was jumping the gun on this poison business."

Charlene grabbed the pizza box out of my hands and sniffed. "Pepperoni? I'm too depressed to eat, but I should keep my strength up. May I?"

I nodded, resigned.

Laying the pizza beside the TV, she opened the box and made a face. "Mushrooms? Why did you have to go and add fungus to a perfectly good pizza?" She shuddered and flicked mushrooms from a slice. "They're slimy, and they've got no flavor." Taking a bite, she pointed the slice at me. "So what are you going to do about this murder?"

"Why would you expect me to do anything about it?"

"You used to be an investigative journalist, weren't you?"

"No."

"But you told me you took an investigative journalism class."

"As part of my English major. That was nearly ten years ago. The police are investigating. I'm sure they'll test the quiche and discover there's nothing wrong with it, and then things can return to normal."

Her face tightened. "Joe's dead. He was a good man, and things will never return to normal."

I stared at my sneakers. "I'm sorry, Charlene. I didn't mean it that way. I just meant you won't be a suspect."

"Because they've never been normal."

"Come again?"

"Things have never been normal in San Nicholas. Not that you would have noticed; you've got your head stuck so deep in that pie shop. You need to get out and look around." She gazed around the room. "Couldn't you find a better hotel?"

"It's temporary."

"Five months sleeping in your office isn't temporary. Where are you keeping all your things? You do have things, don't you?"

Not many, and those that I did have were where I couldn't get at them, in my ex's storage unit. I grabbed a slice and stuffed pizza into my mouth. The storage unit was a sore spot. "It's only been four months, and do you have any idea how expensive rents are in San Nicholas? I can't afford to start up the best pie shop in Northern California and pay for an apartment."

"Staying in this rat trap isn't the answer."

I took a deep breath. Great Buddha, that pizza was good. "Look, I appreciate your concern, but I'm sure the right apartment will come along."

"I've got a place."

"Thanks, Charlene, but I don't need a roommate."

"Neither do I. I've got one of those, whatchamacall'em, tiny houses, up on the bluff. My tenant recently moved out."

My heart beat faster. Could the solution be that easy? "How much are you asking?"

"Hold your horses." Her eyes narrowed, glinting with cunning. "I didn't say you could live there. I couldn't possibly rent out my jewel box of a house overlooking the ocean, ideal for single living, after a man I knew for decades was horribly murdered."

I blew out a breath. "There's no reason to think it was murder."

"That's what you say. The police say otherwise."

"What do you expect me to do about it? And I haven't even seen this so-called tiny house overlooking the bluff."

She grabbed the pizza box. "You drive."

We crammed into my VW. I aimed the car downtown, a collection of restaurants and touristy shops tucked between a swell of green hills and the Pacific.

"Left on Main," Charlene said.

I turned at the stop sign. A police cruiser sat outside Pie Town's brick facade. A CLOSED sign hung in the dusty window of the comic shop. We puttered past antique shops and coffee houses. At the old firehouse, Main Street curved toward the beach, intersecting Highway 1. Eucalyptus trees lined the highway. Wind from passing cars rustled California poppies, flaming amid tall, green grasses.

"Turn left here." Charlene pointed with another pizza slice, and my stomach rumbled a protest.

I reached for the box.

She slid it out of my reach. "You have no idea how many accidents are caused by eating and driving."

Neither did Charlene. Pressing my lips together, I turned up the road, wending through low, emerald hills. "That was my pizza."

"It's delicious, thank you. Turn right here."

"Where?" I squinted, slowing the VW.

"Here! Here!"

A shaded road cut between two eucalyptus trees, and I turned sharply, bumping onto rough macadam. We drove up a steep hillside, the road snaking, narrow. Charlene directed me onto an open space overlooking the ocean and a blue, metal cargo container.

I stopped the car. "Where is it?"

"You're looking at it."

I looked around. Grass, some trees, the container, and a view of the ocean, a bank of fog hovering off the gray line of coast. "Where?"

"There." She stabbed a crooked finger at the container.

"A shipping container? I'd rather live in my office."

"You've been living in that office for the last five months."

"Four months."

"And it's a little sad if you ask me." Unbuckling her seat belt, she lurched from the VW. "Come on."

Exhaling slowly, I followed. With Pie Town closed, I didn't have anything better to do, and the view was spectacular. The faint tang of salt air and local herbs and grasses tickled my nostrils.

I walked around the container and stopped short. The side facing the ocean was nearly all windows. A crisp white awning jutted out above the glass doors, sheltering a picnic bench.

Charlene climbed the two steps to the entrance, unlocked and opened the container.

Wordless, I followed her inside. The polished wood floors glowed. The walls were a soft white. A kitchenette with a surprising amount of counter space anchored the center of the room. A square dining nook stood off to one side of the kitchen. At the other end of the container, a bookshelf blocked off a sleeping area with a pull-out futon arrangement. A desk folded out of another wall.

Charlene stomped to the opposite side of the container, past the bookshelf. "Bathroom's over here."

I blinked, slow, disbelieving, feeling like I'd stepped inside Doctor Who's TARDIS. The container looked a lot bigger on the inside than the outside. But there was a real bathroom, with a separate toilet and shower area. And that view . . . I gazed out the window. I could watch the ocean all day, the lines of foaming waves, the creeping fog.

I swallowed, mouth dry. I had to play this cool. "It is small."

"All my other properties are rented, and you couldn't afford them anyway."

Other properties? Had I employed a real estate mogul? Charlene hadn't mentioned that on her job application. But you couldn't put much faith in job applications. On hers, she'd listed her age as forty-two. "How much are you asking?"

She stopped in front of a gilt mirror, fussing with her white hair. "I told you, I couldn't possibly rent this ocean view gem to a single soul when one of my oldest friends has been murdered, and the police think I might have been responsible."

Resigned to the coming blackmail, I bit my bottom lip. "What do you want?"

"Well . . . I might see clear to renting it to you, if you were the right sort of person."

"What sort of person, exactly?"

"The sort who'd help me find Joe's killer."

Chapter 3

Yawning, I curled up on the lumpy motel bed, remote control in hand. The local news flickered on the TV screen, tinting the room blue. Moonlight streamed through a gap in the grayish curtains, puddling on the carpet.

I'd rather step on a rusty screw than assist my free-wheeling piecrust maker with a murder investigation. But of course I said yes. After all, poor Joe had died of natural causes. And Charlene knew quite well she wasn't a murder suspect. She just reveled in the excitement. Since her name wasn't under attack and no murderer was at large, it would be easy enough to solve the case. It was win-win.

So my conscience was clear. I'd get a new home, the police would figure out what happened to Joe, and I'd made Charlene happy. My motto was to be kind whenever possible, and it was always possible. That's actually from the Dalai Lama, but I didn't think he'd mind if I adopted it.

Someone pounded on the motel room door.

Muttering a curse, I dragged myself off the bed and

peered out the peephole. A veined, blue eyeball stared back.

"Gagh!" Clutching my chest, I willed my heart to stop pounding. "Who is it?"

"It's Charlene. Let's go."

I wrenched open the door. "What?"

Charlene stood on the balcony and glared up at me. "Aren't you ready?" She adjusted the black knit cap over her silvery curls. It glittered with moisture from the night-time fog.

"What's going on?" I asked. The yellowish overhead light flickered, and I shivered.

"You promised to help me investigate."

My brows drew together. This was more than I'd bargained for. Charlene seemed in pretty good shape, but I didn't care for the idea of her crime fighting on her own. She might get arrested or have a stroke. I took in her slim-fitting black track suit, hip-length black knit jacket, and black running shoes. The cat wrapped around her neck seemed to gleam, its white fur shimmering. "You look like a geriatric bank robber."

Her spectacles flashed in the lamplight. "Geriatric! I'm in my prime."

Prime number, possibly. She was seventy-something if a day. "All right." I stepped further into the room, but she stayed outside.

"We're going to find out who killed Joe. Come on."

"Charlene—"

"Don't you want to stop sleeping in Pie Town?"

"Yes, but—"

"You're not going to make me do this alone, are you? I might break a hip."

"I thought you were in your prime."

"I have weak bones!"

"Drink more milk." Grabbing my purse and navy jacket

off the rumpled bed, I followed her down the steps to an ancient, yellow Jeep.

"Get in." Hopping into the driver's seat, she leaned across, unlocking the door.

I had one leg in when the Jeep lurched forward.

"Whoa!" Clutching the grab bar, I swung the rest of myself inside and slammed the door shut. I sputtered.

"What did you say?" she asked.

I took deep breaths, willing my heart to remain in its proper anatomical place. "Where are we going?"

"Joe's house."

"We're not breaking in." I buckled up, my knuckles white.

"Of course not. I have a key."

The Jeep roared around a corner, speeding past a gas station.

"Where did you get a key?" I asked. "I thought you said you were his long, long ago ex-girlfriend."

"Well, yes, but I kept the key. When you're older, you have to watch out for each other in case you trip on the stairs and can't get up. Joe and I knew that if one of us suddenly disappeared, we'd have to check on each other." She chuckled. "Boy was he pissed when I forgot to tell him about my trip to Vegas."

We sped down Main Street, its faux-gas lanterns turning the fog amber. A trio of teenage boys shambled down the sidewalk, their collars turned up, their hair ragged.

Charlene tsked. "I'll bet they're on their way to the cemetery. There's not much else to do in San Nicholas when you're that age."

She turned at a red double-decker bus parked outside a pub and piloted us down a residential street. Slowing, Charlene pulled up beside a white Victorian.

"Is this Joe's house?" I asked.

She arched a brow. "I'm not going to park right in front

of his house. Don't you watch any crime TV? Joe lives a block away." Sliding out of the Jeep, she lifted the cat off her neck and set it on her seat. It rolled onto its back, pawing at the air in invitation. Chuckling, she rubbed its belly.

Clambering out, I shut the door as quietly as I could, and grimaced. How had I fallen in with Charlene's cop and robbers fantasies?

"We'll walk." She backhanded me lightly in the gut. "Now act casual!"

"I am acting casual," I whispered. "Keep your voice down."

"Oh. Right. His house is this way."

The fog slithered beneath my collar, dampening my skin and hair. We passed beneath a misshapen Monterey pine, and I zipped my jacket higher. Streetlamps were few and far between here, and most of the homes were dark. I stumbled over a slab of broken sidewalk and widened my eyes, straining to see.

"Careful." Charlene crossed the street.

I paused in front of a yellow one-story with a gabled roof. A FOR SALE sign sporting my ex-fiancé's leering face sprouted from its lawn. My heart pinched.

Shuddering, I hurried down the block after my piecrust maker. She turned through a gate and strode up the brick walk of a Victorian painted garish purple and orange. The fog seemed to condense around it, covering its shame. Our footsteps clunked, hollow, on the porch.

Charlene jingled a set of keys. "No cops outside the vic's house. They're not taking Joe's death seriously. I knew we had to solve this crime ourselves."

"We are so going to get arrested." And I'd been looking forward to my lumpy hotel bed and grody shower.

"Nonsense. We're here to collect Joe's cat, Mr. Tibbles."

"Joe has a cat?" I sagged, relieved. That was a decent

reason to go inside. I might not spend the night in jail after all.

"No, but we don't have to tell them that. If the cops show up, we'll say Mr. Tibbles ran away."

"Which they'll see through as soon as they notice Joe didn't keep any cat food."

Nose twitching, she shoved the door open. "Please. Do you think that dunderhead detective, Shaw, is going to notice?"

I scuttled after her and shut the door, enveloping us in darkness.

Charlene clicked a flashlight on and shone it in my eyes.

I flinched away. "Aim that somewhere else."

"Oh, right." She directed the beam at the red-carpeted floor and thrust something cold and metallic into my hands. "I figured you'd forget to bring one."

"Forget? I didn't even know we were breaking and entering until about fifteen minutes ago."

"We're not breaking, only entering. Now start looking for Joe's casebook."

I turned on the flashlight and aimed it at the carpet. "Casebook? Was he a private investigator on the side?"

"He and his buddy, Frank Potts, were Sherlock Holmes nuts before Frank died last month. Real obsessive. They called themselves the Baker Street Boys."

"So?"

"Baker Street Bonkers was more like it. They armchair investigated local crimes. That must be why Joe was murdered. He got too close to the truth."

I tucked a loose hank of hair behind my ear. "What local crimes? This is San Nicholas. No one does anything here."

"The worst crimes happen in rural areas. That's what Sherlock Holmes says."

"Sherlock Holmes doesn't exist." Unwilling to leave the security of a quick exit, I wavered in the entryway.

"I know he's fictional. But Holmes was right. There's more going on in San Nicholas than you'd think. You'd be aware of that if you spent a little more time out of that pie shop."

I clutched the flashlight to my chest. "Start-ups take a lot of energy."

She harrumphed and walked down the hall. "You search the front of the house. I'll take the back, and then we'll both check upstairs. Give a shout if the cops turn up."

"I can't believe I'm doing this." But I couldn't retreat now and leave Charlene in the house alone. Seventy-something might be the new fifty-something, but she was seventy-something going on seventeen.

Worried about attracting attention, I aimed the light at the floor and edged into a living room. The decor was Victorian—oil lamps and fringed table runners and heavy, curved furniture made of dark wood. It smelled of pipe smoke and liniment. I picked up a tattered sci-fi paperback, put it down. A floorboard creaked beneath my weight.

I crept through a wide, arched entry into an old-fashioned library. Bookcases ran to the ceiling, covering the walls. On the far side stood a cold fireplace. A local map of the California coast, stuck with pushpins, hung above it. Green and red and yellow pins clustered around San Nicholas. It looked cluelike, which I figured would make Charlene happy, so I snapped a picture with my cell phone.

I wandered to a heavy, wooden desk. A leather-bound journal lay atop it, and I picked it up, opened the cover. Irregular Casebook No. 13.

Eureka! "Charlene! I think I found it."

She appeared in the entry. "Weird. The kitchen door was open, but it doesn't look like anything was disturbed."

"Maybe his cat got out that way."

"There is no cat."

"I might have found the book." Thumbing through it, I made a face. Only the first four pages had brief scrawls on them. Library bd.—sec—the Case of the Bloated Blond.

"You did?" Charlene nudged me from behind. "What does it say?"

"It says it's a casebook, but there's nothing much inside."

She grabbed the book and set it on an end table, shining the flashlight beam on its pages. "His latest casebook. Frank must have died before their next meeting, and Joe hadn't had a chance to finish the cases without him."

A throat cleared behind me.

We turned.

A black-clad figure in a ski mask stared past us. We followed his gaze to the end table.

The casebook.

I dove for it.

The burglar rushed forward, knocking me and the table to the ground. A lamp crashed. The casebook flew beneath an ornate couch.

Red and blue lights illuminated the bookshelves, the armchairs, Charlene's face.

My heart seized. Handcuffs. Jail. Officer Carmichael. What had I done?

Charlene shrieked. "Cheese it! It's the cops!"

The burglar scrambled to his feet, stepping on my hand. He raced from the room.

Charlene grabbed my arm, tugging. "Come on!" She toddled out of the room.

"Wait!" Blood pounding, I stumbled after her and banged

my knee into a low end table. Something smashed to the floor.

Limping, I followed the wandering beam of her flashlight through a narrow hallway and into an ancient kitchen.

Charlene flipped off her light and darted through the open door.

Swearing beneath my breath, I followed her down the steps and into the backyard. The soggy ground sucked at my shoes.

"Turn off your flashlight," she whispered. "Or do you want the cops to catch us? This way!"

Frantic, I hobbled to the end of a yard, and we passed through a low gate. A flashlight beam swept the lawn, and I ducked behind the redwood fence. Through the fog, the moon was a bright, cotton fluff, illuminating twisting eucalyptus trees and a path leading behind the houses. Water splashed nearby.

I moved toward the path.

Charlene gripped my arm. "The burglar went that way. We're going the other." She drew me, stumbling over roots and branches, through the trees and to a shallow stream. Charlene splashed into the water.

"Wait," I said. "We shouldn't be running. We need to tell the police about the burglar." I stepped in after her. The water froze my feet, coiled about my ankles.

"We are the burglars!" She headed north, making her way down the creek.

"But the police need to know. It might have something to do with Joe's murder."

"Do you think they haven't figured out by now that someone was in Joe's house?"

She had a point. "Where are we going?" I asked.

"We're circling back to the car. The stream will throw off our scent."

I stopped, calf deep in the frigid water. "Throw off our scent? They're not sending dogs after us."

"They won't need to the way you're shouting."

"I am not shouting." I'd been whispering loudly. The phone rang in my pocket, and I jumped, slipped on a stone, righted myself.

"You didn't turn off your phone? What sort of a crime fighter are you?"

"The not-a-crime-fighter kind." Wrenching the phone from my jacket pocket, I checked the number.

"Turn it off!"

I answered. "Hello?"

"Valentine Harris?" a man asked. His baritone rumbled through me, sending my heartbeat into a spiral.

"Um, yes?"

"This is Officer Carmichael, from the San Nicholas PD."

Gagh! The police knew where I was.

"I'm calling to tell you that you can open your restaurant tomorrow."

"Oh." I started breathing again. "Oh. Thank you. Did you— I mean, does that mean it was a natural death?"

"I'm sorry, I can't say more than that. But you're open for business tomorrow morning."

"Thanks. I appreciate the call." This was bonkers. I had to tell him the truth. "Officer—"

"Miss H—"

Charlene snatched the phone from me and clicked it off. "Are you crazy? The police are on our tail."

"No, they're not. That was the police, Officer Carmichael."

"What did he say?"

"We can open Pie Town tomorrow, which means there was nothing wrong with that quiche, and you are not a suspect. Mystery solved."

"Mystery solved my Aunt Fannie. Someone killed Joe, and that person probably broke into his house." She sloshed downstream.

My stomach wriggled, uneasy. The timing of the burglary was odd. "Maybe, but we don't know that for sure." Remembering she was my ride, I hurried after her. "I've heard criminals comb the obituaries and target the empty homes of the deceased. Maybe it was just a coincidence a burglar was in there tonight."

"After Joe's casebook? I think not. Besides, there hasn't been an obituary yet."

"Oh. Right," I said, feeling foolish.

We squeezed through a fence, popping out onto a side street. Shoes squishing, we walked to her Jeep.

"Charlene, honestly. We scared off a burglar and got chased by the cops, and you've got a good story for Petronella. Isn't that enough?"

She unlocked the doors. "Mark my words, this isn't over yet. The cops will be watching me even closer now."

Buckling myself in, I attempted reason. "If you were a suspect, the police would be at your house right now."

She laid the limp cat in my lap. "And why are you so sure they're not?"

"Why would you be a suspect? We know the quiche was fine, and no one could suspect we had a reason to be in Joe's house." Beneath my hand, the cat vibrated, purring.

"Did Carmichael tell you the quiche was fine?"

"He told me we could open Pie Town." But I had to wonder what would have happened if Heidi had taken the quiche. I shook my head. No, I'd made that quiche. It hadn't been poisoned.

"Pie Town, Pie Town," she said. "There's more to life than Pie Town."

"Not to my life," I muttered, crossing my arms over my

chest. Had I been focusing too much on the pie and not enough on the town? I should have known Joe better.

"What?" she asked.

"Nothing."

"Whoever was in that house got a good look at us." She turned to me, the furrows in her brow deepening. "I'm sorry, Val. I shouldn't have brought you into this. It's too dangerous."

I dragged my palms down my pant legs. He'd seen us. Or had it been a she? In the dark and panic, the only thing I'd gotten a good look at was the black ski mask. And if Charlene's theory was correct . . . "We need to tell the police."

"What we need to do is plot our next step." She turned onto Highway 1. "The killer's out there, and he thinks he's gotten away with it."

"Which is why we should tell the cops."

"Tell them what? That we broke into Joe's house—"

"You had a key! And what about the cat?"

"There is no cat. We're prime suspects, and we broke into Joe's house. How's that going to look?"

My piecrust maker wasn't wrong. Besides, there wasn't anything useful we could tell the police about the person who'd broken into Joe's house. But I didn't like it. "Why are we driving this way?" My feet were freezing, and they'd started to itch.

"It's called losing a tail."

I clutched my skull. Why had I agreed to come on this looney quest? No house was worth this madness, even if it was overlooking the ocean. "Charlene, no one's tailing us. There's no killer. The burglar was just a burglar, and Joe probably died of a heart attack. It's awful, and I'm sorry for your loss, but—"

"Did that look like a heart attack?"

No, it hadn't. Crumb. I could only delude myself for so long. "Joe had mentioned that things tasted funny to him that morning," I said. And I'd forgotten to tell the cops.

"A funny taste in his mouth? Could be poison. If someone poisoned your quiche, Heidi could have been the target."

"No one poisoned that quiche. It was either behind the glass in the front counter or in my possession. Someone would have noticed if there was any quiche tampering." Unless Charlene or Petronella had sprinkled cyanide on the quiche, and that didn't seem likely.

"Good gad!" She slammed on the breaks.

I flew forward. The seat belt hitched under my breast, my head thunked the windshield, and ten burning scalpels dug into my thigh. "Ow!"

"Did you see that?"

Pain arced through my forehead. Wincing, I detached the cat's claws from my leg. "Augh!"

Frederick twitched his ears.

"See what?" I asked, watching the cat. Had he reacted to my shout? Maybe he wasn't deaf after all. Maybe it was a scam so Charlene would cart him around like a feline prince.

A cleft in the hillside revealed a sandy beach littered with twists of driftwood. The ocean seethed, a gray mass beneath a low bank of fog.

She leaned forward, peering over the steering wheel. "It looked like a jaguar."

"There are no jaguars in Northern California."

"There are in zoos."

I ground my teeth. "Just. Drive." Our adventure in breaking and entering had wound me a little tight, and I soothed myself with thoughts of Pie Town. I'd open it tomorrow, and all would be right with the world. The police now knew that someone had broken into Joe's house and would be on the track of the murderer. So my piecrust maker was more eccentric than I'd thought. No problem. It wasn't as if she was going to kill anyone.

Frederick purred.

Except for maybe me.

Chapter 4

I punched the dough on the stainless steel counter, raising a cloud of flour. "Stupid." Punch. "Useless." Punch. "Gym!" Punch.

A humongous, hand-lettered sign blazed from the gym's window next door: SUGAR KILLS. Talk about insensitive.

It was high noon, and Pie Town was deserted of all but the gamers, huddled in their usual booth. They were good eaters, but they couldn't support the shop on their own. I'd stopped our usual pie production line and sent my assistant pie maker, Hannah, home. As painful as checking out of the hotel had been this morning, now I was glad I'd done it. It was cheap, but I still couldn't afford it for long, especially if sales didn't pick up.

Petronella leaned against the counter and crossed her black-denim-clad legs. "You gonna kill that piecrust or run it through the machine?" She jerked her chin toward the piecrust roller, and the unlit cigarette threatened to slip from her lips.

I glared at her.

"I'm only curious." She shrugged. "Kill it or flatten it, your call. But I don't think it matters much either way."

I knuckled the crust one more time. Petronella was right. Beating an innocent piecrust was pointless. It wouldn't change the fact a maybe-killer had looked me in the eyes, or bring down the sign in Heidi's window. But I could solve at least one of those problems.

"I'll be right back," I said.

Petronella saluted with her index finger, her black nail polish flashing. "I'll hold down the fort."

I whisked through the swinging door. Untying my apron, I dropped it on the counter near the register. After Joe's death, Heidi had to see that a big SUGAR KILLS sign was pretty rude. Maybe she hadn't meant anything by it. Too much sugar was bad for you, sure. Hers was a reasonable point of view. But there was nothing wrong with an occasional slice of pie. A pie shop and a gym could coexist.

I pushed open the glass door to Heidi's gym and pasted a smile on my face.

A girl in a green Heidi's Health and Fitness golf shirt looked up from behind the frosted-glass counter. "Hi! Welcome to Heidi's Health and Fitness! Would you like to hear about a gym membership?"

"No, thanks. I'm Val from Pie Town. Is Heidi here?"

"Wait a sec." She disappeared through a door behind the counter.

Leaning against the counter, I picked up a brochure advertising a colon cleanse. What sautéed hell was this? I flipped through its stiff, glossy folds. For the low, low price of a treasure-house of supplements, I could cleanse my colon, lose weight, and boost my immune system. "I'd rather eat pie."

Heidi bounced out the door. "Valentine! Did you come for the recipes I promised?" She held out a sheaf of papers.

I took them. "Uh, thanks. Actually, it's about the sign in your window."

"Which one?" Her blue eyes widened.

"You might have heard that Joe from the comic shop passed away in Pie Town yesterday."

"Sad." Her lips made an insincere moue of regret.

"Yes, well, the 'sugar kills' sign . . . I was wondering if you could take it down."

She raised her narrow chin. "I have the right to put up whatever sign I want."

I rubbed my forehead where I'd banged it into Charlene's windshield the night before. "Of course you do. I'm asking, as your neighbor—"

Her nostrils flared. "Sugar does kill. America is suffering from an obesity epidemic. It's tragic, and it's our duty to do whatever we can to stop it. Sugar, chemicals—we're jamming our bodies with unnatural substances."

An ache blossomed behind my right temple. "Yes, but only for a few weeks, until—"

"You don't need to be a part of the complex." She leaned across the counter toward me. "You don't have to sell pies. What about selling healthy food?"

"My shop's called Pie Town. I make pies. That's what I make."

"Well, if you're going to keep that awful sign suggesting pies make you happy—"

"It's my motto!"

"Then my sign stays. Is there anything else?"

Yeah, was there anyone out there who wanted her dead? I knew the quiche hadn't been poisoned, but had poison been somehow involved in Joe's death? Joe had said there'd been an odd taste in his mouth all morning. "Have you had any conflicts with anyone lately?"

"What's that supposed to mean?"

"Your newish in town, aren't you?"

"Three months." Her nostrils flared. "I've been here three months."

Not enough time to make someone angry enough to kill her, though I was getting seriously annoyed. And besides, the quiche couldn't have been poisoned, so Heidi couldn't be a target. Charlene's paranoia was contagious. "Good."

"What's good about it?"

"Um. Look, can't you just take the 'sugar kills' sign down for a few weeks, until things calm down?"

"America's in a health crisis. I'm not taking that sign down because you feel guilty about killing one of your customers."

"I didn't—"

Turning, she zoomed into the back room.

"Thanks!" I stomped out of the gym and discovered I'd crumpled her recipes into a crude bow tie. Fine. Just because we were neighbors didn't mean we had to be friends. At this point, I'd settle for frenemies. Blood pounded in my ears, along with a half-dozen pithy comebacks I could have said but hadn't and shouldn't. I'd take the moral high road. So sayeth the woman who broke into a dead man's house last night.

Flinging open the door to Pie Town, I stormed inside.

A uniformed police officer turned toward me. Officer Carmichael.

I stumbled to a halt, heart thudding. Had someone seen Charlene and I at Joe's house last night? I knew we shouldn't have gone. I knew we should have called the police. What had I been thinking? Maybe they'd let me bake pies for the other inmates.

"Miss Harris?"

"Ah . . ."

"I'm Carmichael. We met yesterday?" He held a black computer-looking thing under one arm and a sheaf of wrinkled papers.

"Yes, of course! It's not like I could have forgotten,

because it's not as if people are in the habit of dropping dead here." Shut up, stop babbling. I shut my piehole.

Removing his hat, he ran a broad hand through his hair. The hat had left a dent in its dark waves. "Slow day?"

I looked around the dining area. No horde of customers had flooded in since I'd been at Heidi's gym, getting taken to the woodshed.

Dice rattled across a table. At least the gamers hadn't budged. In fact, they didn't look like they'd moved since last night. They seemed to be wearing the same T-shirts and baggy jeans.

"You could say that," I said.

"I heard you've got great potpies." He smiled, his green eyes crinkling.

My heart beat faster. "We try."

"Have you got Wi-Fi by any chance?"

"Of course!" Tell him. Just tell him the truth.

"Great." He pointed toward a table by the front window. "Do you mind?"

"No! Have a seat. I'll bring a menu." Normally people ordered at the counter, and the coffee was self-serve. But today I wasn't going to draw a line in the sand. And I couldn't help but notice that Carmichael was sexy in a tall, muscular, man-in-uniform kind of way. He was the first guy I'd noticed that way since the Breakup. It had only been four months, and I knew I wasn't over my ex yet. But I enjoyed the new flush of warmth to my cheeks.

Handing him a menu, I grabbed my apron and returned to the kitchen, prodding my chignon for any stray wisps of hair.

I passed through the swinging doors, and Charlene pounced, a pink blur in a knit tunic and faded jeans ripped at the knee. She adjusted her pink cloche hat. "What's a cop doing here?"

"What are you doing here?" I asked. As usual, Charlene

had left Pie Town at nine AM this morning after she'd made
a day's worth of crusts and left them for me in the walk-in
refrigerator.

"I was driving by and saw the cop car. What does he
want?"

"Potpie." Walking to the metal table in the center of
the kitchen, I tied the apron around my waist. Sliced pies
with missing wedges filled one half of the table, divided
from a floured work area by white, ceramic canisters of
utensils and a stack of white plates. Nearby, a tall rack for
dirty tableware stood empty. Aside from the gamers, we
hadn't had any customers to dirty the plates. I never
thought clean dishware would be so depressing.

"You didn't say anything, did you?" Charlene asked.

Petronella strode past with a tray full of fruit pies that
weren't going to be sold.

I tapped her on the shoulder. "Could you take the order
from the cop in the window?"

Her brow wrinkled, her brown eyes reflecting bafflement. "Take an order?"

"Just this once," I said.

"Okaaaay." She hurried past with the tray. If I couldn't
sell those pies, maybe I could donate them to a local
shelter. Was there a local shelter? The state had weird laws
about food donations—would a shelter accept the pies?

Charlene's eyes narrowed. Dragging me into my office,
she shut the door. "Did you tell him?"

"No, but I still think we should."

"It's a bad idea. And I don't buy that he's just here for
lunch. That copper's got an ulterior motive."

"This place is dead," I said. "I don't care what his
motive is as long as he orders pie." And the fact that he
was sitting in the front window for all to see . . . Well, as
long as people saw him eating and not arresting me, I
was happy.

"Watch your step around him. He's new in town."

I raised a brow. The plastic-draped wedding gown fluttered at the corner of my vision. "And that means he's not to be trusted?"

"No, it means he'll do his job. Unlike that numb nuts, Detective Shaw."

Sick of the sight of it, I unhooked the silk dress from the bookcase and looked for a place to stash it. "I know why I don't like him." The walk of shame he'd put my quiche through yesterday had been totally unnecessary and likely the cause of my empty bakery. "But what's your beef with Shaw?"

Turning to the mirror by my desk, she fiddled with her hat. "He's no Detective Goren, I tell you."

"Detective Goren?" How many homicide detectives did tiny San Nicholas employ?

"That nice detective in New York."

"Wait. You mean from Law and Order: Criminal Intent?"

"That's the one. The show went downhill when he left to take care of his ailing mother."

"Ah." I hung the dress on the back of the door. That way, when it was open, which my office usually was, I wouldn't have to see the gown.

"Shaw's the mayor's nephew." She tsked. "Nepotism is a societal rot. Now, I've been going through that book—"

"What book?"

"Joe's casebook."

"You stole it?" My voice rose.

"Borrowed it. Joe wouldn't have minded."

"We have to give it to the police."

"Shaw won't take it seriously unless we can prove it has bearing on the case. We need to follow up on these, figure out what they're about, and then tell the cops."

"Charlene—"

There was a soft knock at the door, and Petronella stuck

her head in. "The cop in the window talks to himself and wants a mini chicken potpie, and there's someone here to see you, Val."

My stomach plunged. A visitor? All my friends in San Nicholas were already in Pie Town. Stretching my mouth into a smile, I walked into the dining area. Officer Carmichael stabbed at his computer-thing with one finger, muttering beneath his breath.

Detective Shaw stood frowning in the center of the dining area, his long arms crossed. He wore an expensive-looking blue suit, and I wondered how he afforded it. My cantankerous piecrust maker would no doubt have a theory.

I approached the lean detective. "Detective Shaw?" I had to tell him about the casebook. "Did you want to see me?"

Carmichael looked up. His lips pressed into a thin line.

"You're open," Shaw boomed, glancing at Carmichael. "And nice to see you supporting a local business, GC. Are you on your break?"

"Lunch," Carmichael said, expressionless.

The gamers watched us, two dice rattling off their table and onto the floor. A pudgy college kid dove for them before they could scatter beneath a booth.

I brushed my already clean hands on my apron and glanced at Carmichael.

He poked the computer screen.

"Someone from your department called and told us we could reopen," I said. "Is there a problem?" Tell him, tell him, tell him. But if I confessed to breaking in, I'd have to tell him about the casebook Charlene had removed, and I couldn't do that to my piecrust specialist. She'd stolen the book. She needed to come clean, and we could fess up together. Still, if it was a clue in a murder investigation, it was my duty to come forward.

Shaw stepped closer, forcing me to crane my neck. "You weren't entirely honest with the police yesterday."

I gnawed my lower lip. Maybe there was a way I could ease into the casebook imbroglio. "You mean, about the cases Joe and his friend, Frank, investigated? I didn't mention it yesterday, because I only just learned about it."

"His little busybody Sherlock Holmes club?" Shaw waved away the idea. "Trivia."

"But maybe he was involved in something that got him killed?"

"Come on. It's not as if those old geezers stumbled across a conspiracy in San Nicholas. Most murders are over money, jealousy, or rage. And then there's negligent homicide."

"Negligent?"

"For example, if someone accidentally put something into a pie they shouldn't have."

"But . . . we didn't! And I heard someone broke in to Joe's house last night. Wouldn't that suggest something?"

"It suggests we've got a local scumbag robbing the homes of the recently deceased."

"But—"

"You withheld some other information, young lady. Something important, and I'd like to know why."

Charlene had pegged Shaw all right. He wasn't taking Joe's cases seriously. And what hadn't I been honest about yesterday? Crikey! Joe and the coffee! "I'm sorry, you're right. I forgot to mention that Joe had complained of having a bad taste in his mouth. But I didn't mean to not tell you. There was so much going on after he collapsed."

"Bad taste? I'm talking about what Mr. Devlin ate. You told me all the victim had consumed was some quiche and a cup of coffee."

"Well, maybe more than one cup. He tended to linger. Wait, victim? Are you saying you found evidence of foul play?"

Shaw's high cheekbones colored. "He ate something

with fruit filling in it. It seems to me that you sold him more than a quiche."

I looked to the counter and its array of rectangular hand pies. "A hand pie?"

"Why didn't you mention it?"

"The day-olds are self-serve. If hc took one, he just dropped the cash in the basket. I wouldn't have known about it."

He sneered. "You wouldn't have known."

"Are you saying it wasn't my quiche, that a pie killed him? That's impossible. Lots of people ate those hand pies yesterday and no one else got sick."

"The hand pies were confiscated—"

"I noticed that, and I'm glad. That will prove it wasn't one of mine."

"And the investigation is still ongoing. Did you have any conflicts with your neighbor?"

"With Joe? No."

"That's not what I heard."

"I liked Joe. He was funny. He came in here every morning for coffee. If we'd had a conflict, he wouldn't have kept returning, would he?"

"So the quiche was a peace offering?"

I laid a hand over my stomach. Not the quiche. It couldn't have been the quiche. "No, Joe and I didn't need to make peace, because we didn't have a problem. I made the quiche for Heidi from the new gym to welcome her to the neighborhood. She said she didn't want it, so Joe took it."

"Heidi, the neighbor you are having a conflict with?"

"That was only fifteen minutes ago! How . . ." Oh, curse my mouth for flapping ahead of my brain. "I met Heidi for the first time yesterday, right before I didn't give her the quiche."

"Only yesterday?" He raised a brow. "It didn't take long for you two to get into an argument."

"We didn't argue." I'd taken her smackdown like a big lump.

"Were you upset, distracted when you were baking yesterday?"

"No! I argued with Heidi after I baked the quiche."

An odd growl emerged from one of the booths, and I twitched. I glanced toward the window booth. Officer Carmichael appeared to be throttling his computer.

"Well, we didn't exactly argue," I repeated in a lower voice. "Heidi suggested I change the Pie Town slogan, that's all, and I said— I don't think I said much of anything. You can ask her."

"I have." He squinted. "Your eyes are pink. Are you on drugs?"

"No!"

"I've heard what goes on in kitchens, all the drugs you chefs take to keep going."

"I'm a baker, not a chef. And I don't do drugs. I didn't sleep well last night." Because I'd lain awake thinking either the killer had been burgling Joe's house and knew who I was, or Pie Town was somehow responsible for Joe's death. Does it make me a horrible person that I preferred the first option? Because if something Joe had eaten here had been responsible for his death, I wasn't sure how I was going to live with myself.

"Guilty conscience?" Detective Shaw raised a brow.

I wracked my brain for a clever retort, but my rusted razor wit failed. My chin lowered, throat tightening. Joe had been an amateur crime solver, had run a comic shop, and had lived in a garish Victorian, and I'd only known one out of three. He'd had loads of life under his belt, and he'd been cheerful, someone worth knowing better. But I'd missed my chance. "But Joe's cases. He kept a casebook—"

"Don't leave town, Miss Harris." Shaw gave me a last long look, as if to impress upon me the gravity of the situation, and sauntered out.

Leave? I couldn't if I wanted to. Short of packing it in and joining a monastery, I had nowhere to go. Everything I had was in Pie Town.

I rubbed my jaw with my knuckles. If there was anything wrong with the quiche, then there were only two obvious suspects—me and Charlene. I couldn't confess our break-in and drop Charlene into the proverbial fire. But I couldn't walk away either, not when we were holding on to potential evidence.

Feeling sick, I plodded into the kitchen. At the central, metal table, I arranged a steaming mini-potpie on a plate, grabbed some tableware, and returned with them to the dining area.

Officer Carmichael mouthed curses at his computer tablet.

I laid the pie in front of him, along with the utensils wrapped in a napkin. "Here you go. The coffee's serve yourself. Feel free to go up and get a refill from the counter."

He didn't look up from his computer. "It wasn't the quiche," he said in a low voice. "Your food's fine."

I swallowed, hoping it was true, wondering why he was telling me. "The pie's hot. Be careful."

He grunted, pecking at his computer with two fingers.

I returned to the kitchen. Walking to a wooden shelf, I straightened the plastic jugs of spices. It wasn't the quiche or a hand pie. I hadn't killed Joe, and Heidi hadn't been an intended target. And Carmichael was sitting in my window. . . . Why? Not just for a convenient lunch spot to abuse his computer. But he wasn't afraid of my baking. His presence in my window booth was sort of a vote of confidence, and after last night, I was glad to have him nearby.

I only hoped passersby didn't assume he was on a stakeout.

Chapter 5

"How well do you know Joe?" I ran a ball of dough through the flattening machine. Sunlight streamed through the skylight, glinting off the metal refrigerator doors, the ovens. I'd turned off the big oven, with its rotating racks that guaranteed an even bake. It was a restored, fifty-year-old behemoth that could bake fifty pies at a time. But there was no sense in wasting energy.

No customers had poured into Pie Town after Carmichael's departure. I baked anyway, using the small ovens, my gloved hands coated with flour, under the premise that if I baked it, they would come.

Except they didn't.

Petronella adjusted the net over her black hair, tucking the cigarette more firmly behind her right ear. I'd never seen her actually smoke. Was the cigarette an affectation or a talisman? "I knew him."

I spread the dough on the lightly floured work island and cut it into rectangles. Since traffic was low, now was a good time to experiment. I'd mix my fresh strawberries with mascarpone cheese for hand pies. "I'm sorry. You really held it together yesterday when he . . . I'm sorry," I repeated, feeling lame.

She blinked. "He went to my parents' church. I didn't know him know him. But I saw him around a lot, especially here, and we joked around. He was a cool guy. Easygoing."

Yeah. My vision blurred, and I blinked. Time to change the subject. "Did Charlene tell you she once dated Joe?"

"What?" Petronella laughed, laying out my piecrust pieces in rows on a baking sheet. "You're kidding. Those two had a thing? I'm glad. Charlene needs someone in her life. Her daughter hasn't been back to visit once since she left for Europe four years ago."

"Not even for the holidays?"

Petronella shook her head.

"Why not?"

"She blames Charlene for her father's death," Petronella said.

"Why?"

"Mr. McCree had a heart attack surfing. Her daughter thought Charlene should have stopped him, that he was too old."

"Wasn't it his choice?" I fed another round of dough into the flattener.

"Of course. Charlene didn't make him go into the ocean. She hates surfing."

I had a low opinion of my father for the simple reason I'd never met him. But this grudge against Charlene didn't seem fair. It did, however, explain why Charlene rarely spoke of her daughter. "How is it that I know you want a degree in funerary services, dream of traveling to Iceland, and have a thing for Russian poets? But I didn't know much about Joe aside from he owned a comic shop, was a widower, and hated the Giants."

She scrunched up her face. "What else do you need to know?"

"Who was he?"

"That would have been a better question for Frank," she said.

"Frank."

We fell silent. Joe and Frank used to sit together in the corner booth. Portly and balding and with the kind of tweed cap taxi drivers wear in the movies, Frank had passed away about a month ago. I'd gone to his funeral, but hadn't known anyone there aside from Joe, Petronella, and Charlene, so I hadn't stayed for the wake. Frank had been quieter than Joe, laughing at his jokes, smiling at the cashiers. But I hadn't gotten very close to him either. I'd been skimming the surface of San Nicholas.

"Well," she said, "if we're gossiping—"

"We're not. Hey, would you mind zesting a lime?"

"I can tell you that Charlene's loaded."

I blinked and had to grab for the round wheel of dough as it emerged from the other side of the machine. That would track with Charlene's comment about other properties she owned. "Then why is she working here?"

She grabbed a lime from a metal basket and scrubbed it along a grater into a striped bowl. "Because she wants to, I guess. Oh, and her husband used to chase me out of their yard when I was a kid. There was a shortcut out by the creek I liked to take." Smiling, she turned the lime, zesting away.

"She doesn't talk about her husband much." And I hadn't prodded, because Charlene was a widow, and I'd sensed his death was still an open wound. "What did he do?"

"A professional—what do you call it?—sommelier."

"Is that why her daughter is in the wine business?" I cut the second piecrust into rectangles.

"Yeah. I wish I could go to France. Or is she in Belgium? She's somewhere with cheese." She handed me the bowl, and I dumped the zest into a larger, metal bowl piled with strawberries and mascarpone. I dropped in an egg, dribbled in agave syrup, and mixed it all with a metal spoon.

"I'm pretty sure they've both got cheese," I said. "What about you?"

She pressed the lime, squeezing the juice into the bowl. "What about me?"

I knew she had dreams beyond Pie Town. But I wasn't sure if she was serious about the degree in funeral services.

The bell above the front entrance rang.

Petronella glanced at me and widened her eyes.

Whoa, a customer!

Peeling off my gloves, I darted from the kitchen. In the corner booth, two more young men had joined the gamers and frowned over sheets of paper covered in arcane charts.

A Eurasian woman about my age stood at the counter, her hand poised above the bell as if unsure about committing. To ring? Or not to ring? That was the question.

"Hi," I said, "can I help you?"

"Maybe. I hope so." Her gaze swept the glass counter, filled with unsold pies. "I'm Joy Devlin, your new neighbor." She had the long, lean body of a gym rat, but the rumpled, black business suit and sensible heels didn't shout free weights and yoga lessons. She yanked tight her ponytail of straight, ebony hair.

"Are you Heidi's partner?" I asked.

Expressionless, she shoved her wire-frame glasses further up her nose. "Who's Heidi?"

So she wasn't allied with my new, bursting-with-health arch-nemesis.

"Joe Devlin was my uncle," she said in a rat-a-tat monotone. "He left me the comic shop, along with his house. I just came from the police station. I don't suppose you serve anything stronger than coffee?"

"Only pie."

Her tawny eyes narrowed. "Strawberry-rhubarb?"

"Would you like a slice?" Strawberry-rhubarb was my favorite, another point in her favor.

"Better bring out the whole pie. It's been that kind of day."

My kind of girl. I handed her a coffee cup and nodded toward the urn. "It's on me. The pie too. I'm sorry for your loss."

"You don't have to do that," she said.

"Yes, I do. Would you like me to heat a slice?"

She nodded.

Joy sat in a window booth, and I warmed a slice of pie, bringing it to her on a plate with the rest of the pie in its tin.

She nodded toward the empty bench opposite. "You were here when it happened?"

I slid onto the seat across from her. "Yes." I hoped she wasn't going to ask if he'd died in pain. I wasn't sure how I'd answer that, because the pain had looked ferocious.

She stabbed at the lattice piecrust, and it broke into flakes. "I suppose that's something. At least he died doing what he wanted, out and about. He and his buddy, Frank, talked a lot about this place. They were thrilled when you moved in." Her brows pulled together. "And now they're both gone."

"I'm sorry. It's so strange not to see them together in their booth." I nodded toward the corner. "I wish I could tell you more," I said. "Detective Shaw seems to be the officer in charge. He was on the scene pretty fast. You might want to talk to him."

She tilted her head, questioning, her ponytail cascading over one shoulder.

"We called nine-one-one," I explained. "Everyone came. Police, fire, ambulance."

"I know. Shaw called me."

"Oh," I said. So why was she asking me?

"Joe was a good guy. He was old, but . . ." Her breath hitched. "I wasn't expecting this."

"Did he have any allergies?"

"Not that I know of."

"Were you close?"

Her shoulders slumped. "I visited most weekends. And in thanks he left me his house and a comic shop I can't sell and will now be forced to run."

"His house?" I never should have let Charlene flimflam me into raiding it. I drummed my fingers on the table.

"It's a run-down Victorian. God knows how much it will cost to renovate. And some jerk broke into it last night."

"Really?" I squeaked. "Was anything taken? Do the police know who did it?"

"I can't tell. The police were useless."

"So why can't you sell his store?" I asked, anxious to change the subject.

"Want to buy a comic shop?"

"Uh, no."

"That's why."

"But why do you have to run it?"

"I've been unemployed for two years now. Strangely, the market for herbalists is glutted in California. A house for me is here. A business is here, and I'll make that comic shop turn a profit or die trying." She frowned at her pie.

"Have you ever run a comic shop?"

She shrugged. "I spent enough time in it with Joe. The accounting is easy enough. His employees are comic geeks—they're familiar with what sells." She took a bite of pie. "This is good, by the way."

"Thanks."

Charlene waved frantically at me from the kitchen.

What was she doing here, again, twice in one afternoon? Watching to make sure I didn't spill the beans? Beans! I'd forgotten to put a vanilla bean into the strawberry-mascarpone mixture.

I rose. "If you need anything, let me know." Leaving it to Joy to decide if I was referring to food or comfort, I hurried through the swinging door.

Charlene grasped my arm and pulled me into my office. Whipping off her cloche hat, she shook loose her snowy hair. "Did you tell Petronella anything?"

"And you say I'm obsessed with Pie Town. Your shift ended hours ago."

"Did you say anything to Petronella?"

"What would I tell her?"

"Nothing. She's a good girl. I wouldn't want to get her mixed up in the conspiracy, not after last night. The fewer people we tell, the better. I realized something when I was looking at the casebook this morning."

I crossed my arms over my chest. So murder and burglary wasn't enough for Drama Queen Charlene, and it was a conspiracy now? "What did you realize?"

"It's not in Joe's handwriting."

"And that means . . . ?"

"It's Frank's casebook, not Joe's. Frank must have written up the cases in the book before he died, and Joe took his book for some reason."

"Nostalgia? As a memento mori?"

Her eyes flashed. "I'll bet Joe investigated the last cases in honor of Frank."

"It's hocus-pocus. You can't twist the facts to fit your theories."

"Why not?"

"Charlene, if you believe the casebook has to do with Joe's death, we need to confess and give it to the police."

"It's kind of you to say 'we.' I'm the one who took the book. I'm the one who dragged you into this mess." She sank against my metal desk, her shoulders slumped. "Do you really think Shaw will listen to anything I have to say? When he looks at me, all he sees is a useless old fool. Maybe he's right. I used to live an interesting life. We all did. And then Joe and Frank were reduced to their little club, and I'm . . . I don't know what I'm doing."

"Charlene . . . That's not . . . You're not useless."

She blew out her breath. "Useless or not, there's no sense in feeling sorry for myself. If Shaw won't take Joe's death seriously, I owe it to him to bring him justice."

"The police are on this. Shaw's investigating Joe's death as a possible homicide."

"He thinks someone in Pie Town accidentally slipped cyanide into Joe's meal."

"Shaw did mention negligent homicide," I admitted. Was she right? Was Shaw so fixated on human error that he was blind to an actual murder?

"You should have heard him questioning me. 'Aren't you a little old to be working with the public, Mrs. McCree?'"

"But—"

The bell above the entrance tinkled faintly.

"A customer?" Charlene asked.

"Doubtful." Today had been awful.

The counter bell pinged.

"Excuse me." I scuttled from my office to the order area and felt the blood drain from my face.

My ex, Mark, stood jammed between two bar stools, his blue suit bunching up against the counter. He ran a hand through his dirty blond hair, trying to tame the shock that always seemed to drift out of place.

I itched to brush it back and clenched my fists, jamming them into my apron pockets.

A middle-aged blond standing next to Mark spoke to him in a low voice. He bent to hear her, laughed.

Another man examined an empty coffee cup. Bull-necked and bald, he wore jeans and a polo shirt, and looked to be in his midfifties. I knew him from somewhere, but I couldn't place him. He wasn't a customer—I'd have remembered that.

I cleared my throat to mask the frenzied banging of my heart. "Welcome to Pie Town. How can I help you?"

Mark turned.

I tried to look surprised. "Hi, Mark. What are you doing here?" My voice wavered, and I twisted my mouth into a smile.

"Hi, Val." He studied a plastic menu. "The place looks great."

"Thanks!"

"Have you, uh, got a minute?" he asked.

I glanced at Joy, my lone, nongamer customer. She took a thoughtful bite of her strawberry-rhubarb.

"You've caught me on a slow day." And because I couldn't bear to look at my ex-fiancé, I stretched out my hand to the blond. "I'm Val Harris."

We clasped hands, hers cool and loose in mine. Her smile was brisk. "Antheia Royer." She motioned to the man beside her. "And this is Jack Sharp."

Mark's face turned a shade darker. "Sorry, I should have introduced you. Antheia's on the library board with me. Jack's on the town council."

"Chairman. And that makes me mayor this year." Sharp shoved his large hands in the pockets of his jeans, multi-tasking a bicep flex at the same time.

"Oh, right. San Nicholas has a rotating mayorship." I glanced at Mark. "When did you join the library board?" My hands bunched in my white and pink apron. Dumb,

dumb, dumb. Now he'd think I cared. But Frank's casebook had mentioned the library board in the Case of the Bloated Blond. And last night's burglar had seemed interested in that casebook. Could Antheia be the blond? The burglar had struck me as bulky, but beneath the right loose-fitting clothing, Antheia might fit the bill. So could Mark for that matter. Or the mayor. Charlene was right. What was the point of telling the police about the burglar when I had nothing helpful to say?

"I joined a couple months ago," Mark said, his expression cool. "A lot has changed for us both, since . . ." He pulled his shoulders back. "I heard about your murder."

"My murder?" My voice snapped an octave higher. "The papers haven't said anything about a murder." How could the autopsy be finished? Because my mother had been under fifty when she'd died, the state had required an autopsy. It had taken weeks before I was allowed to bury her. If Joe's was a potential crime, maybe his autopsy had been fast tracked. But if the police suspected murder, wouldn't they have been more heavy handed with me?

Sharp shot Mark a warning look. "That's unofficial."

My stomach clenched. I couldn't deny it any longer. The burglar, the cops . . . It was murder, and that meant Pie Town might be deserted for a lot longer than a day or two, even if my food wasn't responsible. I didn't want to think about what it meant that Charlene and I were holding possible evidence—the casebook—or that the person we'd run into last night might be the killer. On the bright side, he might have been a run-of-the-mill sleazebag, looking to take advantage of an empty house.

"Are you here for a pie?" I asked.

"Uh, no," Mark said. "We were passing by, and I wanted to stop in. I know you have a five-year lease—"

"You should, since you negotiated it," I said.

"And I've got another client who would love to take it over."

Dizzy, I braced my hands on the pink countertop. I knew my presence made Mark uncomfortable. But I wasn't staying in San Nicholas to annoy him. Leaving would mean losing Pie Town. Mark understood that. "Pie Town opened five months ago." My voice was steady. Good. "We've been doing well, but I'm not ready to expand to a new location yet."

Mark leaned across the counter and dropped his voice. "Val, I understand what this place means to you, but there's no shame in starting over somewhere else. This is a small town. People aren't going to forget a murder in your pie shop. Get out now while you've got an offer on the table."

"Joe might have died here," I said, stung by the betrayal, "but his death had nothing to do with Pie Town."

Joy looked up from her pie.

"Did you know that Joe and his friend, Frank, liked to investigate funny little cases around town?" I asked, all business. Who cared if Mark couldn't stand to see me in San Nicholas? After all, our relationship was over. But maybe the mayor could help us talk to Shaw, convince him the casebook should be investigated.

Mayor Sharp laughed. "What jokesters those two were."

"Jokesters?" I asked.

"Their ridiculous cases. Well, when you get older, I guess you need something to keep busy."

Or maybe the mayor wouldn't help. I slogged onward. "Before he died, Joe was investigating a case having to do with someone who worked on the library board. He called it the Case of the Bloated B—" I stopped. If the blond in question was Antheia, I didn't want to be insulting. "I can't remember. Did you know him, Antheia?"

She glanced at Sharp. "We were both members of the San Nicholas Business Association. You should join."

I nodded. "Did he ever talk to you about—"

"It sounds like you and old Joe were buddies." Mark fiddled with his cuffs.

"We were neighbors," I said. "You know how it is. He came in here nearly every morning for coffee, but so did a lot of people. And when the police figure out what happened to Joe, my customers will return. Are you sure you wouldn't like a slice of pie?"

Sharp patted his washboard abs. "I don't do sugar. But good luck, Val. San Nicholas needs small businesses. I hope to see you at the next association meeting."

"I'll be there," I lied, plastering on a smile. I enjoyed chatting with customers, but networking? No thanks.

Mark pushed his business card across the counter to me. "If you change your mind about the lease."

I glanced at the shiny card. Mark's photo smiled wistfully at me from one laminated corner. He had a new mobile number, but he couldn't have made the change because of me, since I never called him. Our contacts had been limited to monthly, unsuccessful e-mails from me asking to get my stuff out of his storage locker. He always found reasons not to be available. At this point, I wasn't sure why I even bothered. I had nowhere to put my things anyway.

"Thanks for stopping by," I said, and watched them leave.

Joy strolled to the counter and poured herself a cup of coffee. "I couldn't help overhearing—since you were practically shouting—do you really think my uncle was killed over one of those cases?"

"No. I mean, I'm not sure. No. I just wanted to get them out of here. Was I shouting?"

"Speaking loudly. If it makes you feel any better, your ex looked pretty hot under the collar too."

"Did he? How did you know . . ." I trailed off, my toes curling. Small town. Was there anyone in San Nicholas who wasn't in on our breakup?

She lowered her head, gazing at me over her glasses, and stirred sweetener into the coffee. "Joe told me about his cases. I'm not even sure they qualified as petty crimes."

"Did the police tell you they suspected foul play?" I asked.

"They were careful not to tell me much of anything, aside from the fact the investigation is still ongoing, and I can't bury my uncle yet. I learned more in fifteen minutes at Pie Town than an hour at the police station."

"They've been cagey with me too."

"It's obvious they think something's wrong, but murder?" Joy asked. "That's got to be idle gossip."

"But this gossip came through the chairman of the town council."

Joy's brows crumpled downward. "I shouldn't think the cops would be reporting to the town council on investigations. Have you got a box? I think I'll take the rest of the pie to go."

Sliding a flattened cardboard box from behind the counter, I unfolded it. I loved my retro, pink boxes with their white script, an inversion of our logo, even if I'd spent way too much time designing them.

Was Mark right? Was today's drop in customers more than a blip? Had San Nicholas marked Pie Town for death? One thing was for sure—the longer Joe's demise remained unsolved and unexplained, the longer my pies would remain unsold.

A lump swelled in my throat. I'd put everything I had—all my savings, all the money from my mother's life insurance—into Pie Town. I couldn't lose the pie shop, couldn't fail. I'd be failing her all over again.

"Are you okay?" Joy asked.

"Fine." I smiled and boxed the rest of her pie. "Seriously, if there's anything I can do to help, let me know."

"Thanks." Tossing her ponytail, she strode outside.

I walked into my office. A good coupon, that was what Pie Town needed. Buy one pie, get the second half off? No, who wants two pies at once? Maybe a 10-percent-off coupon. Or even 25 percent. I halted in my office doorway.

Charlene snapped a photo of my beast of a wedding dress, which had somehow found its way back to the bookcase. She shuffled away, pursing her lips. "Forget everything that happened last night," she said, not looking at me. "You're innocent in this, and it was wrong of me to drag you into my troubles. Consider our investigation over."

"Does this mean you've decided to take the casebook to the police?"

"I don't know what I was thinking"—she waved her hand, lethargic—"that I could be some hotshot detective? Shaw's right. I'm past it."

"Shaw actually said that to you?" I asked, indignant.

"I called Shaw and told him everything, everything but your involvement. He wasn't interested."

"What?"

"He told me Joe's cases were a joke, and it was my bad luck to run into a burglar."

"But . . . the burglar wanted the casebook!"

"I told him that, but as he pointed out, I couldn't really prove it."

"But I was there too. I saw it. I'll call him."

"Forget about it, Val. The only reason I'm not in jail

is he thinks I'm feeble. If he learns I covered up your involvement, he'll only get suspicious. Of you."

"But—"

"He knows everything he needs to know, and he doesn't care. It's over."

Oh, no it wasn't. Pie Town was empty. Joe was dead. Charlene was giving up. It was wrong, all of it. "The casebook, did you bring it with you?"

She clutched her phone to her chest, forehead wrinkling. "No. What do you want with it?"

"I think it deserves another look."

Chapter 6

I turned the sign in the window to CLOSED. Outside, fog grayed the rooftops. Sunset wouldn't be far behind and neither would Charlene. She'd promised to return with Frank's casebook.

Joining Charlene as the newest Baker Street Boy was probably a cosmically bad idea, but I was all out of good ones.

I unlocked the door and stepped onto the sidewalk. A chill wind blew through me, carrying salt and damp, and I shivered, clutched my arms. Turning the key in the lock, I hurried down the cracked sidewalk toward the comic shop. I halted beneath an ornate streetlamp. A shiny, new, brass arrow proclaimed: FINE DINING. It pointed away from Pie Town.

Was the universe conspiring against me? Where did that arrow come from? It was likely pointing to that fancy new seafood place and not intended to imply Pie Town was less than fine. But I wondered how I could get an arrow that said Pies. I should have thought of this myself.

Shaking my head, I walked into the comic shop. Heat blasted me as I entered.

A shaggy-haired blond with broad shoulders and a beer gut looked up from behind the counter. "Hey," he said.

"Hi." Could he have been the one who'd broken into Joe's house? I didn't think last night's burglar had such a round stomach, so I was probably safe. But I edged between the racks, putting distance between us.

I wandered the gray-carpeted aisles, past shelves of gilded action figures and plastic-wrapped comics arranged in cardboard bins like old records. Thumbing through a bin, I picked up a comic featuring a teenage vampire killer. If I was going to ingratiate myself at the comic shop, I had to buy something, and this beat the other muscle-bound superheroes.

I walked to the counter, laying the comic beside the register. From high on the wall behind it, a row of villain masks glowered.

The clerk grunted. "Good one."

"Thanks. Have we met? I'm from Pie Town."

His cornflower-blue eyes lit. "The pie shop? Man, we were so happy when you opened up." He patted his gut. "I had to cut back though. I've got a weakness for cherry pie."

"You're not alone." And now I would segue into a subtle but incisive question about who might have killed Joe.

And I had no idea how I was going to do that. "I'm sorry about Joe. He was a good guy."

"Yeah."

"You must have known him well."

"He was the boss."

I tried again. "Some people are saying he was murdered," I said.

He rang up my comic. "Murdered? No way."

"But I suppose everyone has enemies."

The clerk gave a short laugh. "Joe? Enemies? Who?"

"That's a good question." I handed him a fiver. "Who do you think?"

"I don't. I mean, whenever a customer got annoyed, Joe would figure out a way to smooth it over. He was really good with that. Want a bag?"

"Sure. Did customers get annoyed often?"

"Comic book readers are lovers, not fighters. I mean, sure, they've got fantasies about being bad-ass superheroes—who doesn't? But inside, they're teddy bears."

"Did Heidi ever come into the shop?" Maybe she'd slipped some arsenic into Joe's coffee as part of a dastardly plot to put Pie Town out of business.

"Who?"

"Heidi. From the new gym next door." Okay, maybe that theory was over the top. But was it so wrong to want her to be the killer?

"Oh, the hot blond."

I straightened. Wait, the gym owner had come in? She hadn't struck me as a comic book person. Maybe she did have some secret, dark relationship with Joe, and—

"Nope," he said. "She never came in here. Want a bag?"

I slumped. Rats.

He handed me my change, then slid the comic into a white, paper bag and laid it on the counter. "Enjoy the vampire slaying."

"Thanks." How had Joe managed his investigations? So far, the only thing I'd uncovered was that I was a terrible detective, and that was no surprise. But I had one suspect—Joe's niece and comic store heiress—and I was on the case. "Is Joy available?"

"Joy?"

"Joe's niece? The new owner?"

"Oh, yeah. Miss Devlin. Yeah. She's here." He stood rooted behind the counter.

"May I see her?"

"Oh. I guess. Wait a second." He vanished into a back room.

Maybe it wasn't me. Maybe this kid was just a tough nut to crack. Oh, who was I kidding? If I couldn't even interrogate a guy selling comic books, I had no business looking into Joe's death.

Joy emerged from the back room, rubbing a palm into her eye. "Who . . . Oh." She slid her glasses from the top of her head onto her nose. "Hi, Val. What are you doing here?"

I raised my plastic bag. "On a quest for reading material. I was closing up and thought I'd drop in, see how things were going."

"Come on in." Turning, she disappeared into the back room.

Cautious, I followed. Boxes teetered in cobwebby corners and atop dusty, metal cabinets. Joy sank into an executive chair behind a scarred, wooden desk. She motioned me to a folding chair, and I sat.

"Rough day?" I asked.

"Joe had things well organized." She sniffed. "But it's weird going through his stuff without him." She picked up a man's tweed cap and laid it atop an old-fashioned, ten-key adding machine. "I don't know what I'm going to do with half the things in the house."

"Do you have to do anything right away?"

"No, I guess not." She nudged a mechanical pencil with the tip of her finger, and it rolled across the desk. Stooping, she opened a drawer, pulling out a bottle of brandy and two shot glasses. "Want some?"

"Okay." I didn't, but I could see that Joy did.

She poured the shots and handed me a glass. "To Joe."

"To Joe."

We clinked glasses. I shot back the brandy and choked down a cough.

She relaxed into her chair, and it creaked beneath her. "I'm still trying to wrap my brain around the idea that Joe might have been murdered. The police wouldn't give me a definite cause of death, but they're keeping Joe's body. They must think his death isn't natural. Is it possible?"

"It looks that way." Joy had been awfully quick to tell me she wasn't thrilled by her uncle's inheritance—a case of the lady protesting too much? But would someone kill for a comic shop and an old Victorian?

"Who would have wanted my uncle dead?" she asked.

"We didn't exactly talk enemies lists."

"What did you talk about?"

"Starting up a business. Baseball. I can't believe he was an A's fan." Oh, hey. Who was interrogating whom here?

"Me neither, but that was Joe." She poured two more shots. "To baseball."

Gulping it down, I winced. The more I drank, the more she'd pour. I gripped the shot glass between my hands, trying to hide that it was empty. "Did your uncle mention any enemies?"

"No. Oh, there were plenty of people he didn't like— mostly politicians, but everybody hates them."

"He didn't say anything about the new gym, by any chance?"

"The gym?" One corner of her mouth moved ever so slightly. "My uncle wasn't a gym person."

Okay. Enough about Heidi. It had been a desperate idea anyway. "What about those cases he investigated?" I asked.

Joy's lips quirked in a tight smile. "His little two-man club was a fine excuse for him and Frank to drink beer and make up stories."

"Make up? So they didn't conduct investigations?" I looked at the stained linoleum floor and chewed my lip, disappointed. Maybe Shaw had been right to dismiss Charlene's confession.

She raised a brow. "I think the point of armchair investigating is not leaving the chair."

That didn't bode well for Charlene's theory that someone killed Joe over a Holmes-style case. But the burglar had seemed interested in the casebook. Or throttling me.

I eyed her. Last night's burglar had looked bulkier than Joy, but I wasn't sure I could trust that impression. And what if she had an accomplice? On the other hand, why would she need to break in to her uncle's house? She had every right to be there.

"It must have been an accident," Joy said. "Maybe my uncle ate something he shouldn't . . ." Meeting my gaze, she flushed.

I sucked in my cheeks, my temperature rising. "You've got no reason to believe me, but there was nothing wrong with that quiche. There's nothing poisonous in Pie Town's kitchen."

"You'd have to be the stupidest criminal ever to poison my uncle in your own pie shop. Besides, the police searched your kitchen for poisons after he died."

"Where did you hear that?" I asked.

"Detective Shaw told me, and that they hadn't found anything toxic."

My face tightened. "That's more than Shaw told me." And it seemed to knock out his negligent homicide theory. Was someone at Pie Town a suspect, or did Shaw simply enjoy watching me twist? I dragged my fingers through my hair, pulling loose my chignon. "I hope that detail makes it into the papers."

"You haven't read the local news today, have you?" She reached into her giant, leather purse on the floor and pulled out a rumpled newspaper. Unfolding it, she slid it across the desk toward me.

DEATH AT PIE TOWN, the headline shrieked.

"Page one," I said weakly. Scanning the article, I sprang from my chair. "They interviewed Heidi? That . . . How could she?" I choked on a dozen ripe swear words, because when you're in the hospitality industry, you have to learn not to curse.

Nothing in the article said that a pie had killed him, but the article was carefully worded to insinuate our guilt. The nail in the coffin was Heidi's lecture on Killer Sugar.

My hands trembled, and a loose insert slid to the floor. I bent to pick up the glossy sheet, an ad for Mark Jeffreys Realty, complete with that stupid photo. Folding the insert, I stuffed it inside the newspaper. "I'm surprised you ordered a pie."

"I grabbed that newspaper after I left. But I know your kitchen is innocent."

Rising, I shook my head. "After this article, you're the only person in San Nicholas who will believe that."

"I'm not sure if anything in there is actually libelous," she said.

I groaned. "It doesn't matter. Even if it was libel, I couldn't afford to sue." I checked the byline—Chet Atkinson, one of Mark's buddies from high school. No wonder Mark thought I was prepping to flee the scene. I held up the newspaper. "Can I keep this? I want to show it to my piecrust specialist, Charlene." My crust maker knew this town. She might have some ideas for handling the negative publicity. I considered asking Mark for help with his journo friend and dismissed the idea. Mark didn't want anything to do with me unless I was signing over a lease.

Joy raised a brow. "Charlene? Charlene McCree? Is she your piecrust person?"

"Best in five counties."

"You are aware that she's nuts?"

"What do you mean?"

She barked a laugh. "You're kidding. She's been working for you, and she hasn't buttonholed you about Roswell yet?"

"Who's Roswell?"

"You'll see."

"How do you know Charlene?"

"She and Joe were friends. I think they even went out on a couple dates. Trust me. Nuts."

I shifted my weight. "Um, you do mean she's nuts in a delightfully eccentric way, not poison-in-the-piecrust way?"

She lifted a brow. "You'll see."

Chapter 7

Newspaper beneath my arm, I returned to Pie Town and locked up behind me. Light from the overhead lamps glinted off the countertops, the empty booths, the checkerboard floor. Devoid of customers, the dining area seemed less whimsically retro and more past its sell-by date. Fog pressed against the windows. Drawing the blinds, I shivered and hurried to my office.

Charlene, seated in my chair, looked up from my desk. The white cat around her neck yawned.

I yelped and scuttled backward. "What are you doing in here? And with your cat!?"

"I've got a key." She lifted her chin, her mercury curls quivering. "And Frederick gets lonely. Don't freak out, we didn't go through the kitchen. Wouldn't do to have cat hair in the quiche." She cackled.

Was Frederick lonely or my widowed piecrust maker? Whatever the case, she looked more cheerful than she had that afternoon. "How did you get a key?"

"Well, I didn't want to wait outside, not when there's a murderer lurking about."

Which didn't answer the question, but at least she wasn't wearing her cat burglar attire. In spite of Frederick, she looked suspiciously staid in a prim white blouse, tailored gray jacket, and straight skirt. "And why are you dressed like an insurance agent?" I asked.

She handed me the leather-bound casebook. "I've been going through Frank's notes, thinking of our plan of attack."

"Charlene, I spoke with Joe's niece today—"

"You did? Good! I'm glad to see you're taking the dragon by the horns."

"Don't you mean 'bull'? And do dragons even have . . . ?"

Charlene glared at me over her glasses.

Never mind. I handed her the newspaper, folded to the DEATH AT PIE TOWN article. "Have you read this?"

"Why would I? No one believes anything in that rag. It's filled with lurid tabloid tosh."

"But Pie Town was practically empty today."

She scooted the chair around the desk and looked me in the eye. "Exactly. That's why we need to solve this crime."

I shook my head, throwing in the dish towel on penetrating her circular logic. "Joy said none of the cases were serious, but—"

Charlene wagged a gnarled finger at me, her brows lowering. "At least one was deadly serious. Joe didn't tell his niece everything, because he didn't want to worry her. People get up to all sorts of skullduggery in this town."

I sat against the desk, dislodging my stapler. "Skullduggery?"

"Not to mention mayhem."

"But . . . San Nicholas is boring!"

"That's why they do it."

"Augh." Tucking my chin, I batted the casebook against my forehead.

"I think we should tackle the Case of the Mysterious Lights and the Mystery of the Thudding Footfalls," Charlene said. "We'll interview the witnesses tonight. The Case of the Whispering Wanderer is a dead end. All we've got there is the case title—not a single note. We've no idea what that one's about. Tomorrow, you can use your feminine wiles and tackle your ex-fiancé at the library board and that handsome policeman about the Case of the Bloated Blond."

I dropped the casebook to my lap. While I could lattice a piecrust like nobody's business, I was no PI. "I don't have any feminine wiles! I'm wileless. And, ew . . . I'm not talking to Shaw unless I'm confessing I was in Joe's house with you. He's a jerk." And there was no way I was going to Mark for help. He'd only think I was trying to get back together. There were so many bad, bad things that could happen if I went to him for help. What if I got misty? Or started having feelings for him? Or he thought I had feelings for him? Ew, ew, ew.

"Don't bother talking to that idiot Shaw. It won't do any good. I was referring to that Carmichael fellow who had lunch in here this afternoon. He's sweet on you."

"Officer Carmichael?" I ran my thumb over the casebook's binding. "No. He's just doing his job."

"Sitting in the window eating lunch for all to see, at a restaurant accused of poisoning its patrons? It was a thoughtful gesture. And he wouldn't do it if he wasn't interested in you."

I rubbed the nape of my neck, my cheeks tingling. "He's probably nice to everybody. And how did you know he was here? You'd already left."

"It's a small town. People talk."

"He might have been eating lunch here because he was suspicious. Maybe he's part of the investigation."

"He's a beat cop." She jabbed an invisible opponent with a gnarled fist. "All rough and tumble, life on the mean streets. Murder investigations are kicked upstairs to the likes of Shaw, and that's our mutual problem."

"Well, if I see Officer Carmichael again, I'll ask if he's heard anything. But I'm pretty sure he'll say it's confidential."

She arched her brows. "And your weasel realtor of an ex-boyfriend?"

"He's not a weasel." I cradled Frank's casebook to my stomach.

"He's a realtor."

"There's nothing wrong with realtors."

Frederick's tail curled on her blouse.

"So are you going to see him tomorrow or not?" she asked.

"Not. It would be weird."

Charlene banged her fist on the desk, rattling the pencils. "Joe's dead! Pie Town's at stake! Not to mention our freedom!"

"Charlene, there was nothing wrong with our pies. Officer Carmichael told me so."

"Ah-ha! So he does have a soft spot for you!"

"But you can't tell anyone about the quiche. It's confidential. The point is, we're off the hook." I didn't like that Shaw thought Charlene had been alone in Joe's house. If I weighed in, would he pay more attention? He hadn't listened earlier when I'd told him about the casebook.

"But Joe's still dead," Charlene said, "and the cops will never find out who killed him the way they're going. Now are we going to investigate or not?"

"Fine," I huffed. "We'll investigate."

Standing, Charlene ripped Frank's casebook from my hands and opened it, flipping the pages. "Here we go then. The Mystery of the Thudding Footfalls. Miss Pargiter is being plagued with trespassers. She lives on a cliff over the ocean—"

"Probably kids."

"What?"

"If she lives near the beach," I said, "it's probably kids."

"No, it isn't. I said she lives over the ocean, not over the beach. You can't swim around those cliffs. There are rocks and tides and no sand at all. So I've called and told her we'd visit her tonight."

"And is that why you're dressed like an insurance agent?"

She smoothed the front of her blouse. "This is the attire of a professional investigator. Do you expect me to wear a deerstalker hat and smoke a pipe like Joe?"

I grinned, delighted by the image. "Did he really?"

"I told you, he was deadly serious about his investigations."

"Because a deerstalker hat doesn't sound deadly serious."

She lifted a parka from the back of my chair and shrugged into it. "Stop your bellyaching and put a jacket on. It's cold out, and we've got an investigation. Someone killed Joe, and someone wanted that casebook enough to break into his house."

"Maybe."

"What do you mean, maybe?"

"Maybe it was just a regular burglar, and when he saw we had the book, he thought it must be valuable, so he wanted it too."

She stared at me. "Seriously?"

"Fine. Sorry. You're right. But I want to check something first." I slid the laptop across the desk and typed poison bad taste in mouth into the search engine.

"What are you doing?" she asked.

"Joe said he had a weird taste in his mouth. I'm trying to see what poisons might have caused it."

"So?"

But there were too many possibilities. "Strychnine, arsenic, bad mushrooms, castor beans—"

"Forget that for now. We're burning moonlight."

"Fine." I grabbed a sky-blue peacoat hanging from the corner of the bookcase and put it on. Why was I still in denial? There was a chance that casebook was a part of his murder. Even if it wasn't, I couldn't let Charlene investigate on her own. She might break a hip. And I'd liked Joe too.

"Better take a scarf as well. It's a damp night."

Going into the closet, I pulled a suitcase from behind my mattress and dug out a thick, cable-knit scarf.

"And a hat," Charlene called.

And a matching hat. I wrapped up, pulling the hat low.

"Mittens might not be a bad idea either," Charlene said.

"I don't have any mittens." Backing out of the closet, I swung a messenger bag across my shoulder.

"No mittens? How can you reach the ripe age of twenty eight—"

"How do you know I'm twenty-eight?"

"It's on your driver's license."

"How did you see my driver's license?"

"How can you not have any mittens?"

"I'm from Southern California, and stay out of my wallet." I strode out of the office and through the kitchen to the rear entrance.

"Well, you're in Northern California now. Find yourself a pair of mittens. Or gloves. Or even fingerless gloves. Though I prefer my fingers covered. Have you seen those fingerless mittens with the little flaps that convert them to real mittens when it's cold?"

"Yes." I opened the door.

An eerie whisper floated through the alley, raising the hair on the back of my neck. I stopped short, and Charlene bumped into me. "Do you hear that?" I said in a low voice.

"Hear what?"

A garbage can lid rattled.

"Crimmmmminal."

I cocked my head, listening. Garbage cans clattered. "Someone's out there." I darted into the alley, stumbling to a halt near Charlene's dented Jeep. If there was someone in the alley, did I want to confront them? I clenched my fists. Yes. Yes, I did. I wanted my control back. I owned a pie shop, and I was in charge, dammit!

Another hiss drifted through the chill air, and I whipped around, trying to track its source.

I didn't see anyone in the alley, but it was dark and there were cars and garbage cans and dumpsters to hide behind. Heart thumping, I edged around the Pie Town bin.

A raccoon waddled past.

Charlene braced a hand on her Jeep. "See, it's only a raccoon. Now, I might have a knitting pattern for mittens. Do you knit?"

"No." Element of surprise gone, I checked behind another dumpster.

Nothing.

Locking Pie Town's alley entrance, I strode to my VW. I opened the passenger door for her.

She edged away. "How old is this car?"

"Um, I'm not sure." It had been my mom's, and she'd gotten it used.

Shaking her head, Charlene got inside. "Well, at least it's dark. I'd hate for anyone to see me in this wreck."

Sighing, I turned the ignition. The Bug rattled to life. "Where are we going?"

"Drive north on Highway One."

I piloted the VW down Main Street. Restaurant windows glowed, inviting, through the fog. We crossed the old bridge over the creek, and I paused at a stop sign, beside a barn-like nursery surrounded by a tumble of flowers. If I moved into Charlene's tiny house, I could have a garden.

"You drive like an old woman," Charlene said.

"You are an old woman."

"I'm in the prime of life. Besides, I've been told by reputable sources that I'm ageless."

"Uh-huh."

"At least I drive decisively."

"It's dark, and it's foggy. I don't want to hit anyone."

"No one's out walking in this weather. And if they are, they'll hear you coming. When's the last time this car's had a tune-up?"

Three blocks later, we were on Highway 1, winding up the coast. At least, I assumed the coast was there. I couldn't see more than ten feet past my headlights in the thick fog.

"Make a left up ahead."

I slowed, peering through the windshield. "Where?"

"Here!"

I turned hard, bumping over the edge of a grassy divider. The tires rolled onto smooth pavement, and I relaxed my death grip on the wheel.

Charlene directed me along winding, residential roads. My headlights illuminated a spooky-looking Victorian with an intricate porch railing. Dark cypresses brushed against the green-painted house. Their spiky branches trailed greenish gray, old man's beard over its gray, gabled roof.

I parked in the gravel beside the picket fence. "The kids must love this place on Halloween."

"Not really." Charlene stepped out of the Volkswagen and shivered. "Miss Pargiter's creepy. Some say she's eccentric, but I say she's nuts. And she smells funny, like old people do." The cat draped around her neck sneezed. "Plus, last Halloween she gave out raisins." Making a face, she giggled. "I'll bet she had a devil of a time getting that toilet paper out of her tree!"

I walked down the dark path, shells crunching beneath my sneakers, and did not ask if she'd TP'd Miss Pargiter. I was starting to understand the ignorance-bliss mind-set.

Something struck the front of my left shoulder, and I gasped, slamming backward.

"Watch that lamppost," Charlene said.

"Ow." There was a freaking lamppost in Miss Pargiter's front yard. Painted black, it was little wonder I hadn't seen it. The four light globes branching from its top were unlit.

Rubbing my shoulder, I followed Charlene up the porch.

She knocked on the front door.

Inside, a light flicked on. Floorboards creaked, as if someone shuffled across them. Something skittered in the nearby bushes, and my shoulders twitched.

"What did I tell you?" Charlene asked. "Creeeeeepy."

Frederick yawned, exposing his pink tongue.

"It would be a little less creepy if the porch light was on."

The door flew open, a squat figure in bulky knits silhouetted against the light. The cord from a hearing aid curled from her right ear. "What!"

"Miss Pargiter?" I asked. "I'm Val Harris. Charlene called and said we'd be stopping by?"

Adjusting her glasses, the white-haired woman looked Charlene up and down. "I don't need any more insurance."

"We're here about the trespassers," Charlene shouted. "You remember? This is Val. The one with the wedding dress?"

"The one who was left at the altar by the football player?" Miss Pargiter squinted at me. "She doesn't look like a sap."

"I wasn't at the altar," I said. "And I'm not a sap. What . . . Charlene, what have you been saying about me?"

"Tweeting." Charlene shrugged out of the parka, managing not to dislodge the cat around her neck.

Frederick's whiskers twitched.

"And if you followed me on Twitter," she said, "you'd know."

"All right." Miss Pargiter stepped back. "You can come inside."

I took a breath and took the plunge, following Miss Pargiter into a blue-wallpapered hallway. It overflowed with knickknacks, the walls lined with old family photos. My shoulder brushed against an overloaded coat tree. It tilted, and I lunged, grabbing it before it could hit the parquet floor.

"Watch yourself," Miss Pargiter said.

I fumbled with the coats. They slipped off the tree, coats hooked atop parkas hooked atop sweaters, and all wanting to slither to the floor.

"Speaking of watching yourself, why don't you turn that light on in your yard?" Charlene asked.

"I can't. Bulbs are burned out."

"Would you like me to replace them for you?" I asked, finally getting the coats straightened.

"No. Want some raisins?" Miss Pargiter nodded toward a tall end table holding a bowl filled with tiny raisin boxes.

"No, thanks." I examined one of the photos on the wall. A young man and woman sat on the railing of what looked to be this house's porch. They grinned, heads together.

Charlene rolled her eyes. "Raisins," she said in a low voice. "She's cracked."

I frowned at my piecrust maker. "We came from the pie shop," I said loudly.

Miss Pargiter spun around. "Oooh, where Joe Devlin got killed? Nasty business. These are dark days in San Nicholas. Not like when we were young, eh, Charlene?"

Charlene's lips pinched. "Some of us still are young."

"Ha!" Hobbling into a living area, Miss Pargiter navigated sofas and chairs and tables overflowing with bric-a-brac. Big square windows, blackened by night, faced west. "Sit anywhere."

"If you can find a place," Charlene muttered. Shifting a stack of National Geographics, she dropped into a faded lounge chair.

"I'll stand," I said. "Charlene mentioned you were having problems with trespassers?"

Miss Pargiter squished between two piles of stuffed animals on a plaid sofa. "If you call Bigfoot a trespasser."

I stepped back, staring, and my calf struck a low end table. "Bigfoot."

"Well, it might not have been Bigfoot, but it was big."

Charlene leaned forward. "As big as a jaguar?"

I made a face at my piecrust maker. Again with the jaguars?

"No," Miss Pargiter said, "this was loud. Jaguars are stealthy, like big cats."

Charlene slapped her thigh. "Jaguars are big cats!"

"Forget the jaguars," I said. "What did you hear, and when did you hear it?"

"I hear it on nights like these." Miss Pargiter looked to the window, an ebony square against the night. "It comes out of the mist, like those pirates in that movie."

"The Fog?" Charlene asked. "Good movie, but the remake sucked."

I clenched my jaw, skull buzzing. I'd done it again. I'd let Charlene suck me into another tidal wave of topsy-turvydom. "Thank you, Charlene. That's helpful. Miss Pargiter, did Joe Devlin come by within the last month or so and ask you about these sounds you heard?"

"Sounds I've been hearing. They keep coming. And yes, he was here three weeks ago, poor man. Do you think he was killed because of my trespassers?"

The burglar had been interested in that casebook for a reason. Could Joe's death have something to do with Miss Pargiter's mystery?

"What did you tell him?" Charlene asked.

"It comes on foggy nights. Big thumps and crashing. But when I go outside, there's no one there."

"You go outside?" My brow wrinkled. "But if it is a trespasser, isn't that dangerous?"

"Not with Betsy. I always keep her loaded." She reached behind the couch and drew out a long, metal barrel.

Sucking in my breath, I pulled away and eyed . . . a weed whacker. "That's a weed whacker."

Miss Pargiter grinned. "Metal tipped. Look." She swung it toward me, and I ducked behind an overstuffed chair stacked with newspapers. A breeze passed above my head.

"Oh!" She laughed. "Sorry. I'm not used to whacking people."

I cleared my throat. "Was there anything else you told Joe?"

"Not told him, no. But I showed him my trampled bushes. He even staked them out that night, but he said he didn't find anything."

So much for sticking to the armchair. Joy had either been wrong or lying. And Joe's investigation here had been recent enough that it might indeed be connected to his death. Had he witnessed something he shouldn't have?

"We'd like to see where Joe held his stakeout." Charlene rose majestically from her chair and slipped into her parka. "Where Joe went, we go. No stone left unturned."

Miss Pargiter's smile widened. "I'll bring Betsy. You'll be perfectly safe."

"Oh," I said in a small voice. "You don't have to do that."

"Nonsense!" She patted the weed whacker. "Betsy and I are a team."

We followed Miss Pargiter outside, the crush of the ocean waves sounding through the darkness. Invisible ants marched up my spine, and I glanced across the street. Fog obscured the house on the opposite side. Was someone watching us? Shaking my head, I buttoned my peacoat, turning up the collar to shield my face.

Charlene nudged my arm. "A stakeout's not a bad idea. This is the sort of night the jaguars would be on the prowl."

I stumbled over a tree root. "There are no jaguars in San Nicholas."

She minced down the brush-covered slope. "Fine. We'll call it Bigfoot."

"And there's no Bigfoot either." A pine branch whipped me in the chest, stinging, and I wheezed. We should have brought flashlights. But silly me, I hadn't known we'd be trekking through the woods on an arctic, foggy night.

"I suppose you're right," Charlene said. "The Bigfoot sightings have all been inland, in the mountains around Shasta."

"That's not true." Miss Pargiter's voice wavered through the fog. "There've been sightings in the mountains by Santa Cruz. That's not far south of here."

"Bigfoot isn't a creature of sand, sun, and sea," Charlene said. "He prefers the shade and solitude of the mountains and forests."

"There are mountain forests five miles east of here," Miss Pargiter called from somewhere in the blackness.

"She's right." I pushed beneath a sticky tree branch. "The tiny house you showed me is in a lovely mountainy area. I'm really looking forward to moving in."

"When the job's done," Charlene said.

"Now mind the cliff." Miss Pargiter's disembodied voice floated through the fog.

I stepped into air.

Charlene grabbed the collar of my peacoat and hauled me backward. "Mind the cliff, she said!"

I clutched my chest, breathing hard. Waves crashed beneath me in the darkened void. Oh. My. God.

Miss Pargiter appeared at my elbow. "There used to be

a fence, but . . ." Whistling, she made a diving motion with her hands.

"I remember this place," Charlene said. "When I was a child, I used to run here at night with my friends, imagining pirates, ghosts, and monsters. It seemed bigger then."

"It was bigger," Miss Pargiter said. "I'm losing a few inches of cliff to erosion every year. Someday my house will be in the ocean, but not before I'm long dead."

"Where are these trampled bushes Joe was interested in?" I asked.

"You're standing in them," Miss Pargiter said.

I looked around. My eyes had begun adjusting to the dark, but I wouldn't be able to detect any broken branches or footprints until daylight. Footprints! I smacked my head with my palm. We'd likely trampled those too. Not that it mattered. Bigfoot hadn't killed Joe, and neither had a jaguar. This was one colossal waste of time.

Charlene sat on a tree stump. "Pargiter, go get us some coffee to keep warm. Val and I are on a stakeout, and it's going to be a long night."

"I'm not your serving girl." Miss Pargiter sniffed.

"I don't think we need to stay here all night," I said.

"Fine then," Charlene said. "You can return to your snug office closet and your comfy, cozy mattress on the floor."

Charlene played hardball.

Crossing my arms over my chest, I sat beside her on the stump. "We do have to open Pie Town in the morning."

"The noises usually come around midnight," Miss Pargiter said.

"There you go. We only have to stay here"—Charlene checked her watch, its blue light illuminating her craggy face—"five more hours."

My chin sunk to my chest. Pulling my scarf higher, I buried my nose in its soft wool. Since we'd taken my car,

I could force the issue and drag Charlene off. But that seemed low-down. Someone had killed Joe, and if it was over one of his cases, then we had to see this through. I jammed my hands into my pockets.

"Told you, you should have brought mittens," Charlene said.

"I'm going to wait inside." Miss Pargiter disappeared up the hill, her footsteps fading.

A specter of fog spiraled past. Above us, a clawlike branch swayed, creaked. My skin prickled. Could Joe have seen something in the fog that had gotten him killed? "We could wait inside too," I said. "If Miss Pargiter could hear the trespassers from her house, why can't we?"

"We're following in Joe's footsteps, and Joe waited here."

A gust of wind spattered my face with mist. I pulled my knit cap lower. It was going to be a long five hours.

Chapter 8

"Val."

A talon grasped my shoulder, and I jerked awake, sliding off the tree stump to the ground.

"What?" I shook my head, groggy. The fog cocooned us in chill and dark, but the time I'd spent studying the backs of my eyelids had improved my night vision. A cypress tree loomed above us, its branches reaching over the cliff, toward the ocean crashing below.

I stood and wiped the seat of my jeans. My palms came away sticky. I should have known there'd be sap on that tree stump.

"Someone's coming," Charlene whispered. Around her neck, Frederick's fur stood stiff, his blue eyes wide.

A stick snapped. A thin stream of rocks and dirt rattled down the hill.

Pulse rabbiting, I looked for a place to hide and spotted a low juniper bush. "Quick, under there," I hissed.

Charlene grabbed my sleeve. "I'm not hiding in a juniper. They make me itch."

The footfalls grew heavier.

"We don't have time—"

A roar cut through the air. Charlene shrieked and dodged behind me, gripping my shoulders.

Light blinded me, and I squinted, shielding my face with my arm.

The light dropped.

Blinking, I rubbed my eyes.

Miss Pargiter stood before me, weed whacker whirring in her hand. Her lips peeled into a snarl. "What are you doing here?"

"Miss Pargiter?" I edged backward. "It's Val and Charlene. We're on a stakeout?"

"Oh. Right." She lowered the weed whacker.

A plastic blade thwacked the hem of my jeans, and I yelped. "Turn off the weed whacker!"

"I heard someone out here." Miss Pargiter cut the battery and silence fell, punctuated by a backbeat of ocean waves.

Charlene emerged from behind me. "Pargiter! You know we're the ones out here."

"Of course you are. I heard someone else."

"Then you're hearing things," Charlene said.

"Did you surprise Joe when he was on a stakeout?" I asked.

"I might have given him a start," Miss Pargiter said. "I was bringing cocoa!"

Not for us, I thought sadly. "Okay. Thank you. If we learn anything more, we'll be in touch." Stiff necked, I lurched up the hill, one foot skidding on the loose soil. This had been a fool's errand from start to finish.

"Val! Wait!" Charlene hurried after me.

"I think we've solved this mystery," I said. "It's late. I'm cold. I'm going home to Pie Town."

"Joe thought enough of this problem to stake out Miss Pargiter's cliff."

"Miss Pargiter attacked me with a weed whacker!"

"That's not much of a weapon."

"It's metal tipped," Miss Pargiter said.

I raised the hem of my jeans, displaying the tear in my cuff.

"It's almost midnight," Charlene said. "Let's stay a bit longer."

"We've made enough noise to scare off any trespassers," I said.

"She's right, Char." Miss Pargiter hung her head. "I'm sorry. I blew your stakeout."

"That's all right," Charlene said. "We'll return on the next foggy night."

I ground my teeth. Oh, no we wouldn't. Figuring out who killed Joe was one thing. But the solution to that mystery did not lie in Miss Pargiter's backyard. No house was worth this, even if it was an adorable jewel box with an ocean view.

"Don't you worry," Charlene said. "We'll find out who's terrorizing you."

Rubbing my sticky hands on my jeans, I stopped beneath a cypress tree. "Is that how you feel, Miss Pargiter? Scared?"

"Well, it's not very nice, knowing someone's out and about who shouldn't be." Her voice wobbled. "I'm all alone in that house. Not even a cat."

Charlene patted the sleeping Frederick. With the cat as a neck warmer, little wonder she hadn't complained about the cold.

Miss Pargiter clutched the weed whacker to her chest. "I've called the police, over and over, and they tell me it's kids and not to worry. But whoever it is, they're in my yard. What if one of them fell off the cliff? What if they're not kids at all?"

My chest squeezed with guilt. "Okay. If someone's out there tonight, I think we've scared them off. But we'll come back, and closer to midnight next time, so we don't have to spend quite so much time out in the cold."

"I'll make hot cocoa." Smiling, Miss Pargiter pinched my cheek.

We saw her inside the Victorian. She waved at us from the window, and we piled into my VW. Buckling up, we puttered off, creeping through the fog.

Headlights flashed behind us. Squinting, I adjusted my rearview mirror.

Charlene tsked. "She's lonely. When you get old, your friends start dying, and young people don't want to talk to you. She should think of sharing a house with other women her age, or going to one of those independent-living facilities."

I glanced at the piecrust maker. Was Charlene lonely? Was this the real reason she'd dragged me into her madcap detecting these last two nights? "At least Miss Pargiter is still mobile and independent."

"For now. Did you see how she was leaning on that weed whacker? I think it's more crutch than weapon."

I frowned. No, I hadn't noticed that. I glanced in the rearview mirror. The car's headlights had fallen back. I pressed the accelerator, speeding up.

"If I ever go the way of Miss Pargiter," she said, "I want you to put me on an ice floe and push me out to sea. Let the elements have me. I'll be one with nature, floating."

"There aren't any ice floes in California, and you'll never be like Miss Pargiter."

"Why not?"

"You've got Frederick." I reached over and scratched the cat's head, resting on her shoulder.

Frederick yawned.

"So assuming I kick off in a blaze of glory," Charlene said, "then I'll have a Viking funeral. A flaming boat, sinking into the sunset."

"That's got to be illegal."

"It's my dying wish!"

"You're not dying."

"It's important to plan ahead," Charlene said. "Joe was good about that sort of thing. Poor man. His spirit won't rest easy with a murderer at large, and tonight was a complete bust."

"Not complete. We've proved Joe was here on a stakeout only a few weeks ago. He thought enough of the case to sit on that cliff on a foggy night." We hadn't seen anything tonight, but he might have witnessed something important and not told Miss Pargiter.

I turned the VW onto Highway 1. The headlights behind us followed, vanishing into the stream of cars. "What do you think of Miss Pargiter's hearing? Could she be imagining the footsteps?"

"Joe didn't think so."

"What if the burglar was looking for something in Joe's house aside from the casebook?"

Charlene gave me a hard look. "That burglar tried to get it away from us. But if you insist on checking Joe's house for more clues, I'm always up for a spot of B and E."

"B and E?"

"Breaking and entering."

I tugged at my scarf. "I thought it wasn't breaking in if we had the key. Besides, his niece is living there now. At least, I assume she is. She told me she inherited the house."

"Did she now? She's awfully free with her information when talking to the woman who might have killed her beloved uncle."

"I'm not a murder suspect." But I pressed deeper into my car seat and wondered if Charlene was on to something. "Joy told me she wasn't exactly happy about inheriting the comic shop."

"She ought to be happy. That place is a gold mine."

A pickup zipped behind us and flashed its high beams. It whipped around my Bug, buffeting the car with its wind.

"Really?" I asked.

"Are you kidding? Those Silicon Valley engineers love their comics."

"But we're not in Silicon Valley."

"We're close enough. And Joe's comic shop has got a name. It's the comic shop on the Peninsula. The engineers come here for the comics and stay for the microbrewery."

I smiled. It had been ages since I'd been to the microbrewery. Not since Mark and I had broken up. I wondered if they still made those beer-battered artichoke hearts.

"Pie Town's getting a name too." Her lips pursed. "Or at least it was until Joe's death. Now it's getting a different sort of reputation."

"Between us and the police, we'll figure this out." My grip tightened on the steering wheel. If this went on for much longer, Pie Town wouldn't survive.

"It feels right," she said, "carrying on in Joe's name. The new Baker Street Boys. We'll have to think of a new name though."

"How about the Baker Street Leftovers?"

She wrinkled her nose. "Do you always think in terms of food?"

I checked the mirror. There was no one behind us. "Yes."

Dropping Charlene off at her house, I returned to Pie Town and spent a restless night dreaming of empty booths and bank accounts.

I was not bright eyed and bushy tailed the next morning. Not that it mattered. Unwanted pies filled the glass display case, unused coffee cups sat upon the tables, unoccupied bar stools bellied up to the counter.

I'd told Hannah not to bother coming in today and hadn't bothered to turn on the big oven. On the bright side, I now had plenty of time to design my coupons.

Petronella slammed into the kitchen, her black hair spiking into the air. "Will those gamers just order something? All they do is hog up the booth and drink coffee."

"Yeah, I feel I should reward their loyalty. They do buy pie."

"Not enough." She folded her slim arms across her apron. The pink and white blazed against her black T-shirt.

"I'm going to talk to them."

Her eyes widened, and she clutched my arm. "You can't. They're gamers. They're not like you and me."

"Pie is the great equalizer."

"Nooooo."

Exiting the kitchen, I approached the gamers' booth. Four shaggy heads huddled over a table littered with books and papers and dice.

"You can't do that," one of them said.

I cleared my throat. "Hi."

Four pairs of eyeballs swiveled to regard me.

"Is there anything else I can get you?"

They stared, a frozen tableau of gamers.

"Some pie? On me?"

"Seriously?" the bearded redhead asked.

"Seriously."

They looked at each other, wary. "Usually no one comes to the table," the redhead said. He seemed to be their leader.

"Business is a little light today. You don't have to eat anything. Stay as long as you want. I only thought, since it's so slow, and since you're here so often, I might offer you all a free slice of pie. As a thank you."

"Well, cool! I'll have a cherry," their spokesman said.

I took their orders. The bell rang above the door, and I

turned. Officer Carmichael strode to a window booth. He sat and set up a computer on the table.

I knit my lip. What would he say about the mysterious casebook?

"Hssst!"

I looked to the kitchen.

Beside Petronella, Charlene stuck her head through the window and made a shooing motion toward the cop.

The clock over the counter read noon. Charlene had left work hours ago. What was she doing at Pie Town? Again?

Ignoring her, I glided to his table. "Hi, Officer Carmichael. How are you?"

He frowned at his computer. "I thought you didn't take table orders."

"Desperate times. Desperate measures."

"Then I'll try a mini curry-chicken potpie."

"Sure thing." I hesitated, then headed to the kitchen.

Petronella and Charlene sidled up to me as I passed through the swinging doors into the kitchen. "Well?" Charlene asked.

"He wants the curried chicken. The gamers' orders are a little more complicated." I handed Petronella the gamers' ticket. She nodded and walked into the kitchen.

"I don't care about the cop's dining choices." Charlene adjusted the hem of her black yoga jacket. "What did he say about the murder?"

"I didn't ask."

"Well, find out. You've got a police officer right there sitting in your booth, and a good one, too."

"A good booth?"

"A good cop!"

"I thought you said he was new here. Why do you think he's any good at his job?" Heading into the kitchen, I grabbed a curried potpie from the center island and stuck it in the toaster oven to warm.

Charlene trailed behind me. "He may be new to the SNPD, but he grew up in San Nicholas. Carmichael moved away for college and never looked back, until now."

"You seem to know a lot about him," I said.

"His parents were always yammering about how smart he was, which was really annoying. But he couldn't help being son to Mr. and Mrs. Bragalot."

I eyed her. No one could accuse Charlene of boring the populace with tales of her far-off daughter. Time might heal the wound between them, but how much time did Charlene have left?

"Fine," Charlene said. "I'll admit he was a smart kid. Driven."

"Why do you guys care about that cop?" Petronella asked. "He talks to himself, and he's always hanging around here."

I had no good answer for that. "Why are you here?" I asked Charlene.

"I forgot to collect my paycheck."

I looked at the cooling racks, laden with pies that wouldn't be sold, and my stomach knotted. Pie Town had finally managed to break even the month before Joe's death, but I'd eaten through all my resources to get there. Now my pie shop was at square one—worse than square one. We'd had more customers when we first opened than I did today.

Someone rapped on the back door, and Petronella went to open it.

"What's wrong?" Charlene asked in a low voice.

"Nothing." I smiled tightly. "Your check is in my office. I'll get it."

"I can wait," she said. "Now go and gather some intel."

"Charlene, he can't talk about an ongoing investigation. Not with me."

"Would that have stopped Magnum? Now get out there. All he can say is no."

"Or 'you're under arrest.'"

"For being a concerned citizen? Nonsense."

The timer dinged, and I removed the potpie. "Good-bye, Charlene." I swished out the swinging doors into the dining area. A cup of coffee sat at Carmichael's elbow, so at least he was down with the self-serve concept. I slid the pie onto the table. "Here you go."

"Thanks."

I hovered, trying to figure out a casual way to slip in my questions, and wondering why my blood seemed to be fizzing.

He looked up. "Is anything wrong?"

"Can I ask you a question?"

"Not about the Pie Town case. Even if I could talk about it, I'm not on it."

My cheeks warmed. I'd known he wouldn't talk to me. "Is that what they're calling it?"

"No comment."

"I heard someone tried to break in to Joe Devlin's house the other night."

"Can't talk about it."

I slid into the seat opposite him. "Do you know Miss Pargiter?"

His green eyes crinkled. "My kindergarten teacher?"

"Possibly," I said. "She's been having trouble with nighttime trespassers. She told me that she's called the police station repeatedly, and they've told her it's kids and not to worry about it. But it's unnerving for her to hear people in her yard, especially so late at night."

One corner of his mouth edged down. "And the dispatcher told her not to worry about it? Or was it another police officer?"

"She didn't say. But Miss Pargiter's a little eccentric. Maybe the police aren't taking it seriously for good reason."

Petronella entered the dining area, a tray of pie slices balanced on one hand. Shooting me a curious look, she placed the pies before the gamers.

"I haven't taken any of her calls," he said, "but I'll ask around."

"Thanks." I returned to the kitchen.

Charlene waited for me inside the swinging doors and followed me into the kitchen. "Well?"

"He couldn't talk to me about the case."

"You were talking about something."

"Miss Pargiter's trespassers." I leaned a hip against the sparkling, stainless steel countertop. It should have been dusted with flour, Hannah and I bumping shoulders as we filled pies. I sighed. There was no sense baking if no one was buying.

"Nice job, Mata Hari. Now Carmichael will talk to Pargiter, and he'll know we're investigating Joe's death. Then he'll report us to Shaw. And if Shaw doesn't arrest us for murder, he'll throw us in the clink for impeding an investigation, and then Joe's murder will never be solved."

"But if she's having trouble with trespassers, we can't do anything about it aside from call the cops."

Charlene threw up her hands, her mouth twisting in disgust.

The bell rang above Pie Town's front entrance, and my heart leaped. Another customer! "Excuse me."

"You're only going to spoil them with all this service," Charlene said.

Ignoring her, I walked into the dining area.

Joy stood in the entry, a long, camel-colored coat draped over one arm. A matching purse dangled from her hand. Tossing her black hair over her shoulder, she marched to Officer Carmichael's booth and stuck out her hand.

"I'm Joy Devlin," she said in that flat voice, "the new owner of the comic shop next door."

He shook it, his expression wary. "Carmichael."

"May I join you?"

"Sure."

Petronella gathered up some empty coffee cups from the gaming table and walked into the kitchen, shaking her head.

I strolled to Carmichael's booth. "Charlene's warned me I'm spoiling everyone with table service, but there's not much else to do today. Nice to see you, Joy."

"They told me Joe died from a heart attack brought on by castor bean poisoning," she said, "and it couldn't have been from anything he'd consumed here. Even if it had been, normally the castor beans wouldn't have killed him. Not that fast. I guess Joe had a bad heart."

"Castor beans?" I asked.

"They?" Carmichael asked.

"Detective Shaw," Joy said. "He wanted to know if my uncle was into any alternative medicines. But Joe was more of a better-living-through-science type of guy."

Carmichael's lips pressed into a white slash. He bent his head to his computer.

"Did he say anything about the break-in at Joe's house?" I asked.

"Since nothing was taken, he said it's low on their list of priorities."

"But . . . it might be connected to your uncle's murder!"

"Shaw didn't think so," she said. "He said thieves will strike the empty houses of the recently deceased, and news of Joe's death got around town pretty fast. Can you believe people could be so awful?"

"Yes," I said. "But I don't believe the break-in was a random robbery."

Carmichael gave me a look, his green eyes piercing. I shifted to face Joy.

"You might want to submit a press release," Joy said, "so the rest of the town knows what really killed my uncle."

"Don't," Carmichael said. "The less the killer knows about the investigation, the better."

Frustrated, I scrubbed a hand across my face. "Look around. This is ruining me."

"It's important," he said.

I knew he was right, but civic duty was falling fast on my list of priorities. "Fine," I said in a strained voice. "Can I get you anything, Joy?"

She looked at the chalkboard above the counter. "How's the mini pumpkin potpie? Aren't pumpkins out of season?"

San Nicholas was a big pumpkin-producing town. The full-grown pie, baked in a pumpkin shell, was a big hit during the season. But it was early March, and fresh pumpkin was three months in the rearview mirror. "I froze some pumpkin, which I realize makes it sound not as good, but it's yummy in the potpie. Until I run out, it's my Wednesday special."

"I'll take one," she said.

"Coffee's on the counter." I nodded toward the urn and returned to the kitchen, thinking hard. They weren't taking the break-in seriously. Would anything I could tell them change that? I couldn't wait and hope. I had to do something.

Carmichael hadn't seemed happy about Joy's knowledge of the poison. Had Shaw messed up? As heiress to the comic shop and house, Joy should be a suspect. Maybe she had an alibi that put her out of the picture, but I'd read enough mystery novels to understand that the benefit of poison as a murder weapon is delay. The killer doesn't have to be on the scene when the victim drops. He could sneak poison into something the victim usually ate or drank—such as a castor bean into a bag of coffee beans, waiting to be ground. What did castor beans look like anyway? And even if the real cause of death was a heart attack, if it had been triggered by castor bean poisoning, it was still murder.

Charlene waited inside the swinging doors, tearing open an envelope. "I found my check."

"Good."

"What did he say?"

"He didn't. Joy told me her uncle was poisoned with castor beans, but he died from a heart attack."

"Nasty. That's what they make ricin out of."

"Where did you learn that?"

"The Internet."

"There's something else. You were right, they don't think the break-in at Joe's is linked to his murder."

"Like I said, it's up to us, my girl."

"But if I tell Detective Shaw the burglar wanted the casebook—"

"I already told him. You keep your mouth shut, missy. It's bad enough Joe is dead. I don't want to spend my golden years visiting you behind bars for withholding evidence. Do you have any idea what prison is like? Gang fights and shivs and trading cigarettes for favors."

"If he didn't arrest you, he won't arrest me."

"You sure of that? Shaw thinks I'm old and harmless. What's your excuse?"

"Youthful stupidity?"

"What else did Carmichael say?" she asked.

"Not to tell anyone that Joe was poisoned with castor beans." An order I'd just violated. Striding to the rack of potpies, I weighed Joy's mini-potpie in my hands. It was still warm from when I'd baked it this morning.

She stuck her tongue in her cheek. "Makes sense. If the killer thinks Pie Town's being blamed, he might drop his guard and make a mistake."

Which meant Pie Town wouldn't be cleared until someone caught the murderer. Dammit. "We should check out the mysterious lights on the docks next."

"You should go talk to your ex about the library board and that bloated blond."

"I saw Mark yesterday," I said. "It will make him suspicious if I see him two days in a row. The docks make more sense."

Charlene sighed. "You can't avoid him forever. I'm surprised you've avoided him as long as you have."

I wasn't. My world was Pie Town. Mark knew it and avoided my shop, which was his loss. I sniffed. The pumpkin potpie's sweet/spicy mélange mixed with the other kitchen scents, and my stomach rumbled.

Leaving the pie at their table, I strained my ears for other nuggets of crime-solving info. But Joy sipped coffee, asking Carmichael about the local business association. Meh. Passive listening was not going to cut it if I was going to be a successful Baker Street Leftover.

I grimaced. Charlene had been right. That name was no good.

Chapter 9

"What about the Baker Street Bakers?" she asked as we whizzed down Highway 1.

"Oh, I like that one." I slowed at a stoplight, moving into the left-hand turn lane. The sun, a plump tangerine-orange, floated on the horizon. I lowered the visor, squinting at the stoplight. A truck filled with garlic rumbled past, rocking my VW.

"I think the name's got pizzazz," she said. "It's more marketable, really says something about our sleuthing brand."

We turned toward the docks, driving past restaurants and a boutique hotel. Boat masts pierced the horizon, rose-gold streaked with cobalt.

The cat's stomach growled. He lay crumpled in Charlene's lap, and she ruffled his fur.

So far, I hadn't seen him move of his own accord, aside from the occasional yawn.

"Did you need to bring the cat?" I asked.

"Frederick gets lonely."

"How old is he?"

"Five years. I got him when he was a scrawny kitten, mewling on my front porch."

"He doesn't move very much."

"Of course he doesn't. He's got narcolepsy. You have no idea how difficult it is for him between the narcolepsy and his deafness. If I left him at home, he wouldn't have any social interaction."

The cat stretched, claws extended, and went limp. Narcolepsy. Right. Frederick was lazy and knew a good thing when he had it.

"After we hit the harbor, what's say we stop at the microbrewery for dinner?" Charlene rubbed her hands together. "Pumpkin ale!"

"It's probably out of season." My current finances were veering me dangerously close to my college ramen diet. I glanced at her. She leaned forward in the car seat, grinning. "But why not?" I said. "It's been ages since I've eaten there."

I pulled into the harbor parking lot. Charlene draped Frederick over her shoulder, and we walked to the harbormaster's office, a gray clapboard building overlooking the small bay. The sunset reflected off its square windows.

Charlene knocked on the door and strode inside without waiting for a response. "Loomis! Where are you, you old dog?"

A bearded, white-haired man swiveled in his seat. He rose, gripping a harpoon, his frame somehow broad and gangly at the same time.

I stiffened, imagining him in a black ski mask. But it was broad daylight, and even though we were alone with him, and he brandished a weapon, I'm sure we were perfectly safe. Perfectly. Safe.

"Char! What are you doing here?" He kissed her on the cheek. "And how's my favorite cat?"

Frederick's ears swiveled toward him. Deaf my eye! The cat knew when he was being discussed.

"We're looking for information," Charlene said.

"You and Frederick?" The blade of his harpoon glittered, wicked, beneath the overhead lamp.

"Me and Val. She's assisting me with my investigation."

I waved a limp-wristed greeting. Assisting? It was clear who thought she was the Sherlock Holmes and who the Watson was in this relationship.

"Information's not free, lass," he said.

Charlene peered at him over her spectacles. "It had better be today."

"What investigation?" he asked.

"We've heard there have been strange lights spotted over the harbor," I said. "What can you tell us about them?"

"I go home at six o'clock."

"So you know the lights appear later at night," I said.

"They wouldn't be much of a story if they happened during the day," he said. "But you got me, I've heard about the lights in the sky."

"What exactly have you heard?" I asked.

He rubbed the back of his neck with one wrinkled hand. "Fish stories, I reckon."

"UFOs?" Charlene asked.

I stared at her. My jacket suddenly felt too tight, and I shifted my shoulders. UFOs?

"I couldn't say about aliens," he said. "Most of the harbor activity takes place in the early morning and day-time. There's a bit of night fishing that goes on, and a class that runs night dives, rain, shine, or fog. They're at slip thirty-eight now, getting their equipment ready."

"Did Joe Devlin stop by and ask about the lights?" I asked.

"Not of me."

We thanked him and crossed the parking lot to the pier, waves lapping at the pilings.

"It's 1947 all over again," Charlene said, stopping beside

a red and gray fishing boat. "Strange lights in the sky, a coverup."

"1947?"

"Roswell! A UFO crashed in New Mexico at Roswell, and the government covered it up."

Uh-huh. "If Joe didn't talk to the harbormaster, maybe he spoke with the night divers," I said, refusing to engage in one of Charlene's conspiracy theories. UFOs. Ha. I chafed my hands together to warm them.

A point of heat flushed the skin between my shoulder blades.

Stomach knotting, I looked to the parking lot, then down the dock. I knew that feeling. We were being watched.

My breath caught. My ex, Mark, walked toward us on the pier, his hands in the pockets of his khakis. His navy fisherman's sweater stretched tight across his chest. Either he hadn't spotted us or he was pretending he hadn't, staring down at his loafers as he neared.

Blowing air into my hands to hide my face, I hunched my shoulders, turning away to examine a tugboat thick with barnacles. Had he seen me? Or had someone else been watching us?

"What's wrong?" Charlene asked.

"Um, are you sure Frederick's warm enough?"

"Well, if you're thinking of dumping him on that nasty tugboat to warm him up, you can think again."

Mark's footsteps thunked past us, and the muscles between my shoulders relaxed.

"Of course not," I said. "I was admiring the lines of this boat. The wharf area is beautiful." That, at least, wasn't a lie. The sky had turned bluish purple, and the boats gleamed, bobbing in the softening light.

"All San Nicholas is picturesque," she said. "Haven't you seen the postcards? Come on."

I followed her to slip thirty-eight, where a tall motorboat with a blue awning docked.

Charlene hallooed.

A bronzed Poseidon in a surfer T-shirt, his hair thick and blond, stepped onto the deck. He grinned, teeth gleaming, and his gaze traveled from my head to my sneakers. "If you're here for the dive, you're a couple hours early."

"No, I'm Val Harris. This is my friend Charlene McCree."

She nodded. "We're here to ask you about the UFO—"

I coughed. "A friend of ours, Joe Devlin, was at the harbor a few weeks ago asking about some strange lights. You might have heard he died recently. We're following up for him on some unfinished business." Which made us sound like a pair of ghost hunters, laying an uneasy soul to rest. I shuffled my feet, torn between embarrassment and suspicion. I had to stop suspecting every person I met was a potential robber/murderer. It was exhausting.

"Oh, yeah, killed in that pie shop." Squinting, he tugged on his ear as if there were water in it.

"Did Joe Devlin speak with you?" Charlene asked.

"He came out with us one night into the bay. Didn't dive, just sat on deck. He said he wanted to enjoy the night air. But it wasn't the best night for stargazing."

"Stargazing?" I asked. So he had come into contact with Joe.

"That's what it looked like he was trying to do, staring up above the cliffs, except it was overcast."

"Do you remember when this was?" I asked. From the bay, Joe could look up at the cliffs by Miss Pargiter's house. Were the lights and her trespassers somehow connected? But what did that have to do with his death?

"Must have been a Wednesday. That's when we do all our night dives."

"How late were you out?" I asked.

"We usually return right after midnight."

"Did you see any odd lights that night?" I asked.

He laughed. "I was underwater with half a dozen night divers. All the lighting was odd."

Charlene pushed her glasses up her nose. "How much—"

"Thank you," I said, "you've been a big help." Taking Charlene's elbow, I hauled her up the pier.

"What are you doing? We can surveil the cliffs from his boat!"

"Or from one of the opposite cliffs." I could only imagine what a boat trip would cost me.

She frowned. "Joe used a boat."

"I get seasick."

"There are pills for that," Charlene replied.

"How about a beer?"

"Oooh, can we get the fried artichoke hearts too?"

"I'm counting on the fried artichoke hearts." If I was going to blow a week's worth of dinner money, I might as well live it up.

We got a table on the patio with the other pet owners. Warming ourselves beside a snapping fire pit, Charlene and I discussed the case in low voices.

Wary, I watched the entrance to the patio. No one had seemed to have followed us to the microbrewery. Had I imagined someone watching us at the docks, my paranoia running amuck?

"If Joe thought he had a serious case," I said, "would he have told the police about it?"

"Would Shaw have listened? No one listened to Pargiter when she complained about trespassers."

"What are you saying?"

"Old people might as well be invisible in this town," she said. "No one takes them seriously." She sipped her beer. "Granted, Pargiter is a weirdo."

"All right. What if it's Joy?" I asked. "It sounds as if she spent a lot of time at Joe's house. She could have slipped a castor bean into his coffee bean supply, figuring it would kill him, and waited for him to die. She said she thought he was in good health, but she could have known he had a weak heart."

"Joe did love his morning coffee. But we don't know that's how the castor bean was administered. And she wouldn't have broken into Joe's house. She had a key." She fed Fredrick a morsel of chicken breast.

He ate it, his eyes shut, then rolled onto his back, a Roman emperor waiting for his stomach massage after a rich meal.

"Maybe the cops are right, and the break-in and case-book don't have anything to do with the murder," I said. "It's a little strange, Joy's spending so much time at Pie Town, since that's where her uncle died."

"Maybe she's trying to be nice to you."

A seagull alighted on the glass patio wall. Fluttering to the brickwork, it snatched up a crumb by our table. A terrier barked at the bird, and it lifted off, flapping into the darkness.

"Joe's Victorian has got to be worth something," I argued.

"At least a cool two mil."

I choked on my beer. "Two million dollars?"

"You've seen the housing prices in this part of California. His house is old, but it's big and you can see the ocean from the second floor. It's only a sliver of blue, but it's there, and that's what counts."

Sparks shot from the fire pit, vanishing high into the air.

"I've been looking at rentals," I said, "not places to buy." Because I'd known I wasn't anywhere near to being able to buy a house. But two million bucks for an old Victorian? What was the plumbing like? "Had Joe remodeled recently?"

Charlene laughed. "That old cheapskate? No way. But he's had realtors sniffing around. That place is worth money."

"So Joy does have a motive."

"Not to break into her own house wearing a ski mask."

I waved aside her dissent. "So our suspects are Joy and person or persons unknown, someone Joe might have encountered in one of his investigations."

"Like your ex-boyfriend, Mark. He's blond, and he's on the library board, don't forget. And he's a weasel."

"But he's not bloated. And he said he only joined the board recently. Even if there was something hinky going on there, it's not likely he'd be involved."

"I'm glad you don't hold a grudge. But that boy was a liar when he was a kid, and I don't trust him now," Charlene said.

"When he was a kid?" He'd certainly told me a lot of lies. Most of it had been stupid stuff to impress me, and I'd let him off the hook when I'd found out his real age, his real income, his real family status. And there were the white lies, told, he said, because he wanted to make me happy. But then came the big lie—he'd never wanted to marry me, even though he'd been the one to ask. Why had he proposed? Had he been carried away by the moment?

Charlene licked beer foam from her upper lip. "Oh, yes, I've got Mark Jeffreys's number. He busted my window playing ball and tried to blame it on his little sister, but I'd seen what happened. We need to learn what his game is."

His game? Thoughtful, I sipped my beer. San Nicholas was a quaint beach town. It was awfully small for someone with big plans, like Mark. Why had he insisted on returning here? Was it the lure of being a big fish in a small pond? "All that may be true," I said, "but it doesn't make him a murderer."

"Still, all the more reason for you to talk to him tomorrow."

"I've already spoken with him, and he didn't know anything."

"You spoke with him in public, in front of other library board members. He's not going to give up the dirt under those circumstances."

"But—"

"Talk to him."

"Wouldn't you rather manage the interrogation?" There was no way I was going to talk to him by myself.

"Uh-uh. You two have things to discuss. Alone. Find out what Joe was doing with someone on the library board."

"I'd rather slam my fingers in the walk-in fridge."

"That can be arranged."

Chapter 10

I sat in my VW outside Mark's realty office and gnawed the inside of my cheek. He worked on a shady side street in a blue and white, craftsman-style bungalow. A picket fence caged its garden, bursting with flowers. They shimmered in the light from the lowering sun.

My stomach churned. As much as I hated the idea, I needed to talk to Mark. Aside from the gamers, Pie Town had been empty again today. And the library board had been the only other viable trail in the casebook to follow.

A seagull landed on the picket fence and dug his beak into his wing, picking at a ruffled feather.

Blowing out my breath, I told myself to get out of the car. Mark wasn't an ogre. It was better that we'd broken up before the wedding than after. I just wish he would have told me his misgivings before I'd staked my future on San Nicholas and Pie Town. But I'd been having second thoughts too. I'd pushed them aside, pretended they were normal prewedding jitters. Why had I ignored my instincts? Had it been insecurity? Desperation? Denial?

I stepped out of the car, not bothering to lock the door. In spite of Joe's murder, San Nicholas was still the sort of place where you didn't need to worry much about crime.

Passing the wooden sign advertising the realty office, I walked up the steps and knocked. A black cat uncurled from a patch of sunlight beside a wide-leaved plant and yawned.

A slender woman in a red wrap dress and Miss America hair opened the door. She flashed her teeth. "Why, hello! Come on in. How can I help you?"

"My name's Val Harris. I'm here to see Mark."

The corners of her cupid-bow mouth turned down. "He's on the phone right now. If you take a seat, I'll tell him you're here as soon as he's free."

So Mark had a receptionist now. That was new. "Thanks." I sat on the leather couch and checked out the home improvement magazines on the coffee table. One heel bouncing on the floor, I picked up a magazine and thumbed through photos of bathrooms.

The receptionist made a call. "Mark? Val Harris is here to see you." She paused, flicked a glance at me. "I see. Yes." She hung up, her expression less friendly. "He'll be with you in a moment."

"Thanks." I stopped on an article about paint colors and mood, pressing my hands harder on the slick paper.

Mark leaned out of his office. He ran a hand through his blond hair and every strand sprang back into exactly the right place. The man used more hair product than I did.

He smiled. "Hi, Val. Come on in."

Ache speared my chest. I faked a smile in return, following him into his office.

He shut the door behind us. Bookshelves lined the walls. A leather couch sat on one side of the room, facing a coffee table and two matching wingback chairs. His desk stood near the opposite wall, its back to a window overlooking a shady yard filled with ferns. I concentrated on the view. It hurt to look at him.

He motioned me to one of the chairs, and I sat on the couch.

Mark took the chair he'd offered me. "So what can I do for you? Have you changed your mind about that lease?"

"No. I can't afford to move Pie Town, and I like my location."

"The location isn't doing much for you now."

"We have had a few slow days since Joe's death. But Pie Town wasn't responsible for that. Once the police find out who killed Joe, customers will return."

He raised a brow. "So, Val, what do you want?"

I wanted his help. I wanted to edge into the question of the library board. I wanted to run, shrieking. "I want to get my stuff out of your storage locker."

He shifted in his chair. "Now's not really a good time."

"Just lend me the key. I won't take anything that's not mine, if that's what you're worried about."

He made a face. "Come on, Val. You know it's not. Things are jammed in there, and you'd have to dig through it to get to your stuff. Something might fall on you and get broken."

"Or break me?"

"Right."

I propped my head on my fist. "When will be a good time to get my things? I've found a new place to live, and I need them."

He shifted some papers on his desk, not meeting my gaze. "Maybe in a couple weeks. Things are busy. The real estate market is heating up. Look, I'll call you."

I stiffened. What the blasted blue blazes was the problem? I admit having someone else pay to store my junk had seemed like a bonus when I was living in Pie Town. Money before pride is my motto. But how long did it take to open up a storage locker and point out my boxes? I didn't have many.

"Why was Joe involved with someone on the library board?" I asked.

His blue eyes widened. "I didn't think he was."

"Then why might he have been investigating someone on the library board?"

"Investigating?"

"Joe was murdered," I said. "I told you, Joe and his buddy Frank were armchair detectives, and the notes on one of their investigations mentioned the library board. Ergo, he might have been killed because of his investigation."

"You've got to be kidding."

"Someone killed him."

He sputtered. "Are you accusing me of killing him?"

"Don't be absurd," I said. "You only joined the library board recently—not enough time to become part of a murderous cabal."

"The library board isn't a cabal! Have you been inside our new library? It's architecturally stunning. The board has a lot to be proud of, especially since the library is self-sustainable." The statement sounded canned.

"The new library is a temple to the written word and the envy of three counties." As a committed logophile, I found the new library was my favorite escape. "But Joe's notes state he was conducting an ongoing investigation of the board."

"There's nothing to investigate at the library board."

"You haven't noticed anything odd since you joined?"

"It's a library board! They manage a library, where people borrow books. There's not even any money exchanged to embezzle."

"Embezzle? Why would you bring that up?"

"I didn't. I just—what are you accusing us of?"

"I'm not accusing you of anything." I gazed out the

window. A breeze stirred the ferns, and a hummingbird paused to sample a hanging fuchsia.

Mark was right. What dark deeds could Joe have investigated at the library? The only crimes committed there were literary. So if he hadn't been looking at the library board, maybe Joe was investigating someone who happened to be on it? Someone whose name he didn't want to write down for privacy reasons? "How does the board work?" I asked.

He rolled his eyes. "We meet every two months. Board members are appointed by the town council and serve four-year terms. We oversee the library's policies and procedures and help out with the fund-raising."

"You're doing a helluva job. The new library must have cost a mint."

"That was a bond measure, before my time. Look, it's a library board. I understand why you're desperate to clear Pie Town's name, but there's nothing here."

"You're probably right, but the board members must have lives outside the library. I'm assuming they're on the board because they're prominent members of the community?"

Mark puffed out his chest, and I realized I'd accidentally complimented him.

"The board members are good, hardworking people," he said. "If they weren't, I wouldn't be involved with them."

That was true. Mark knew networking, and he would hook up with winners who could give him a boost. "Then maybe Joe and Frank were conducting an investigation on behalf of someone on the board?"

"Maybe," Mark said, his eyes dulling.

"Where can I find that board member you were with the other day? Antheia Royer?"

"You're not going to bother her with your insane theories."

I crossed my legs, tapping my foot in the air. "Right

now, I've got no theories, insane or otherwise. I only want to ask her why Joe had a note in his journal about a case at the library board."

"Didn't you already ask her that?"

"But I didn't ask her who, if anyone on the board, might have introduced Joe to this so-called case. I'm sure she'll want to help. When we met, she seemed sympathetic," I lied.

"I'm not letting you bother her."

"It's no bother. But don't worry about it." I rose. "I can find her on my own."

"Wait."

I paused, hand on the doorknob.

"We have a committee meeting in thirty minutes," he said. "If you come with me now, you can ask her about Joe."

And Mark could try and control the conversation. Annoying, but I'd set myself up for that. And if it was a more than two-person committee, I'd be able to meet some other board members.

"Fine," I said.

We drove in separate cars to the library, its exterior dark, polished stone with faux fossils embedded in the walls. Tall windows glittered in the setting sun. Mark met me at the tinted-glass front doors and led me through wood-paneled halls. Heads bowed over desks typed at sleek computer keyboards, hushed, reverent.

"Second floor," Mark said.

A slender, dark-haired man in a business suit intercepted us by the wide staircase. He looked like a young Bela Lugosi, pale, with deep-set, dark eyes. His nose wrinkled. "Mark! How nice to see you. And this is . . . ?"

"Val Harris," Mark said. "She needs a quick word with Antheia. Val, this is the head librarian, Hunter Green."

"Hi," I said.

The librarian checked his watch and frowned. "I'm not sure about bringing a visitor. The meeting's about to start."

"We'll be done before that," I said, tugging Mark up the stairs.

We climbed to the second floor, and Mark led me to a glass-walled meeting room. The librarian trailed behind us.

Antheia looked up from her e-book reader and stuffed it into a quilted, lipstick-red purse. Smoothing her red blazer and pencil skirt, she tucked a stray, silvery-blond hair behind her ear. "Good evening, Mark, Hunter. And . . ." She cocked her head, questioning.

"Val." I put my hand out. "We met the other day at my shop, Pie Town."

She shook my hand, her grip limp and unpleasant. "Oh. Yes. Of course." She glanced at Mark. "No one told me we were going to have guests for our committee meeting."

"We're not," Mark said. "Val had this idea that Joe was working for someone on the library board and wanted to ask you if you had any idea who that might be."

I glared at him. That was not what I'd said, but okay, it was a conversation starter. "As I mentioned the other day, Frank or Joe may have been doing some detective work," I amended.

"Detective?" Antheia gave a short laugh. "I thought you were joking. I can't imagine who would hire them."

"Can you imagine why someone might be interested in the board members?" I asked.

"Val!" Mark glowered at me. "She didn't mean it like that," he said to Antheia.

He'd scolded me like a child, and my face heated with anger and shame. In fairness though, my question hadn't exactly been subtle, and I forced my fists to unclench, my breathing to slow. This was his board, and he wanted to impress the members. I needed to cool it.

Antheia's smile was brittle, not reaching the fine lines around her eyes. "That's all right, Mark. As far as I'm aware, none of us are cheating on our spouses. And if we were, we'd be more likely to hire a real detective, not a Baker Street Boy."

"Their notes mentioned a blond," I said.

"Mark and I are the only blonds on the board. And I certainly didn't hire Joe or Frank." She checked her watch. "We really should start the meeting. I'm afraid you'll have to go now, Val."

"We can't start without Turner," the librarian said.

"That man is always late." She scowled. "I don't have time to wait for him." She stood. "I'm sorry, Mark, Hunter. Please give my regrets to Turner. I've got to go."

"But we were going to review the bylaws." Mark's brows sloped downward. "You're our lawyer."

"And I have to reschedule. Sorry!" She scooted out the door. The glass panel whispered shut behind her.

Weird.

Mark whirled on me, hands on his hips. "You had to bring up cheating spouses. Three months ago her husband left her for an aerobics instructor."

"But I didn't bring that up."

"Yes, you did."

"No, I didn't." I appealed to the librarian. "I didn't!"

He folded his arms, expression stony.

"You need to leave before Turner gets here," Mark said.

"Turner Morris, the board's treasurer?" I'd been doing my Internet research and knew who the board panjandrums were. I'd also discovered Antheia was the board's secretary. Frank's notebook had said, Library bd.—sec—the Case of the Bloated Blond. Was Antheia the sec in question? Because she was certainly blond.

"Go!" He hustled me out of the meeting room, down the stairs, and out of the library.

I stomped to my VW and got in, breathing hard. The ejection from the library prickled my insides with embarrassment. Had I gone too far questioning Antheia? Or not far enough? I could return inside and try to catch Turner, but I doubted I'd get far with Mark snarling in the background. Why had Antheia run? Had I struck a nerve asking about Joe, or was it just bad memories of a broken relationship? I glanced at Mark's green BMW, parked beside my car.

Okay, let's assume the bloated blond was a client of Joe's rather than a suspect. If Antheia was going through a nasty divorce, an investigator could come in handy. But if she wanted to take any evidence to court, Antheia was right, a real PI would be a smarter choice than two enthusiastic amateurs. Also, Antheia didn't look particularly bloated. Maybe Frank's case note had nothing to do with her at all. So why had she fled under my lightweight questioning?

I needed more information about Antheia.

Bam-bam-bam.

I yelped, banged my knee against the steering wheel.

Through the window, Charlene grimaced at me.

I opened the door.

"How did it go?" Charlene leaned into my car, Frederick dangling rakishly over one shoulder.

I rubbed my knee. "Were you following me?"

"No, I saw you and Mark in the library with the head vampire and decided to wait for you in the parking lot."

"Head vamp . . . You mean the librarian?" So I hadn't imagined his Bela Lugosi vibe.

"Who do you think?"

"You do know he's not really a vampire."

She goggled at me. "Well, of course not! Everybody knows real vampires don't swan about in the daylight."

Duh. I hunched my shoulders.

"And who would name their child after a color?" she asked. "Hunter Green indeed. Either it's a bad alias, or his parents were evil. And that can only mean one thing."

"It can?"

"The apple never falls far from the tree. That means the librarian's evil too. Did your ex-boyfriend take you to a library board meeting?" she asked. "That seems promising."

"No, a committee meeting. I asked Antheia about Joe, and she suddenly remembered she had somewhere else to be."

"Suspicious. Antheia's not the sort to ditch on her responsibilities."

"Oh? What sort is she?"

"The boring, reliable type."

A seagull swooped down and landed on the hood of my VW. I made shooing motions. It sat and made itself comfortable.

"Antheia Royer must be the blond," Charlene said, "but it's hard to peg her for a murderer. If she didn't kill her husband—who everyone knew was stepping out on her—then what could Joe have done to make her snap?"

"She did run away when I started asking questions. Mark said I hurt her feelings because her husband ran off with an aerobics instructor."

"Antheia's emotions are running high with the pending divorce. Last week I caught her sobbing over an avocado in the Grab and Go. I wanted to cry too when I saw the price." She chuffed me on the shoulder. "You look as if you've had a rough day. Why don't you come over to my place and watch some Stargate? That always cheers me up. I've got all ten seasons, plus Atlantis. Not that Stargate Universe though." She wrinkled her nose. "Too dark."

"Thanks, but I've got to stop by the print shop."

"Why the print shop?"

"For the Pie Town coupons." I'd submitted the design online, and the coupons would be ready to pick up tonight.

"Coupons aren't going to save Pie Town. Good, old-fashioned detective work is what we need. Come to my house, and we'll plan our attack."

"I don't know—"

"Go pick up your coupons and come over."

"Maybe we can strategize while we cut the coupons." Hiring the print shop to slice the coupons into trim rectangles would have cost more than the actual printing.

She held up her hands in a warding gesture. "Hold on, missy. That would be overtime. Besides, I've got arthritis. I can't use scissors."

"Fine. I'll do them on my own." It wasn't as if I lacked spare time.

"So you'll come?"

"I'm really tired—"

"I've got Oreos. Mint flavor."

"Okay."

Chapter 11

Rubbing my eyes, I stumbled out of my office in my pajamas. I started the coffee urn and set water to boil to poach some eggs. Last night, after Charlene's sci-fi marathon, I'd picked up a pack of bacon and a bag of frozen hash browns on a whim. Now I stared at the bacon, parked inside my walk-in fridge. There was no way I was going to eat an entire package of hash browns on my own. And bacon?

Feeling reckless, I tore both open and fried a few slices with the potatoes. My bedroom might be a closet, but the Pie Town kitchen was a palace of high-end utensils, industrial refrigerators, and sparkling metal countertops. I might never go hungry, but I needed my own place and a life outside Pie Town that didn't involve Charlene and a DVD player.

Carrying the urn to the front counter, I poured myself a cup of java. I turned, mug to my lips, and froze. Through the blinds, I saw words in drippy black paint splattered the front windows. I read them backward: KILER GO HOME.

I swayed, staring through the window at the fog-shrouded street. Killer? I didn't know whether to laugh at the misspelling or scream. Someone actually believed I was a

killer? What next? Would a posse of townsfolk march on
Pie Town brandishing torches and pitchforks?

And my window! My hands trembled.

Carefully, I put down the coffee, got dressed, and called
the police station. A sleepy-sounding dispatcher promised
they'd send someone over.

I hung up. Was I making mountains out of molehills? It
was only graffiti. But it was graffiti because of a crime that
had been committed here, in Pie Town. If it hadn't been
worthy of telling the police about, the dispatcher would
have told me, right?

I dumped my cold coffee into the kitchen sink. Pouring
myself a fresh cup from the counter urn, I sat in the front
booth to wait.

A black-and-white glided through the fog and halted
in front of my shop.

I unlocked the front entrance and stepped onto the brick
sidewalk. Barbells clashed faintly in the gym. The light
streaming through its windows barely penetrated the thick,
morning fog.

Frowning, Officer Carmichael stepped out of the squad
car and stared at the graffiti. "Not the best way to start your
morning."

"No. I wasn't sure if I should have called the police or
not," I said. "It's not an emergency."

Drawing his cell phone from the breast pocket of his
uniform shirt, he snapped a picture. "Under the circumstances, you were right to call. When did you find this?"

"This morning." Last night I'd returned around midnight, parked in the alley, and came in through the rear entrance. "But it could have happened any time after I'd
closed up Pie Town around five o'clock."

"It was probably some bored kids, but I'll make sure
there are extra night patrols past your shop."

"Thanks." The idea of patrols made me feel a bit better.
"I don't suppose you have any tips for removing graffiti

from glass? I want to get this paint off before we open."
Not that I was expecting a lot of foot traffic this morning,
but I wanted the graffiti gone.

He winced. "Paint on glass is tough. Try dish soap and
warm water. Spread it on the window with a sponge and let
it sit a few minutes to loosen the paint. Then you'll have to
go after it with a glass scraper. Have you got a glass
scraper?"

"No."

"The hardware store will, but they don't open until
nine."

My shoulders sagged. How many people would see this
before I was able to clean up the vandalism?

He gave the windows a speculative look. "I have a glass
scraper in my garage. If you want, I can get it and lend it
to you. I only live a few minutes away."

"Would you? I'll owe you one."

"No, you won't." Returning to his black-and-white, he
drove off.

I trudged to the kitchen and filled a bucket with soapy
water. Someone hammered on the rear entrance. I checked
my watch. Charlene. I walked to the heavy door and let
her in.

Darting inside, she rubbed her biceps, bunching the soft
fabric of her emerald-colored tracksuit. "Brrr. Chilly out
there. So how many crusts do you think for today? Down
to a quarter of the usual again?"

"Bring it down to ten." The local charities couldn't
accept my pies—nothing personal, it was the law. I'd
frozen what I could for our own use later, but we were still
wasting a grotesque amount of food.

"Ten! Business has got to be getting better."

I nodded to the dining area. "Someone painted graffiti
on the front windows last night."

"What?" She stormed out of the kitchen.

Carrying the bucket, I followed her into the dining room.

She stopped short, staring at the window. Her cheeks pinked. "That is it. I have reached my limit."

My hands grew clammy, and I tightened my grip on the bucket. "You're not quitting?" Keeping Charlene with business so slow squeezed my bank account, but the thought of her abandoning Pie Town twisted my gut.

"Quitting? Don't be ridiculous. No more Stargate until we catch Joe's killer. We should have been on a stakeout last night instead of watching TV." She motioned toward the window. "We'll never get that off!"

Water sloshing in the bucket, I lumbered to the glass door and unlocked it. "Officer Carmichael said it's tough but doable."

"Johnny Law was here?"

I told her about my chat with Carmichael and soaped the outside of the windows. The water was warm, but the air was cold, the fog a sullen gray drift obscuring the opposite side of the street.

She snorted. "Kids! That's wishful thinking. It was the killer. Kids would have written something rude. The killer wants us to stop investigating."

"The graffiti says go home, not stop investigating. And they didn't even spell killer right."

"Trying to make it look like kids did it, so the police don't look too closely at the vandalism. Not that there aren't some rotten kids in San Nicholas. That Freddy Brinks is always scuffing up my picket fence."

Heavy footsteps padded up the sidewalk toward us.

"And Achilles Kopeckni—any parents who could give their kid that name deserve what they get. But when he messed with my petunias, it was a bridge too far. And don't get me started on—"

A man in a blue jacket and khakis emerged from the fog.

I tensed. For a moment I registered only his bulk, that Charlene and I were alone and vulnerable, and no one would hear us if we screamed. Then I realized I knew him, and my muscles slackened. "Mayor Sharp."

The librarian, looking miserable in a rumpled trench coat and thick scarf, followed behind him.

The mayor stopped in front of our windows, his lips pursed, and tugged on the brim of his blue baseball cap. "Ladies. What's going on here?"

"Only some graffiti," I said.

The librarian's eyes flashed. "Kiler go home? I expect better from our schools. Poor quality education is a crime."

"It's a crime against our window," Charlene said.

"According to town code," the mayor said, "graffiti needs to be removed within forty-eight hours. If you leave it up, it will only attract more."

"What does it look like we're doing?" Charlene asked. "We don't carry buckets of water around to build muscle tone. That's what the gym's for. What are you doing out here?"

"Hunter and I were out for a morning walk," he said. "If I have to talk city business, I may as well get some exercise."

A police cruiser pulled up to the curb, and Officer Carmichael stepped out. He nodded to us. "Ladies. Mr. Mayor. Mr. Green."

"If you're here," Sharp said, "you should take a report on this before they wash it off."

"I already have." He handed me a paint-spattered glass scraper. "Here. This should help."

"Is that city property?" Sharp asked.

"No, it's mine. I'm lending it to Miss Harris so she can clean her window. There's a forty-eight-hour rule on removing graffiti."

Sharp grunted and walked away. The librarian wandered after him.

I repressed the urge to stick my tongue out at their departing backs.

A pickup truck crept past, its tires whooshing on the damp street.

Charlene sniffed. "'Never trust a man who looks like Bela Lugosi,' my mother always said."

"Did your mother know many men who looked like Bela Lugosi?" I asked.

"Only Lugosi. She never trusted him. And I don't trust anyone who pals around with that librarian. The only reason Sharp got elected is no one cares about local elections." Charlene sniffed. "The whole council is a pack of sharks."

"Shoal of sharks," I said absently. Could Charlene's mother have actually known Bela Lugosi?

"People should care," Carmichael said. "Most interactions between citizens and government happen at the local level."

"And on that note," I said, "thanks for the glass scraper. That falls into the above and beyond category."

He shrugged. "It's just a glass scraper. I'll come by later to pick it up."

"Men are so jealous of their tools," Charlene said. "I think there's a phallic connection between their tools and their—"

"Yes, Charlene," I said, my face going hot. "Don't you have some piecrusts to work on?"

Grumbling, she stomped inside.

Carmichael grinned. "Never a dull moment with Charlene around."

"She said she knew your parents," I said, wanting to prolong the conversation for reasons I didn't understand.

"Probably. My parents know nearly everyone in San

Nicholas." A shadow crossed his face. "Or at least they used to. Since they've gotten older, they seem to have turned inward."

"They're still in San Nicholas?"

"Mm." He nodded. "That's a twenty-four-hour gym. I'll talk to the manager. Maybe someone in there saw your vandal. We don't have a citizen's watch here in San Nicholas, but since the gym is open all night, they could be a good neighbor."

I forced a smile. "Great idea. I should reach out to the owner." On a cold day in Hades. Heidi still had that SUGAR KILLS sign in her stupid window. But . . . We were neighbors. We didn't have to be friends, but maybe we could help each other out.

Officer Carmichael strode inside the gym, and I got to scraping. There was something oddly satisfying about removing the black paint. In this small way, I was setting things to rights.

An hour later, I stood back and rolled my stiffening shoulders, examining my handiwork. This was going to take forever. Bits of black paint remained streaked on the windows, but you could no longer tell what the graffiti had said.

Two gamers walked into Pie Town, heads bowed, hands in the pockets of their thick jackets. The bell above the front entrance jingled. Had I put the coffee on? My heartbeat slowed. Yes, I had.

Petronella pushed past them to stand beside me. "Charlene told me what happened." She ran her fingers through her spiky black hair. "We don't see much vandalism in San Nicholas. Someone TPs Miss Pargiter's house every Halloween, but no graffiti."

"Probably because there's a forty-eight-hour rule about removing it." I attacked a thin line of paint with the scraper.

"Is there? What happens if you don't get it off?"

"A fine, public flogging, the stocks. That sort of thing."
She pursed her lips. "Is it okay if I take the day off?"

I paused, clutching the scraper to my chest. Was she taking time off to job hunt? My stomach twisted. If things didn't pick up soon, I would have to let someone go. I drew a slow breath. "I guess so. Business has been slow lately."

"Thanks." She shifted her weight, gazing at the streaky window.

Three more gamers slouched into Pie Town, glossy, hardbound gaming books beneath their arms.

"At least we've got some dedicated clients," I said.

Petronella snorted. "I'm not sure they even noticed anyone died here. Not that that's a reason not to come to Pie Town," she added quickly. "Well, I should get going."

"See you later." I hoped.

I attacked the window with renewed vigor. Another hour later, shoulders burning, I tossed the paint scraper into the bucket. You had to look hard to find any stray flecks of black. For now, that was good enough. The fog had lifted, the end of Charlene's shift was nigh, and I couldn't ask her to stay longer to manage the kitchen while I worked outside.

I lugged the bucket into the dining area. The gamers didn't acknowledge me, their heads bent over piles of books, papers, dice.

In the kitchen, I chucked the dirty water down the drain and cleaned the scraper. Charlene sat in a chair, reading a tabloid. The front bell rang.

"You should check on that," she said.

I changed aprons, smoothed my hair, and pushed through the swinging kitchen door to the counter area.

Joy poured herself a cup of coffee from the urn, a newspaper tucked beneath the arm of her gray suit jacket. "Now I understand why my uncle and his buddy hung out here every morning," she said in her flat staccato. "The coffee's not bad, and no one bothers you. I thought not having any waitresses was weird, but American waitresses are revoltingly chipper."

"They have to be," I said. "Most of their income comes from tips."

"True. But I like the atmosphere here."

"Today the atmosphere is dead." And speaking of dead, what had happened to Joe's friend Frank Potts? He'd died about a month before Joe. Everyone seemed to assume it was an accident, but was there a connection?

"About that." She tossed her hair. It fell in a black curtain behind her shoulders. "I realize playing detective is a bad idea, but the police here are useless."

"Oh?"

"Not only have they gotten nowhere on whoever broke into my uncle's house, not to mention his murder, but this weird, old, homeless guy has been hanging around the comic shop. When I asked that cop who was in here the other day about it, he said I could refuse service and tell him to leave."

"Did he?" So her chat with Carmichael had been less of a tête-à-tête and more a banal business meeting. My insides warmed.

"Well," she said, "the homeless guy did leave. If he hadn't, I could have charged him with trespassing, which is a misdemeanor. Your cop is a fount of information, which I think he uses to keep from having to actually do anything."

"I'm not sure that's—"

"Anyway, Joe never mentioned problems with homeless people hanging out in the store. Hopefully, creepy guy is a one-off. But since the police are useless, I've been going through my uncle's things. Maybe I can find the reason why someone killed him."

I bit my bottom lip. The police weren't useless. Well,

maybe Shaw. And though he might not care about the case-book, Joy might. It rightfully belonged to her. Or did it? It had originally been Frank's. At some point, we were going to have to return his casebook to someone. "Have you found anything?" I asked.

"Not yet." She scanned my empty shop. "What's happening to your business is really unfair. Is there anything I can do?"

I nodded toward the gamers. "Right now my only business comes from your customers. They shop at your comic shop and then come here to play."

"I thought they looked familiar. Maybe I should expand our game inventory. I hear board games are coming back."

"There is one thing—how late were you open last night?"

"Until eight. Why?"

"Someone painted graffiti on my front window. Did you see anyone suspicious when you locked up?"

"No, but there's a lot of activity on the street after eight because of those restaurants. I can't imagine someone hitting you until later, when the diners have all cleared out and things have quieted down. What was the graffiti? A gang sign?"

"No."

"So what did it say?" She leaned forward, moistening her lips.

I edged away from the counter, unwilling to tell her the full text of the message. "It said, go home."

"That's it? Go home? Weird."

"Yeah, right?" I swallowed. Charlene was right—Joy hadn't put on a ski mask to break into the house she'd just inherited. But there was something odd about her.

"Well, I'll keep an eye out for vandals." Strolling to a window booth, she sat, unfurling her paper.

I swiped a cloth across the gleaming counter and re-turned to the kitchen, flooded with the scent of baking fruit pies. I liked having a customer, but what was Joy really doing here?

Charlene folded her paper. "There's going to be a thick fog tonight, perfect conditions for our stakeout at old lady Pargiter's."

"What else can you tell me about Antheia Royer?"

"You're not weaseling out of our stakeout?"

"No, I'll do it. But Antheia was avoiding my questions. And aside from Mark, she's the only blond on the library board."

"Okay, let's see, Antheia . . ." She looked toward the ceiling. "Nasty divorce."

"We already knew that." I went to the fridge and pulled out the ingredients for chicken potpies.

"But did you know her husband is suing her for alimony? He spent the last ten years finding himself with his so-called jewelry-making business, and she supported him. Now after cheating on her, he wants her to keep on paying."

"That doesn't seem fair." Should I even bother baking full-size pies, or stick with the minis? People did take home the large potpies for the family, but the minis were a popular lunch item. I nodded. I'd stick with the minis.

"Fair? It's a travesty! In my day, men worked. They took pride in supporting their families. Not that there's anything wrong with women in the workplace. I'm all for independence. But he's a moocher."

"What kind of law does she practice?"

"Wills and trusts. She did mine." Charlene grinned. "She undercharges."

"Where does she work?" I laid out the basil and vegetables—carrots, celery, onion, and snap peas—and unhooked my favorite chopping knife from its wall hanger.

"Now? Out of her house, I think. She's semiretired."

Charlene stood, and her bones cracked. "What's say I surveil her? See who's coming and going?"

"No, I don't think we need to go that far. Besides, it's broad daylight. If she sees you, she'll get suspicious." I chopped the celery.

She raised her chin. "I'll have you know I'm a master of disguise."

"Oh? What have you disguised yourself as?"

"I was Cleopatra last Halloween, and everyone told me I was her spitting image."

"Cleopatra? For you, that seems a little passé."

"I was going to be a jaguar person, but the clerk at the costume shop got things mixed up and gave my costume to someone else. It was either Cleopatra or a vampire. And vampires are so last decade."

I chopped veggies, and we arranged to meet at Miss Pargiter's for our next stakeout.

"I'll call and tell her we're coming," Charlene said, "so she doesn't go after you with the weed whacker."

"I'll take care of it." I wanted to drop a pie off for her after work. Miss Pargiter had looked thin beneath her bulky sweater, and I wondered if she was eating well. Maybe I'd bring two pies. It wasn't as if there was a shortage.

"Right-o. Oh! And I'll bring you season two of Stargate. They really get going in that season. You'll love it." She barreled out the back door, waving over her shoulder.

I put the pies in the oven and went to sit in a window booth with my laptop. Joy had vanished, likely back to the comic shop, and I figured the more people on display, the better. Could I ask the gamers to move to a window booth? No, best let gaming gamers lie. They were my most consistent customers, and I wanted to keep them happy. I sensed happy meant "undisturbed."

I searched for Antheia Royer online. If she had a page for her legal practice, I couldn't find it. Charlene had said

Antheia was semiretired. Maybe she didn't feel the need to keep up a Web site? Her bio on the library board page was brief and unenlightening. The Internet was failing me. How had private investigators researched people in the days before the World Wide Web? WWNDD? What Would Nancy Drew Do?

Thoughtful, I returned to my office and dug through a stack of business cards wrapped in a rubber band. Ripping a card from the deck, I called my lawyer.

He picked up the phone himself. "Robert Arnold."

"Hi, Robert. This is Val Harris from Pie Town."

"Val! I heard about the trouble at your shop. How are you doing?"

"Um, business is a little slow, but I'm doing okay. I was thinking of getting a will made, and wondered if you could recommend anyone."

"Is the death in Pie Town making you ponder your own mortality?" The lawyer chuckled. "Well, it's never too early to make a will or trust. There's Pete Dickson. He's good, and he's local."

"Pete Dickson . . . What about Antheia Royer?" Oooh. Subtle.

"She knows her stuff, and she's inexpensive, but she's also semiretired, working out of her home."

"Oh? Can you give me her contact info?"

"Sure, wait a sec . . ." Pens rattled, and something rolled across a desk. "Here it is." He gave me Antheia's telephone number and address, not far from the center of town. "But I'm not sure if she's taking new clients. Hold on, let me ask Renee. I think she's still doing some legal secretary work for her."

Over the phone there was a muffled shout and conversation.

"She's cut way back," the lawyer said, "but Renee says she's still working."

"She must have done well for herself to take an early semiretirement." Antheia hadn't looked much beyond fifty.

He chuckled. "Doubtful. She undercharges. I think she's always been in it more for the love of the work. If you can't get her, Pete's fees are quite reasonable."

"Thanks. This is a big help. Is Renee only working for you part time?"

"She works part time for a lot of the lawyers around town. Between you and me, Renee does most of this town's legal legwork."

"I'll bet she knows where the bodies are buried."

He barked with laughter. "Not that she's talking."

Renee could be an interesting person to chat with.

I thanked the lawyer and hung up. He was the second person who'd told me Antheia undercharged. If she wasn't taking many new clients, where would she get the money to pay alimony? Did her husband know something I didn't, or was he just a cockeyed optimist?

Chapter 12

A shadow fell across my table, and I looked up. A rotund gamer wearing a black superhero T-shirt loomed over me.

He cleared his throat. "Uh, we wanted to ask you something."

I glanced at the booth with the gamers.

They watched us, silent.

"Sure," I said.

"Are you going to be making breakfast pies, like that guy said? Because those sound good."

Bless the lad and his selective memory. He remembered the fateful quiche, but not that it had been accused of killing a man. "Do you guys want one?"

His stomach growled.

"I could make a breakfast pie," I said, "but it will take an hour."

He hustled back to the table and conferred with his fellow dragon slayers. They nodded. "We can wait," he said.

"Maybe with bacon?" I asked.

They agreed, enthusiastic, and I motored into the kitchen. Fortunately, I was a breakfast person. I had enough bacon, eggs, and Gouda cheese for a pie. And of course, plenty of piecrust at the ready.

I let a few strips of bacon fry while I whisked eggs, spices, and milk in a bowl and thought about Joe. Frank's notebook bothered me. Why had Joe held on to it? For nostalgia? Or had he suspected something had been wrong with Frank's death? It seemed an odd coincidence that the two Baker Street Boys had died within a month of each other. A memory niggled at me. I mentally reached for it, but it slipped away.

Setting the bowl on the metal counter, I diced green onions, shredded cheese. The motions soothed me, as they always did. Bacon crackled, its scent filling the air. I checked the pan. The bacon looked nicely crunchy. Laying the strips on a paper towel to drain, I added to the egg mixture cheese, onions, and the bag of uncooked hash browns. The latter had somehow ended up in the walk-in refrigerator rather than my freezer, and the mistake worked in my favor. They needed to be thawed for this recipe, and these spuds were already soft. I dumped the mixture into a pie pan, lined with one of Charlene's crusts.

Dusting off my hands, I slid the pie into an oven and set the timer.

Joe's buddy, Frank, had died at home, but the details eluded me. Maybe there was some information in the online paper. I walked to my office and flipped open my laptop. Online, I found a short obituary, saying he'd died at the age of seventy-nine after a fall down the stairs in his home. His death could have been an accident. Or not.

I rubbed my forehead. I'd been spending too much time with Charlene. Everywhere I looked now, I saw treachery.

I drummed my fingers on the metal desk. The obituary also mentioned Frank had been survived by a daughter, Tandy Potts. I remembered pressing her hand at the funeral, but we hadn't spoken. A Web search of her name turned up lots of mentions, but no addresses or phone numbers. Charlene would know if she was local. I reached for the phone and snatched back my hand. Did I want to get Charlene involved?

The oven timer pinged. Hurrying to the kitchen, I slid the quiche from the oven and wove the remaining, uncooked bacon on top, making a lattice. It smelled fantastic, a cheesy, bacony, buttery blend, and my stomach growled. Would the gamers be willing to share?

Brushing maple syrup over the bacon, I reminded myself I wasn't hungry. I put a pie shield over the crust and returned the quiche to the small oven, raising the temperature and setting the timer.

I needed to learn more about Frank's death. Mark wasn't going to help me, and even if he was willing, I wouldn't ask. Not after our last encounter. Though I still wanted my stuff back, especially the giant spiral fossil a friend had brought me from Morocco. I really liked that fossil.

I shook my head. Forget the table decor. I could ask Officer Carmichael about Frank, but then he'd guess I was looking into Joe's death. Apparently, law enforcement frowned on outsider involvement in investigations.

There was a shout from the diner. "Aw, come on! My orc can't be dead."

I leaned one hip against the counter. I could ask Joy. She'd seemed down with my amateur sleuthing. Which was odd, since the two proper reactions to amateur sleuthing are laughing or running.

Joe might have talked to his niece about Frank's death, and Joy was right next door in the comic shop. Besides, maybe she'd stumbled across her uncle's casebook. If Frank and Joe had been murdered, the killer had been inside both of their homes—someone they knew? Joe was smart. He wouldn't let a potential killer inside, unless that killer was someone he trusted, someone like his niece. Maybe the killer had planted the castor beans in Joe's kitchen before he'd had time to grow suspicious. Or maybe Joe hadn't been suspicious of anyone, because he hadn't been investigating Frank's death.

This was all speculation. Great galloping gum boots, I was turning into Charlene.

The oven timer pinged from the kitchen.

Removing the quiche from the oven, I tilted it carefully to pour off the bacon grease, then set it on the cooling rack. The bacon lattice had pulled away from the edges, making a perfect circle atop the pie. I sighed, inhaling, and my muscles relaxed. Bacon makes everything better. Beneath the lattice, the quiche—sorry, breakfast pie—was golden yellow and firm to the touch. Maybe I should branch out into breakfast? Sell quiche by the slice like my other pies? Mini-quiches?

I blew out my breath. If I didn't turn things around, I wouldn't be baking anything. Pie Town would close, and I . . . I had no idea what I would do. There had never been a plan B. Everything I possessed had gone into plan A.

I tasted something sour in my mouth. By my estimates, I had a month to get Pie Town back on track before I'd be visiting my lawyer about bankruptcy proceedings. After that, I'd have to throw myself on Mark's mercy and see if he could get me out of the lease. The thought turned my stomach.

When the quiche was cool enough, I cut it and brought it to the table with a stack of plates.

The gamers shoved aside their books, papers, and dice.

"The pie tin is still hot," I warned, sliding trembling slices onto the plates.

They watched, unspeaking. Candied bacon has that effect on people. "If you like Pie Town," I said, "tell a friend. I could use the business."

The redhead forked a bite of quiche into his mouth. His eyes rolled back. "Genius," he mumbled. "Where did you learn to bake?"

I paused, surprised. The gamers usually didn't engage in conversation. "My mother. Most of the recipes are from her family, Pennsylvania Dutch. The others she modified from old magazines. She was always trying out new recipes."

He tucked into his pie, and I left, feeling I'd been dismissed. But in a good way. I had a great product. Now if only I could get more customers in here to taste it.

Officer Carmichael stopped by for lunch, claiming his window booth and ordering a beef potpie.

Feeling weightless, I brought him the steaming, minipotpie and his glass scraper. I scooted onto the seat across from him, my jeans squeaking on the pink faux leather.

"Your neighbor has said she'll keep an eye out for any vandals," he said.

"Who? Oh. Great. Can I ask you a question?" After all, I wasn't investigating. I was asking questions. There was no law against questions, was there?

"That depends on the question," he said.

"Joe and his friend, Frank Potts, had some sort of Sherlock Holmes club. They solved cases together, from their armchairs. Frank died a month ago, and now Joe's dead, murdered." My heart beat faster. I wasn't admitting to having the casebook, but I had to make sure the police were on the right track.

"What's your question?"

"Do the police think there's a connection?"

"Do you think there's a connection?"

"The thing is, Charlene showed me one of Frank's casebooks—"

"Are you playing detective? Because if you were, I'd

have to tell you that you could be guilty of impeding an investigation."

My mouth went dry, and I pressed one hand to my heart. "No! That's crazy talk. I heard some things and am reporting them to you, so the police can look into them."

"I'm not the investigating officer. If you know anything, you should tell Detective Shaw."

I must have made a face, because he continued, "Shaw's not that bad."

Shaw didn't seem that good either. "Charlene told detective Shaw about the casebook. He wasn't interested."

"There you go then."

"I heard Frank fell down the stairs," I said.

"Yes."

"In his home."

"Yes."

Well, namaste, Mr. Talkative. I met his gaze. "He and Joe met here for coffee every morning. When Frank died, it really upset Joe. Do you think he could have been investigating Frank's death?"

"If you have any information, you need to talk to Shaw."

I looked at my hands, palms flat on the Formica tabletop. Should I call Detective Shaw to back up Charlene's story about the burglar grabbing for the casebook? The last time I'd encountered Shaw, he'd practically accused me of murder. "I don't think Detective Shaw wants to hear anything from me."

"He wants to close this case."

"Charlene doesn't think much of him."

His lips quirked. "Charlene doesn't think much of anyone. Shaw did peg Joe's death as a possible homicide, and he was right."

And a little too quick? Joe was elderly. The signs of poison hadn't been obvious. He could have had a seizure. Why had Shaw jumped to the death-by-poison solution?

"What's wrong?" Carmichael asked.

"Nothing." I slid from the booth. "I'll talk to Shaw. Enjoy the pie."

The gamers left at four o'clock, and I closed the shop. No one else was coming to Pie Town today. Heat warmed the back of my eyelids, and I rubbed my face.

I wandered down the sidewalk to the comic shop. Pale young men in saggy clothes browsed the aisles. Joy sat behind the counter, gnawing on a pen and staring at a laptop computer screen.

"Hi, Joy."

She pointed to a far corner with her pen. "Action figure sale is over there."

"It's me. Val."

Looking up, she brushed a chunk of black hair behind her ear. "Oh. Sorry. How's business? I would have come by for lunch today, but . . ."

"You can't eat pie every day. It's okay. I get it. How well did you know Frank Potts?"

"Joe's buddy? Not very well. Why?"

"Doesn't it seem weird that Frank would die falling down the stairs, and then someone poisoned his fellow investigator a month later?"

"Maybe." She ground the tip of her pen into the wooden counter. "What's your point?"

"Frank and Joe kept casebooks, notes on their investigations. Have you found any of your uncle's? If he's got notes on Frank's death, then that means he thought it was suspicious too. Maybe he was investigating."

She gave me a long look. "I found some old notebooks in his office. Come on." Rising, she turned toward the back office.

"Um, you've got a few customers." I rubbed the back of my neck. "I can come back later."

She glanced over her shoulder. "I'll be in the back room," she yelled. "Steal anything, and I'll rip your throat out."

We seemed to have differing philosophies on customer service. "Or you can do that." I hurried after her.

The office looked as I'd seen it last, boxes stacked in the corners. For a supposedly organized guy, Joe had a disaster zone of an office.

Hands on the hips of her gray slacks, Joy stood in the center of the cramped room and turned. "I saw them in one of those filing cabinets." She pointed at a set of dented cabinets, piled high with boxes and bracketing a copy machine. "You take that one." She wove around a garbage bin to another tall set of metal drawers.

Wary, I edged toward the cabinet, my eyes on the teetering boxes. If Joy was plotting my death by comic books, it would be an easy sell in this mess. I tugged on a drawer. It stuck, and the boxes on top wobbled. I pushed the latch, tarnished by decades of fingerprints, and slid open the drawer. It was filled with manila folders. I opened the drawer beneath and the one below that.

"Here they are," Joy said.

Gently, I slid the drawer back, eyeing the boxes quivering above me, and edged away.

She handed me a classroom style, spiral-bound notebook.

I flipped through its pages. They dated back years, cases of lurkers in bushes (the grocer, sneaking a smoke), stolen surfboards (unsolved), and lost dogs (returned to owners unharmed). They read like stories, and I chuckled over the Mystery of the Footsteps in the Garden. "This is too old," I said. "We need his recent cases."

"I think this is it." She handed me another flimsy notebook. As in Frank's book, the case details were sketchy—the Case of the Thudding Footfalls, the Case of the Harbor

Lights, and the Case of the Bloated B. Why hadn't he spelled out *blond*? Had Joe a less flattering word for Antheia Royer? It was a good bet the *B* didn't stand for *Baker*. I flipped forward to the fourth Chapter heading. Two words: *Frank Potts*.

Heart racing, I flipped through the rest of Joe's casebook. It was as empty as Frank's had been. "He was investigating Frank's death, or at least he thought it was worth investigating." I frowned, hunching over the book. "But there are no actual case notes."

"He only wrote up the notes after the case was solved."

"But there was a case." Something fluttered beneath my breastbone. "Frank Potts was a case. Frank might have been murdered too."

Chapter 13

Joy hung up her office phone. An overhead fluorescent flickered.

"What did Shaw say?" I asked.

She tucked a strand of hair behind her ear, her glasses glinting in the light from her orange, seventies-era desk lamp. "He thanked me and said he'd keep it in mind."

"He doesn't want to see the casebook?" I slumped in the folding chair.

"He didn't ask for it."

"But, that's . . ." I sputtered. Shaw wasn't taking this seriously.

"Look," Joy said, "Shaw told me Frank's death was an accident."

"Your uncle didn't think so." I crossed my arms over my chest.

"We've done all we could. We've given Shaw the information. If he thinks it's worth following up on, he will."

Yeah, if he thought it was worth it, and it seemed he didn't. I rose. "Right. My duty here is done. Um, can I borrow this book?"

She hesitated. "I've got a photocopy machine. I can copy the pages for you."

"Thanks."

It didn't take long. There were only four pages to copy.

Photocopies in hand, I said good-bye and walked to my car, parked in the alley behind Pie Town. Shaw was an idiot. I got into the car and locked the doors. Could I take this to Officer Carmichael? Maybe, but he was beneath Shaw in the chain of command. And as he'd told me, it wasn't his case.

Frank had been a case, and my mind dizzied at the ramifications. Had someone killed Frank because of Antheia or mystery lights or Miss Pargiter's trespassers? And what about the Whispering Wanderer? That wasn't in Joe's book, only Frank's. Or had someone killed Frank for another reason? There were six cases now, and I wasn't sure where to start. The Baker Street Boys had been busy.

I started—Antheia. She had called Joe a Baker Street Boy. She knew more about his investigating than she'd admitted. And my questions about Joe had unnerved her. They said poison was a woman's weapon. Maybe pushing an old man down the stairs wasn't outside the realm of possibility for her either. Antheia wasn't bloated, but she was no waif. She could manage it, especially with surprise on her side. My hands tightened on the wheel. She was either guilty, or she knew something. We needed to talk.

I pulled up beside Antheia's house, a craftsman-style bungalow painted moss green with white trim. A wooden sign was stuck in her front yard, and I sucked in my breath, half expecting to see Mark's grinning realtor mug. But the sign advertised her legal services.

The front windows were dark, impossible to see inside.

I checked my watch. Five-thirty. Was confronting a potential murderer a good idea? The answer to that was easy: no. Was I going to do it anyway? The VW's metal frame ticked, cooling, contracting. I drummed my fingers on the steering wheel.

Yes.

I reached for the car door handle.

No.

I pulled away and folded my hands in my lap. At the very least, someone should know where I was before I leapt into the proverbial breach. Sighing, I dug my phone from my purse, dialed. I only had one person to call.

"Charlene?"

"Hi, Val. If you're calling about the stakeout, I'll pick you up at eleven. Be sure to wear warm clothes this time. I'll bring the snacks. Would you prefer sweet or salty?"

"Sweet." Stepping out of the car, I walked down the brick path to Antheia's porch. "I'm outside Antheia Royer's house. Since she didn't answer my questions the last time I tried, I figured I'd try again."

"Do you want me to meet you there? I'm good at drawing people out."

I climbed the porch steps. "I'm here already. If our last encounter is anything to go by, she probably won't even let me in." I knocked on the white-paneled door. It swung open beneath my fist. I froze, hand raised, scalp prickling.

"If all else fails," she said, "maybe you can suggest sponsoring a library event. It wouldn't be a bad idea for Pie Town, and the jaguars—"

"The door's open." Either Antheia was one of those free-wheeling types who always kept it unlatched, or something was wrong.

"What?"

"Her front door's open," I said. "Hold on."

"Do not go inside. Do not—"

I lowered the phone from my ear and leaned inside the small, square foyer. "Hello? Antheia?" The walls were cream colored, large white-painted beams running from floor to ceiling. The floor was blond, natural wood, none of that laminate stuff. Low bookcases created a break between the foyer and an office area to the left, with a wide, wooden desk, and a living area on the right. "Hello?"

Ignoring Charlene's squawks, I sidled inside. "Antheia?"

I walked down a step, hovering at the entry to the office. One of the curtains hung loose, allowing waning sunlight to slice across the floor. The rest of the room was in shadow. Something seemed odd, out of place, and the open door had my heart jumping. No bodies lay on the pink and ivory oriental-style carpet. No bloodstains puddled on the wood floor behind the desk. No Antheia slouched in the leather executive chair.

Maybe she'd gone shopping and had forgotten to close up? As a good neighbor, I should leave and lock the door. But the sense of wrongness weighted my shoulders, tightened my neck.

I took another step down into the home office. Okay, I'd take a quick look around to make sure everything was okay. That was neighborly, wasn't it? And since the door had been open, I wasn't breaking and entering. Just entering.

I walked to the desk, scanning the room. A woman's sensible blue shoe stuck out behind it, toe pointing toward the ceiling. Groaning, I edged around the desk.

Antheia lay on the floor, her eyes wide and blank. Her face was bluish, mottled. A thick green and gold cord knotted around her neck. Her blond hair was rumpled. Her skirt rose up around her thighs.

I stood staring, nauseated. I should move, take charge, help. But no sensible plan of action burst into my brain.

Charlene's tinny shouts recalled me. Dropping to my knees, I felt for Antheia's pulse, found none.

She stared at the ceiling.

Antheia was dead.

I put the phone to my ear. "I found Antheia. She's dead. Murdered. I have to go."

"What?"

Hanging up, I called 9-1-1, then went to the front porch to wait. I sat on a swing chair and rocked, mindless. The swaying turned my stomach. I stood and leaned against the railing, jammed my trembling hands in my pockets.

A siren sounded in the distance, grew louder.

I thought of the thick cord around her neck. It was a curtain tie. She'd been killed in her home. Had the killer been one of her clients? Or had someone snuck in and surprised her? There had been no signs of breaking and entering at the front of the house, but I hadn't explored further than her office.

A squad car stopped across the street. Officer Carmichael stepped out, and a measure of my tension leaked away.

He strode onto the porch. "What happened?"

"I found Antheia in her office, inside. She's dead." My voice shook, and I cleared my throat.

"Wait here." He went into the house.

I waited.

A few minutes later, he emerged. "Did you touch anything?" His tone was hard, impersonal.

Had I? I struggled to remember. "I knocked on the door, and it opened, so I didn't touch the knob. And then I went inside. I might have grabbed the desk for balance when I checked her pulse."

"You touched her? Did you touch anything else?"

"I don't think so. I called nine-one-one on my phone and then came out here to wait."

"Okay." He nodded. "What are you doing here?"

For a brief moment I considered lying, but that wouldn't fly. Too many people knew I'd been asking Antheia about Joe's case. And I couldn't ask Charlene to cover for me.

"Val?" he asked.

"Sorry. Today Joy and I found another casebook, but of her uncle's. He and his buddy, Frank, were armchair detectives, investigating local mysteries for fun."

"I know. You told me at lunch."

I cleared my throat. "In the casebook, we found an entry about Frank's death last month, as if it were a case Joe was investigating. And he had an entry about someone on the library board, called it the Case of the Bloated Blond. Antheia and Mark are the only blonds on the library board, so I came here to ask her if she knew anything about it."

His lips whitened. "What time did you arrive?"

"Around five-thirty."

"Did you see anyone or anything unusual?"

"No."

"We'll need to take your fingerprints to separate them from any others we might find inside. Stay here. There will be more questions."

An ambulance and fire truck arrived at the same time, followed by another squad car and a blue, midsized sedan. Shaw got out of the sedan and stretched. He spotted me, and his eyes narrowed.

An icicle pierced my heart. It didn't take a psychic to see a trip to the police station was in my future.

The police released me three hours later, and I stumbled down the station's brick steps. Fog coiled on the dark street, light from the streetlamps reflecting off the sheen on the macadam. A Jeep flashed its high beams at me. I hurried down the sidewalk and opened the passenger door.

Charlene leaned across the seat. "I always knew it would come to this."

"Always?"

"One of us, in jail. It's the fate of the misunderstood investigator."

"Sounds like a title from one of Joe's casebooks. How did you know they'd let me out?" I got inside and buckled my seat belt.

Frederick, draped around Charlene's neck, raised his head. He regarded me, his blue eyes heavy with disdain.

"I've got someone inside the station," she said. "My source told me they'd taken you away in a police car and you might need a lift. Now we still have time for that stake-out at Pargiter's—"

I groaned, rubbing my forehead.

"But maybe not tonight. You're not dressed for it." She handed me a short, black leather tube with a red button on top.

"What's this?"

"Pepper spray. It's past its sell-by date, but they just use those expiration dates to get you to buy more."

I massaged my temple. "Of course."

"So what happened inside the station?" she asked. "Did Shaw give you the third degree?"

I handed her the pepper spray. Knowing my luck, I'd end up spraying myself. "The phrase *obstruction of justice* was used. Repeatedly. I told them I was in Joe's house with you."

She pocketed the spray. "But he didn't charge you."

"No, because he doesn't believe there's anything Sherlock Holmes–mysterious about Frank's death." Shaw had actually seemed to think it was sweet I'd indulged my piecrust maker's home invasion. The worst of it was, I had sort of gone to Joe's house to pacify Charlene. Was I guilty of patronizing the aged too?

"What happened at Antheia's house?" Charlene asked.

I told her about Antheia and the drapery cord, the case-book Joy had found, Joe's investigation of Frank's death.

"I knew Antheia wasn't a killer." Charlene started the Jeep. "She must have had some information on the real murderer."

"Were she and Frank acquainted?"

"He was a semiretired CPA, and she was a semiretired estate attorney. Of course she knew him. This is a small town, and those two professions work hand in glove."

"At least we know her murder doesn't have anything to do with Miss Pargiter's trespassers or the lights in the harbor."

"Untrue," she said. "Joe's murder is connected to Antheia—her death proves that. But for all we know, it may be linked to the other cases as well. We can't leave any loose threads hanging. They may all have a bearing on Joe's death. Now, where's your car?"

"I left it parked in front of Antheia's house."

Pulling away from the curb, she turned onto Main Street. The restaurants and boutiques were closed at this hour, their windows blank, black eyes. I shuddered, remembering Antheia's dead gaze.

"We can't even be sure Frank was murdered," I said, "only that Joe thought it was worth investigating."

"Falling down the stairs." She made a clicking noise with her tongue. "I should have known something was wrong."

"What can you tell me about Frank?"

"He was my accountant, the quiet type. But he was friendly once you got to talking. A good man. Solid. Honest."

"Accountant . . . Could he have discovered some wrong-doing on the part of one of his clients?"

She turned onto a residential street. Cypress trees reached across it, their branches forming a dark tunnel. "He was semiretired. His clients were all small potatoes at the end, folks like Miss Pargiter. And if they did do anything wrong, they'd be fools to tell him. Accountants aren't lawyers. They're not covered by privilege, and Frank was a stickler for doing things right."

"Miss Pargiter was one of Frank's clients?"

"Most of the over-fifties were with Frank. He was a San Nicholas institution."

"Who can we talk to about his death? You said you had a contact in the police department?"

Her eyelashes fluttered. "Oh, I couldn't abuse my source."

"Charlene . . ."

"I can't! I only get so many favors, and then that's all she wrote."

Augh. "There must be someone we can talk to."

"He had a daughter. I think she lives in San Francisco." Charlene pulled behind my VW, still parked in front of Antheia's house.

"Tandy Potts?" I asked.

"That's the one."

"Frank's daughter it is. Thanks for the ride." I yawned and stepped out, shutting the door.

The passenger window glided down, and Charlene leaned across her seat. "No problem. I'll call Miss Pargiter and tell her we'll come tomorrow night instead."

I watched her drive off. She was not going to let me escape the Pargiter stakeout. But at least she hadn't mentioned the mysterious harbor lights. UFOs—ha!

Who was I kidding? Right now, a UFO abduction would make a relaxing getaway.

Chapter 14

Carmichael did not make a lunch appearance the next day. I must have fallen out of his good graces after "obstructing an investigation." Which was a lot of nonsense. I'd told Shaw about every bit of evidence I'd found. Was it my fault they'd ignored the clues until someone else was killed? I wasn't sure.

Now I sat in Carmichael's empty booth, the afternoon sun warming my shoulders, and researched library board members on my laptop. I found nothing suspicious. It was a library board. Nothing bad ever happened at a library.

I paused, gnawing my lower lip. Had it been my fault that someone had murdered Antheia? If I'd verified Charlene's story about the break-in earlier . . . But even after I'd confessed last night, Shaw hadn't given it any credence. The break-in wasn't the sole root of my guilt, however. By following in Joe's footsteps, had I, like Joe, stirred up a killer?

Dice rattled in the corner booth. "Yes!"

My hands stilled, poised over the computer mouse. Should I stop looking?

A gamer howled. "No way."

I moused on, but everything I turned up seemed routine—the library board thanking a local donor for a gift of five thousand dollars, the library board hosting a bake sale. The biggest news was the new library, completed a year ago, and the bond measure to raise funds for its construction. People had had to vote on the bond. That meant opinion pieces pro and con, the mayor making speeches about the importance of literacy, etc., etc. Aside from a couple odes to the historic architecture of the old library in the paper's Letters to the Editor section, there'd been no real opposition to the library funding.

Moans of despair rose from the corner booth.

I glanced the gamers' way, then returned my attention to my laptop.

Would my coupons bring people into Pie Town? Manic, my brain bounced between crises. I blew out my breath, scraping my fingers through my hair. My research was going nowhere.

A shadow fell across my table, and I looked up.

The redheaded gamer shuffled his feet, his T-shirt untucked from his loose jeans. In fairness, given the size of his beer gut, it was unlikely tucking it in would have had any lasting effect.

"Can I get you anything?" I asked.

"Our sea hag had to go. Want to finish the game?"

I parsed that through my gamer-to-English translator. "You lost a gamer and want me to take his place?"

His bushy brow furrowed. "That's what I said."

I looked around the dining area, forsaken by all but me and the gamers. "Sure."

We'd been at it about an hour when a customer came in—an out of towner, was my guess—and ordered a blueberry pie to go. I sold her the pie and returned to the game. I'd already lost one round, and was going for two out of three. The boys turned out to be engineering students. They were decent guys, even if I didn't get all their jokes. I lost the next two rounds, and was on the verge of winning the fourth (we were on four out of seven now) when Charlene strolled in. Frederick lounged over one shoulder, depositing white cat hairs across her purple, knit tunic.

Hoping the gamers wouldn't notice the cat, I checked my watch. It was past closing time.

"Monsters and Madness?" Charlene adjusted her glasses. "That stuff will rot your brain."

I straightened, indignant. "It's a game of strategy. Sorry, guys," I said to the gamers. "I've got to close up."

"Sure thing, Sea Hag." The redhead, whose name was Ray, chuffed my shoulder.

The gamers left, and I cleaned their table. With only one table to clean, closing up was a breeze. "You can't bring Frederick into the dining area."

Charlene sat on a bar stool, swiveling back and forth. "He's a comfort animal."

"Oh, that is the most abused excuse. . . . He is not."

"Is too!" She checked her watch. "Besides, it's after hours."

I glanced at the clock again and frowned. "Hold on, it's only six o'clock. Our stakeout isn't until after eleven."

"I thought you might want to get out, go to dinner. There's a great new pizza place in the mini-mall. The crust is perfect—thin and flaky. The owner uses fresh herbs he picks himself."

"I was thinking of taking a potpie over to Miss Pargiter's." And I'd planned on going alone.

"Why?" Charlene asked.

And that was why I'd planned to go alone. "It didn't look like she was eating too well."

Charlene hopped off the bar stool. "You may be right. I can't stand it when old people get old. Okay, Pargiter's it is. Bring the turkey, that's my favorite."

I boxed one up, along with a strawberry-rhubarb pie for

dessert. The few remaining pies I put in the freezer. We'd dropped way off on pie production, so I didn't have the waste of those first two days. One of the staff members would eat the pies eventually. Still, it killed me to see my freezer full of perfectly good pies.

Charlene drove, the pies in my lap. We took Main Street, passing the bright pink feed store and the cutesy herbal apothecary. It would be Saturday tomorrow, bringing the weekend tourist hordes and clots of traffic. I couldn't wait. Tourists meant business, and I hoped news of Joe's death in Pie Town hadn't reached far beyond our borders. Silently, I prayed for sunshine and surfers and families with screaming children, looking for a place to rest.

"I've been thinking about Antheia." Charlene slowed at a red light, drifted through it.

I bit back a comment. "Me too. I spent the day researching people on the library board, but I couldn't find anything."

"Most murders are committed by spouses. Maybe her husband figured instead of alimony, he'd go for the whole whack by knocking her off."

"But why would Joe and Frank investigate Antheia, or conduct an investigation on her behalf? From what everyone's told me, they investigated local petty crimes. They weren't PIs, peering through windows and trying to get the goods on cheating spouses. His note specifically mentioned the library board."

"Have you ever been on a board?"

"No."

"I have. And while we all had fantasies of killing our fellow board members, it's only a board. The meeting ends and you go home with boring tales to gripe over."

"But what if there was some funny business on the board?" I asked.

"What sort of funny business?"

"Misuse of funds or embezzlement or something."

"The library board reports to the town council," she said. "All budgets are approved there. It would be tough for someone on the board to get away with anything."

"Oh." But there was always a way, wasn't there? People got away with it until they got caught, and then everyone wondered how it went on for so long. "Do you still have Frank's casebook? I want to take another look at it."

She snorted and turned onto Highway 1, joining the flow of traffic. "Thinking he wrote a message in invisible ink?" Headlights from a car passing in the other direction cast Charlene's face into a gargoyle scowl. "Knowing Frank and Joe, he might have. I hear lemon juice works."

"Lemon juice?"

"As invisible ink." She snorted. "Weren't you ever a kid? To read it, all you need is to apply a little heat."

"Don't set our biggest clue on fire without me."

"I won't set it on fire."

Arguing amiably, we pulled alongside Miss Pargiter's house. I slid out of the Jeep, balancing the pie boxes in my hands, and pushed the car door closed with my hip. The old-fashioned streetlamp in her garden was on tonight, and light streamed across the porch of the green Victorian. We crunched up the driveway, our footsteps creaking on the worn porch steps.

The front door opened, framing a masculine silhouette. I took a step back. "Officer Carmichael?"

He tugged at the collar of his fisherman's sweater, and my heart turned over. Carmichael looked good out of uniform, in his jeans and hiking boots.

"Who is it? Who's there?" a querulous voice called from inside the house.

"It's Miss Harris and Mrs. McCree," he said over his shoulder. "What are you two doing here?"

Charlene's expression grew solemn. "We're on a mi—"

"We wanted to bring Miss Pargiter some pies," I said loudly. "I had a few extra. It seemed a shame to let them go to waste."

Miss Pargiter appeared behind him, her oversized gray sweater and skirt sagging on her narrow frame. "Pies? What kind?"

"Turkey potpie and strawberry-rhubarb," Charlene said.

Miss Pargiter clapped her hands together. "How lovely. Come in, come in." She backed into the hall.

Carmichael stood aside.

"Officer Carmichael fixed my outside lamp," Miss Pargiter said.

"I didn't know you and Miss Pargiter were friends," I said in a low voice.

Charlene bumped past us.

He grimaced, taking the boxes from my hands. "I came by to talk with her about the trespassers. I thought . . ." He flushed. "I decided to make her dinner."

"Oh." Wow. Cops did that? "The pies will freeze. I can leave instructions—"

"Do you want to join us? You and Charlene, I mean."

Heat radiated in my chest. "Sure! Sounds fun." I stepped back and bumped into an umbrella stand. Wait, did this mean he hadn't stopped by Pie Town because today was his day off? Not that it was realistic to come into the same place for lunch every day. But maybe he wasn't annoyed with me after all.

"As long as you don't ask me about the case." He shut the door behind us.

"Oh. Right. Sure. Hold on, only one case? Does this mean the police believe Antheia's murder and Joe's death are linked?"

He pressed his lips together and gave me a look. "Tell me you've stopped your little investigation. After Antheia's death—"

"I'm not investigating. And I won't ask about the case," I said. I followed him down the cramped hall, through the doily-splattered living room. Miss Pargiter and Charlene huddled on a couch, heads together, whispering.

Officer Carmichael led me into a kitchen straight out of the fifties. Mint-green tiles lined the walls. The refrigerator was ancient, with one of those locking doors. I shuddered, remembering my mother's stories about kids getting locked inside and suffocating.

He laid the pies on the white tile counter, beside a bunch of spinach, a cardboard basket of mushrooms, and a tub of mascarpone. "Please tell me that wasn't a dead cat on Mrs. McCree's shoulder."

"Not dead, deaf. That's Frederick." The kitchen smelled of chicken and melted cheese, and my mouth watered. "He's also got narcolepsy."

"A deaf, narcoleptic cat? Are you sure he's not lazy?"

"It's possible. In fact, probable."

I leaned against the counter. Warmth emanated from the oven. A pot of water simmered on the stove. I wracked my brain for a conversational gambit that did not include deadly refrigerators. Unfortunately, most of my conversations lately had started with, "What can I get you?" and ended with "That will be . . ."

Conversation, witty conversation . . . Witty conversation might be aiming too high tonight. Right now, I'd settle for stilted intercourse. Discourse! I meant discourse!

"I have coupons now." I reached into my jacket pocket and handed him two—25 percent off any size pie.

"Thanks."

I winced. I have coupons? What kind of conversation starter was that? "Have you always been a cop?"

"Since I graduated from college."

"So what do you enjoy about police work?" And that sounded snarky. Tonight I was a reverse Oscar Wilde.

"Nights like this are the reason why I got into policing—to help people. Unfortunately, most of the time I end up dealing with lying scumbags." He rubbed the back of his neck. "It's made me cynical, but it's also made me value honest people like you."

Honest people like me. My appetite evaporated. Charlene and I hadn't quit our investigation. I'd flat-out lied to him about it, because it was easier than telling the truth. I was as bad as . . . Mark.

My throat thickened. "It must be hard to trust people when you see so much of their dark side."

"Some days it seems like everyone's lying—the witnesses, the accused, the lawyers. It's nice to come to a home like this, have a quiet meal with good people, and remember why I became a cop."

"Why did you return to San Nicholas?"

"My parents are getting older. My dad's been having a hard time, and my mom hasn't been able to cope. It was time for me to come home."

"Well, I'm glad you did. And thanks for sitting in my window this week when nearly everyone else is staying away. You're a good guy, Officer Carmichael."

"Call me Gordon."

"So that's why Shaw called you GC. I thought most cops called each other by their last names."

He folded his arms across his broad chest, his expression pinched. "They do."

I waited a beat, confused by the unexpected, crackling-ice tension. Mine hadn't been the most sparkling conversation, but I didn't think it had been that awful.

"And you?" he asked. "What do you like about Pie Town?"

"Baking, the people, having my own place," I said, relieved we'd moved on to a safer topic. "In fact, I love pretty much everything except the hours." And the murder.

The hours, at least, I could fix. I'd been thinking of closing on Mondays. Now seemed a good time to make that switch. "But I've always loved baking," I said, "ever since I was a kid making a mess in my mom's kitchen. And I love the independence of being my own boss." I'd been so proud when I'd opened Pie Town. My mom would have loved it, with its kitschy, 1950s feel and all the old family recipes. My eyes grew damp, and I blinked. "So how can I help?"

He gave me a startled look.

"With dinner," I said.

"You can wash the spinach."

I set to it, watching him rinse the mushrooms and pat them dry with a paper towel. He sliced them expertly, dropped them into a bowl, and scooped the mascarpone on top of them, then set them in the microwave.

"You're—seriously?" I asked.

"Don't knock it until you've tried it," he said. "These mushrooms are my secret weapon."

"In the microwave," I said, disbelieving.

"Ten minutes and mascarpone. It's all you need."

"And the spinach?"

He dumped the whole leaves into the boiling water and stirred with a wooden spoon. After a few minutes, he pulled the spinach out and ran cool water over it in a strainer. He squeezed the water from the leaves, then mixed them with a packet of Japanese seasoning.

"Where'd you get that?" I asked.

"Japanese grocery store."

The joys of living near San Francisco. I peeked in the oven. A casserole bubbled inside, its edges browning. "I take it there's no ethnic theme to this dinner."

He laughed. "The theme is: stuff I can make."

"It smells fantastic. And your casserole looks done."

He removed the casserole from the oven.

I watched, skeptical, as he took the mushrooms from the microwave. Then I stopped staring and set the table for two more.

It had been ages since I'd sat around a dinner table in a real dining room, and nostalgia swamped me. Gordon had us in stitches with stories of his policing, and the mushrooms could have come out of a French kitchen. Too bad I was rebound girl and a big fat lying liar, because I could really like Gordon.

Who was I kidding? I did like Gordon. He was funny and handsome and cooked for elderly ladies. Unlike my ex, he seemed to care about the difference between truth and a lie. Unlike my errant father, he cared about family obligations. He made mushrooms that tasted divine, even if they did come from a microwave. He smiled at me, and my insides quivered in response.

Stupid rebound.

Chapter 15

After dinner, we ate the rhubarb pie with Gordon's ice cream melting into the lattice crust.

"Watch this." Charlene exhumed a laser pointer from her purse and zipped the pointer's red light around the Persian carpet. Frederick deigned to open one eye and tracked it, his ears twitching.

"Impressive," I said. "Good job, Frederick."

Curling his lip, he feigned sleep.

Charlene fixed Gordon with a gimlet eye. "So, young man, when are you going to make detective? I heard you took the exam."

My insides writhed. Did Charlene have no personal boundaries?

"San Nicholas is too small a town for two detectives," he said. "It doesn't have the budget."

"You should be the detective," Miss Pargiter said. "So many interesting crimes in San Nicholas."

Would Miss Pargiter spill the beans about our stakeout? I shifted in my cushioned chair, looking for a diversion. "That photo behind you, who is it?" I raised my chin toward a framed picture on the wall. The same young man I'd seen pictured in the hallway mugged for a close-up.

Miss Pargiter twisted, squinting at the black and white photo. "My brother. He's gone, I'm afraid."

"I'm so sorry," I said.

"Oh, he didn't die. He left. We had a tremendous fight about one of his girlfriends, and he left town. I haven't seen him since. Never saw her again either." She shook her head. "Such a silly thing to cause so much pain. I think about him every day."

"By now he's probably dead," Charlene said.

I glared. "Charlene!"

"Well, why else wouldn't he call?" Charlene asked. "This isn't the dark ages. Even Pargiter's got a cell phone."

We cleaned up and said our good-byes, and Miss Pargiter urged me to call her Emily.

I got into Charlene's Jeep. Fog swaddled the windows, and I tightened my jacket against the cold.

"Officer Carmichael is a nice young fellow," Charlene said, her expression sly. "I heard he was detective at his last job. He must have had a good reason to return to San Nicholas and take a demotion."

He wanted to take care of his parents, the way I'd taken care of my mother at the end. "Hm. I'm glad he spoke with Miss Pargiter about her trespassers, but talk about bad timing. What are we going to do about tonight's stakeout? Come back later?"

"We'll have to." She waved at Gordon, standing on the porch, hands on his lean hips. "Officer Carmichael is too much of a gentleman to leave before making sure we're safely on our way."

She revved the Jeep, and we drove to a white-washed adobe restaurant and bar, its Spanish roof tiles darkened with damp. Waving to the hostess, Charlene led me down a set of wooden stairs to a patio bar overlooking the ocean cliffs. I ordered cups of coffee, and Charlene grabbed two folded blankets from a bin. A couple rose from a swinging bench, blankets in hand, and we snagged their abandoned seat.

"We have to sit outside, if you don't mind." She pointed to the cat draped over her shoulder. "Can't bring him into the restaurant bar."

"I don't mind." Even if it was cold, there was something magical about the muted roar and salty scent of the ocean, hidden beneath the fog bank.

"I suppose this place is called the White Lady because it's white?" I asked.

"Oh, no," Charlene said, "because it used to be a speak-easy. Bootleggers smuggled alcohol up from the ocean. And of course, it's haunted."

I groaned. "Let me guess, the ghost of a bootlegger's girlfriend?"

"I think she was the bartender's girlfriend. She threw herself off this very cliff when she caught him with another woman. The dimwit should have known better. He was the local lothario—not worth all the fuss if you ask me."

I shivered, wrapping the soft blanket around me tighter. "You knew him?"

She laughed. "Hell, no. That was well before my time. There's also a naughty male ghost who likes to hang out in the women's restroom."

"Good to know."

"And speaking of naughty men, that Officer Carmichael likes you."

My cheeks warmed. "He brought Miss Pargiter dinner, not me."

"But he was happy to see you there."

"I'm not interested in Gordon."

"You ought to be. He's handsome, smart, and kind to cats and old people." She sighed. "It's hard to believe I'm not a teenager anymore."

"Come off it. You'll never be old."

"And you'll never have a boyfriend if you turn your nose up at someone like Gordon Carmichael."

"I'm not turning my nose up. I'm just not ready."

"The best way to get over an old love is to find a new one."

"Yeah, but that usually doesn't turn out well for Rebound Guy."

"Gordon Carmichael strikes me as the sort who'd be willing to take that chance."

"Forget it, Charlene."

"Hard to forget a man like that." She leered. "He sure knows how to fill out a uniform. Ha-cha-cha."

"Charlene?"

"And he looks good both coming and going. Did you get a look at his a—"

"Charlene!" I cleared my throat, desperate for a change of subject. "I'm turned around. Does this cliff face Miss Pargiter's house?"

She shrugged. "No, she's behind us on the south side, facing the harbor."

The swinging of the bench soothed me. I huddled beneath the blanket. I couldn't think of a better place for a stakeout. Plus: drinks and a bathroom. Even if it was haunted by a pervy ghost, it beat a sap-covered tree stump. "Too bad we can't sit here and watch for her trespassers with a pair of binoculars."

"Alas, no. But after all this is over, if you want to go ghost hunting—"

"That's okay. And there's no such thing as ghosts."

"Legend says that on foggy nights, you can sometimes hear the White Lady's sobs."

"Cut it out, Charlene." The branches of a cypress creaked above us. The back of my neck prickled.

"It's no joke," she said. "Lots of people have heard her."

"It's probably just the sound of the ocean."

"And if you see her, it means you're going to diiiiii-ieeee. . . ."

A cold hand clutched my shoulder, and I shrieked, jerking off the bench.

Mayor Sharp guffawed beneath his scarf, wrapped high about his neck and mouth. His bald scalp shone as if polished above the navy blue wool. A matching peacoat stretched tight across his muscular arms and chest. "Sorry," he said, not sounding very regretful. "Did I scare you?"

Glaring, I picked up the blanket I'd dropped to the tiled patio. What the heck was the mayor thinking, grabbing me from behind? We barely knew each other. "Charlene was telling me a ghost story."

"Charlene's full of stories," he said. "I wouldn't believe most of them. Has she told you about the leopards?"

"Jaguars!" Charlene swatted at the air. Frederick twitched one ear and growled.

"Right, Charlene. Jaguars." He braced his hands on the back of our bench, stilling its motion. "Now, what's this I heard about you interfering with a police investigation? Are you two following up on Joe and Frank's little game?"

"Where did you hear that?" I asked.

His brows rose above the scarf. "I really can't say. How did you learn about their recent investigations?"

"I really can't say." I wrapped the blanket around my shoulders.

"Ah-ha, so you admit it." He wagged a thick finger at me.

Good grief, even his fingers were muscular. And I admitted nothing.

"I see what's going on here," he said.

"You do?" Charlene arched a brow.

Oh, cripes. I gazed longingly at the cliff and its long

drop into the fog. The White Lady might have had the right idea.

"I've noticed business has dropped in Pie Town since Joe's death," he said. "You're trying to clear Pie Town's name. I don't understand why the police have been so slow to release information the public is demanding, but never fear. I've made a statement to the press, and there will be an article in the weekend edition of the San Nicholas Times exonerating Pie Town."

I blinked, my heart lightening. "There will?" I'd thought the police were trying to keep things under wraps, but I wasn't going to argue.

"Small businesses are the lifeblood of San Nicholas," he said. "We need to help them, not hurt them. By all accounts, you did everything you could to save Joe. You should be rewarded, not censured."

"Well, thanks. But all I did was call nine-one-one." I curled my hands. Could I have done more?

He clapped me on the shoulder. "I'll see you for lunch at Pie Town tomorrow. That should help get the word out that your pies aren't fatal."

"Thanks," I said.

He strode into the adobe restaurant.

I stared after him, hope fluttering in my chest. An article in the local paper? Would that do the trick?

Charlene snorted. "Well, it took him long enough."

"I don't care how long it took, do you think it will work?"

"That depends on what you expect to happen."

"More customers in Pie Town." I sat up straight, bouncing my toes on the paving stones. Pie Town was saved!

"Oh, that? Probably."

"This is fantastic! We should celebrate. Let me buy you something stronger."

"Not before a stakeout," she said.

"But . . ." I gnawed my bottom lip. The stakeout was a moot point now that Pie Town had been cleared of murder.

"But what?" Charlene asked.

But Miss Pargiter was expecting us tonight. She'd be disappointed if we didn't return. And Antheia was dead, and my questions might have been the cause.

"But the stakeout's not for another two hours," I said, plaintive.

"All right then." She patted my knee. "Maybe just one peppermint patty."

"What's that?"

"Hot chocolate with a shot of peppermint schnapps. It goes down smooth on a cold night like tonight."

I couldn't say no to that, so I got one for each of us from the patio bar and brought them back. Sitting beside her, I took a sip. The drink warmed me in all sorts of ways. "Frank's daughter, Tandy."

"What about her?" she asked.

"I couldn't find any contact information for her. Do you know how we can find her?"

"No, but Joy might. They were the same age. Now, here's what I think we should do this week—"

"I'm thinking of closing on Mondays," I said.

She sat forward, her knuckles whitening on the mug. "You can't close Pie Town! The mayor said he'd make a statement!"

"No, no, only on Mondays. It was crazy for me to have Pie Town open every day of the week." When I'd started up, I didn't have the cash to hire an assistant manager, so Pie Town was all me, all the time. In the excitement of opening my pie shop, I hadn't minded the long hours. Later, Pie Town had given me somewhere to put my energy after the breakup with Mark. But if the mayor's press state-ment got us back on track, I might recruit Petronella to be assistant manager. I'd ask Charlene to take the job, but she'd placed clear boundaries on her hours from the start. She was piecrusts only. She also lacked a certain maturity.

Her shoulders sagged. "That's a relief. Pie Town's about the only job I could stand."

"So, why do you think there are jaguars in San Nicholas?"

"You can hear them calling at night, and their tracks are sometimes found in the mountains."

"But jaguars aren't native to Northern California."

"Of course they're not native. A family of Spanish rancheros brought them to San Nicholas. They used to have bull and bear fights at the ranchos, and the rancheros thought bringing in jaguars would spice things up."

"You're kidding." A gust of wind buffeted us, tossing the branches of the cypress trees. A strand of loose hair whipped my face.

"It's in the history of San Nicholas. Check the library." She blew on her drink.

"And the jaguars escaped?"

"No, they were killed in a fight with a bear and a bull."

I squinted at her. "Wait a minute, these aren't ghost jaguars, are they?"

"It's said that people who see them diiiiiieeee."

"Oh, for pete's sake." She'd had me going for a moment, and I smiled into my mug. When my hair silvered, I wanted to be a hell raiser like her. I sniffed. The hot chocolate and peppermint mix was a steaming cup of awesome. If I'd had a thermos, I would have ordered three more to go.

Ten minutes before eleven o'clock, we left the White Lady, and Charlene drove us to Miss Pargiter's. The fog had thickened, forcing us to creep along the winding roads lined with cypresses. We seemed to have entered a no-streetlight zone, and most of the houses were dark. The Jeep's headlights struggled to cut the fog.

Charlene pulled up and stopped.

"Are we here?" Unclasping my seat belt, I squinted out the window but was unable to make out the looming shapes.

"That's funny." Charlene leaned across me and rummaged in her glove compartment. "Pargiter said she'd leave the porch light on for us. The garden lamppost is out too."

"She must have forgotten and gone to sleep." I swallowed, uneasy, and realized I was still clutching the seat belt. I released it, and it clattered against the metal frame.

A gust of wind opened a gap in the mist, revealing Miss Pargiter's tall Victorian. A swirl of fog dashed in to fill the void, and the house disappeared.

My flesh pebbled. Though there were houses and people nearby, a sense of vulnerability and isolation descended.

Charlene removed two flashlights and shut the glove compartment. "I knew having that hot cop over would be too much excitement for her. Come on." She stepped out, peering into the fog. No light winked on in Miss Pargiter's house.

Flashlights aimed at the sodden ground, we found the rough dirt path and picked our way down the slope.

"What if Gordon decided to hang around to try to catch the trespassers himself?" I whispered.

"Then be sure to identify yourself fast and drop anything you're holding so you don't get shot."

"That isn't funny." I slid on the hill's loose soil, skidding a few feet before catching myself. A branch whipped me in the thigh.

"I wasn't trying to be."

"What if he sends an extra patrol around? He offered to do that for Pie Town when we were vandalized."

"You're right. Better turn the lights off. We don't want the coppers to mistake us for trespassers." She clicked off her flashlight. I heard a stumble, a crash, a curse.

"Charlene?" I swung my flashlight beam about, but all I saw was mist.

"I'm all right," she said. "Stupid log!"

"We should be close to that cliff. You'd better use your flashlight, at least until we find that old tree stump."

"What do you think I tripped over?" She aimed the light down at the stump.

Finding a section to sit on that looked free of ants and sap, I squatted beside Charlene. We clicked off our lights and sat in silence. Fog cocooned us, blotted out the stars. After twenty minutes, I began imagining we were marooned on an island surrounded by a sea of fog.

A low moan raised the hair on my neck.

"What was that?" I hissed.

"The lighthouse. Sometimes you get odd air inversions, and the sound carries farther than normal. This time of night, toward the witching hour, the world quiets. You see and hear things you wouldn't normally see—"

"Charlene—"

"Unseen worlds come to life. It's said that ghosts—"

I heaved a sigh.

"Lighten up. Didn't you ever tell ghost stories around a campfire?"

"I grew up in campfire-free Orange County."

"Not even a campfire at the beach? Kids these days. You're so used to having all your entertainment spoon-fed into your brain, you've lost your creativity."

"I am too creative." Digging into my pockets, I pulled out a 25-five percent-off coupon, and handed it to her. "I designed that coupon myself."

Her flashlight flicked on, off. "You call that a font? Use something a little more interesting than Times New Roman! And that's not the kind of creativity I was talking about."

"I know what you meant, and you're right. The world's changed and not all for the better."

"It's mostly for the better. Refrigeration, air-conditioning, being able to get a credit card without my husband's permission. That's all better."

A light appeared in the fog, about one hundred yards off the cliff.

I rubbed my eyes. The light was still there, hanging in space. It drifted, erratic, an eerie golden orb tracing a meaningless pattern.

Goose bumps rippled my flesh. "What's that?" I whispered.

Charlene hissed and grabbed my arm, pinching.

"Ow."

Leaping to her feet, she fumbled in her jacket pockets and drew out her phone, aimed it at the light. The camera clicked, and she checked the screen. "It's no good. I need someone to give it perspective. Val, stand over there, closer to the cliff."

I didn't budge, my legs numb, paralyzed. "What is it? I can't orient in the fog. It looks like it's hanging out in space." My laugh was high pitched, thin, and I clutched my hands together, jamming them between my knees.

"It is hanging out in space. It's Roswell all over again!"

"Roswell?" I squeaked, my hands turning clammy. "You mean UFOs? Even if there were such a thing as UFOs, why would they and ghost panthers—"

"Jaguars!"

"—and all sorts of other weird stuff happen in San Nicholas?"

"I have no idea. Now are you going to stand over here or not?"

I gulped. Here's the thing. UFOs scare the bejeezus out of me. They have ever since I was a kid, and age and rationality had done nothing to erase the primal fear gripping my throat.

But I was an adult now, and aliens were not going to zip

me away to another planet. Forcing myself to stand, I edged in front of her. I scuffed my feet on the loose earth, unsure where land ended and a hundred-foot plummet to stone and ocean began.

"A little to the left. Now a little bit more. Smile!" She took the picture and looked at the screen. "You aren't smiling. Let's try another. This one for Twitter."

I grimaced, and the cell phone clicked.

She checked the screen. "Great photo of the UFO. You, however, look constipated. But we have evidence!" She danced an awkward jig. "Take that, men in black. The truth is out there, and it's on Twitter!"

The uncanny light was probably from a boat, its light distorted by the fog and the angle of the cliff we stood on. I said nothing, nails biting into my palms, and we watched its slithering movements. We stood there for what seemed like ages, the lighthouse calling, mournful, and then the light blinked out. The tension in my neck and shoulders released.

Charlene checked her watch. "I guess the show's over. It's past midnight and no trespassers. Do you want to call it a night?"

"May as well." We'd seen an odd light, and I hadn't been sucked into a spacecraft for a joyride around the Milky Way. What had Joe made of the light, if he'd seen it at all? I didn't think it was connected to his murder—Antheia's death pointed to the library board. But it was disturbing, and we'd promised Miss Pargiter we'd help.

We plodded up the hill.

"I don't suppose you know Antheia's husband?" I asked.

"You want to question him about her murder? Good thinking." Nodding, she released a branch.

I ducked, and it skimmed the top of my head. "The

spouse is the most likely suspect, especially since they were in the midst of a rough divorce."

"And he's exactly the sort to strangle his wife with her own curtain tie. I'll bet he was too lazy to get a murder weapon of his own."

"Mm." This investigation was sounding less appealing. "He probably won't talk to us."

"He'll talk to me. We'll go to his house tomorrow morning, show up on his doorstep, and use the element of surprise."

I staggered into Miss Pargiter's yard. "Um, maybe we should call ahead. And it's going to have to be a quick interview. Pie Town opens tomorrow at noon." Since we weren't serving breakfast (yet), Pie Town opened at twelve o'clock on weekends. I liked to use those extra hours to power-nap. These were desperate times, but I'd been looking forward to sleeping in. As much as I loved Pie Town, I was starting to feel battered.

"Fine." She stomped to her Jeep and unlocked my door. "I'll be there to pick you up at seven forty-five, sharp."

Charlene drove me to my gym and dropped me off.

I showered and changed. Skin glowing, I hoofed it toward Pie Town. The streets were silent aside my footsteps echoing on the sidewalk. I stopped, stilling my breath, ears straining. Another footstep sounded, halted. It was only an echo, but I hurried on, lengthening my strides, until I reached Pie Town's front entrance. My reflection wavered in its windows, rectangular, black chasms. The dull clink of weights sounded from inside Heidi's gym.

Unlocking the door, I scuttled inside and threw the lights on in the dining area. The night had spooked me, the combination of fog, mysterious lights, and Charlene's stories spiking my adrenaline. Did she ramble on about the supernatural to get a rise out of me, or did she really believe that stuff? Maybe it didn't matter. Charlene enjoyed her wild theories, and tonight had been more fun than my last five months of self-imposed alone time. I walked a hasty recon through my pie shop, flicking lights on and off as I went, assuring myself that I was truly alone.

Chapter 16

At seven o'clock, I rolled out of bed. Standing in the narrow lane between the mattress and the closet wall, I stretched, luxuriating in a good night's sleep. As much as I loved the sunrise, I didn't need to see it every day.

One more stretch, and I wriggled into jeans and a black knit top while standing on my mattress. Charlene's tiny house would be a sky-high step up from living in Pie Town. I edged out of the closet and into my office. Light streamed from the skylight, illuminating spirals of dust motes, glittering off the paper clips on my old desk.

Coffee. Binding my hair into a ponytail, I slouched into the kitchen, grabbing a mug from an industrial drying rack.

The bell in the dining area tinkled.

I started, then released a breath. The bell had fooled me before, but I was alone. I still hadn't gotten used to the tremors caused by passing big rigs that sometimes jangled the bell and the kitchen's hanging knives.

Someone pounded on the door. My muscles spasmed, the cup slipping from my hands. Grabbing for it, I bounced it off my fingertips and caught the mug, gripping it to my chest. I raced into the dining area.

Joy stood on the other side of the glass, her long hair cascading loose about her shoulders. Her mouth pinched, and lines formed between her dark brows. She wore black yoga pants and a matching jacket with a white stripe down the sleeves, and a sense of betrayal stabbed at me. Was she using Heidi's gym? I shook myself. So what if she was? It was a free country, and I needed to get over my issues with Heidi. So what if my neighbor was a powerhouse of evil?

Unlocking the door, I pulled it open.

Joy pushed past me. "You're closed?" she asked, her voice neutral. "I know business has been bad, but I didn't think it was that bad."

"We open at noon on weekends. We're only open earlier on weekdays because the locals wanted a place to drink coffee."

"Oh." She blinked through her round glasses. "Sorry. When I saw closed, this time of day, I assumed it meant you were . . ." She removed her glasses and polished them on the hem of her yoga tank. "But that would have been a different sign."

As in Out of Business? How many other people would think we were on the road to shutting down for good when I changed the sign to say we were closed on Mondays? I still wasn't sure closing Mondays was a good idea. But I couldn't afford to pay staff if there were no customers, and Mondays had always been slow.

"I'm still here," I said, "and there should be an article in the local paper this morning clearing Pie Town." I needed to get a copy.

"That's a relief." She stared at me. "You're here early. What time do you start baking?"

"Around nine. I had some . . . stuff to do."

She leaned a hip against one of the booths. "It never

ends when you're self-employed. Joe was organized, but there's so much to go through."

"Coffee?"

"Sure."

"I'll be right back." Ambling into the kitchen, I boiled some water, dumped it into my French press. The scent of coffee wafted through the room.

I brought the press and two mugs to the counter and poured. "Creamer and sugar's on the counter."

She pulled a pink packet from one of the sugar holders and shook it, tore it open. "So Pie Town's off the hook," she said, stirring her coffee with a plastic spoon.

"We've been off the hook for days, but the police decided not to inform the public." Which Joy already knew. Was she fishing for gossip, or making idle conversation?

"Does this mean they've found my uncle's killer?"

"I don't think so." I told her about my encounter with the mayor last night and the promised vindication. "Maybe there'll be some info in the article."

She glanced at the slim, gold watch around her wrist. "The paper should be out by now. I'll go check." She darted outside, the entry bell ringing in her wake. A few minutes later, she returned, flipping through the local newspaper.

Which meant the Pie Town article wasn't front-page news. My heart nose-dived.

"Here it is." Opening the paper to page four, she smoothed it on the counter.

Page four? That made it a second-tier article. Most people probably wouldn't even read it. After less than a week, was Joe's murder already old news?

Stepping around the counter, I read over her shoulder.

"Poison administered by person or persons unknown," Joy read. "You were right. They still have no idea who did

it. So how can they say Pie Town . . . ? Oh, here it is.
Poison administered hours before he died. Here's a quote
from the mayor. 'In spite of the heroic actions and quick
thinking of the Pie Town staff, emergency personnel were
unable to revive Mr. Devlin.' Well, it doesn't say your pie
wasn't at fault—"

"Quiche."

"But it does say the poison was administered before he
got to Pie Town." She frowned.

"But it doesn't tell us if they're any closer to finding
Joe's killer."

"No." She folded the paper in quick, violent motions,
and dropped it on the counter. "That means no one in your
shop would have seen anything."

"Well, no, but . . . Wait, is that why you've been spending so much time here? To interrogate the staff?"

A flush crept across her cheeks. "Some detective I am.
Your staff is never around to question."

"So you were investigating?"

"Of course. Joe knew me better than my parents did. I
want whoever did this caught."

"I do too. Look, do you remember Frank's daughter,
Tandy?"

"Yeah." She picked up her mug and turned it in her
hands. "I mean, we played together when we were kids, but
I don't see her too often."

"Maybe we could talk to her about her father's death.
Judging from that casebook we found, Joe thought there
was something suspicious about it. He might have spoken
with her. Could you set up a meeting?"

She licked her upper lip. "I guess. As I said, we kind of
lost touch, but I think I've still got her number. Last I
heard, she was living in San Francisco."

"Do you think I can entice her to Pie Town with a free
potpie lunch?"

"Throw in a slice of dessert, and yeah. When do you want me to bring her by, assuming she's available?"

"As soon as possible."

"If Pie Town is off the hook," she said, "what's your interest in my uncle's death?"

Should I tell her? The bell over the front entrance jingled. Charlene stalked in, wearing a nubby, sand-colored tunic, leggings, and sneakers.

"Are you ready?" Charlene asked.

I checked my watch. "Oops, sorry, Joy. I've got to go. You can take the coffee. I'll get the mug from you later."

"Cheers." She walked out, nodding to Charlene.

"Where's Frederick?" I asked.

"Antheia's husband is allergic."

"You got in touch with him?"

She nodded. "He wasn't happy about it, grumbled about the hour of the call. But I told him we had some important information about Antheia's death. He couldn't say no to that, even if he is a horse's ass."

"My car's in the alley."

Wincing, she patted my shoulder. "Let's take my Jeep. It's sturdier on the back roads."

There were no back roads on the way to Mr. Royer's home. Antheia's husband lived in a mother-in-law's cottage behind a monstrous, white, saltbox-style house.

Charlene parked in the driveway and led me around the side of the saltbox to the cottage beside a stand of eucalyptus. Sun and blue sky sparkled through the silvery leaves. The air seemed luminous, and I congratulated myself for leaving my jacket at Pie Town.

Charlene banged on the door, and we waited.

"You'll love the garden." Charlene knocked again. "They hired a landscape designer, the owners of the house did, I mean. Antheia's husband is too cheap to spend his own money."

We waited some more.

Charlene shifted her weight, rang the bell. "He knew we were coming, and his car's here." She pointed at the vintage, black BMW in front of the cottage.

I strained my ears, listening. Nearby, a creek splashed.

Charlene snorted. "He can be hard of hearing when he wants. Either that, or he decided to go back to bed. You go around to the yard. He may be in the garden."

"But that would be trespassing."

"Nonsense! We were invited. He's expecting us. Go check in the garden."

I thought about that. It still sounded like trespassing.

"Go on, go! Wouldn't you feel terrible if he'd slipped and broken his hip and was lying there, starving to death?"

I glanced into the cloudless, blue sky. "I don't see any circling vultures."

"Will you go? I'll stay here in case he shows up." She pressed the bell. It pinged, faint, from somewhere inside the cottage.

"Fine." I walked around the side of the cottage, along a brick path edged with ivy. The sound of the creek grew louder. Turning the corner, I entered a dappled garden. Brick walks wended around raised boxes for vegetables. I passed a cluster of sunflowers starting to sprout. Lavender, sage, and rosemary bushes swayed in the light breeze. I ran my fingers along the rosemary, enjoying the scent of the leaves' heady oil. An azalea bush burst with carnation-colored flowers.

"Mr. Royer?" I called out.

A metal wind chime tinkled in response.

A brick walk led away from the cottage and toward a low tumble of green shaded by more eucalyptus trees. Calla lilies sprouted in small groupings, growing wild. At the rear of the yard, beside the path, three clumps of white-plumed pampas grass waved in the breeze. I inhaled, luxuriating in the fresh air and imagining my own, future garden.

"Mr. Royer?" It was obvious he wasn't here, so I had no excuse to look at the creek. Except I wanted to see the creek, so I kept walking, my footsteps soft on the mossy brickwork.

I passed the tall clumps of pampas grass. Their whiplike leaves needed trimming, and I edged sideways to avoid getting sliced. I stopped at a set of earthen steps cut into the hill. They tumbled down the bank to a narrow creek, splashing over smooth rocks. I stood, soothed by the sound. Something drifted, pale and limp, in the water.

I cocked my head, studying it, and my breath caught. Floating in the creek was a white hand.

Chapter 17

Bushes rustled behind me. Someone struck the small of my back. I pitched forward, unable to stop myself.

I gasped, plummeting down the hill. I grabbed at ivy, tearing it from the earth, shredding leaves in my fists. Splashing into the icy water, I rolled to a stop. I sat for a moment, too stunned to do more. Something brushed my leg, and I jerked away from the floating hand. Struggling to my feet, I turned toward the steps, my fists clenched in a futile, defensive posture.

No one was there.

Around my ankles, the creek splashed. A breeze stirred the branches above me.

Chest heaving, I stood, my feet numbing with cold. A man lay face down in the water, his white dress shirt and gray trousers soaked through.

My brain snapped into gear. Whoever had shoved me down the bank was out there with Charlene. I wavered, torn, and attacked the immediate crisis.

"Charlene!" Movements jerky, I grabbed the man's shoulders and dragged him backward. Huffing and screaming for Charlene, I hauled the top part of his body out of the water. "Don't be dead. Please don't be dead."

But his eyes were wide and staring, and his neck canted at an odd angle. Nausea swamped me. Staggering, I sat hard on the bank. I fumbled in my pockets for my phone and pulled out a fistful of 25-percent-off coupons.

Charlene appeared at the top of the bank. "Did you find him?"

"You're okay." I sagged, scrubbing my wet hands across my face.

"Why wouldn't I be? And what happened to your clothing? You're all wet. Did you fall?"

"Someone shoved me down the hill. I found him, he—"

"That creep! I told him we'd be coming to his house. Now he'll claim he thought you were a trespasser."

"I don't think so." I motioned to the body on the muddy creek side.

Her eyes widened, her mouth opening, closing. "Did you try mouth to mouth?" she asked in a small voice.

"He's dead." On shaky legs, I walked up the steps. "Would you call the police, please? I left my phone at Pie Town."

She nodded. Extracting a phone from the pocket of her tunic, she made the call. When she hung up, she said, "You should beat it. You're in enough trouble as it is with Detective Shaw."

"My footprints are all over the place. I can't pretend I wasn't here." I'd also left a second trail, parallel to the steps, of torn ivy where I'd slid down the hill. "Besides, someone was hiding behind those pampas grasses and shoved me into the creek. The police need to be told." I shuddered. Had I encountered the killer?

She sighed. "You are not going to jail for a crime you didn't commit, and right now, your presence here looks rotten. We found him together."

"Charlene, I just confessed to lying to the police once. I can't do it again."

"Then don't confess."

"But—"

"Did you kill the man?"

"No, but—"

"Then what does it really matter who was first on the scene? Telling them the truth will just muddy the waters, and we'll never find Joe's killer. We need a cover story. Collecting for charity? No, no one would believe it. Did you bring those coupons?"

I nodded.

"Quick, give me some."

I handed her a fistful, and she trotted off. Five minutes later, she returned. A siren wailed in the distance. "We're putting coupons on windshields," she said. "We started on this block, because I wanted to show you Roy's garden."

"Roy?"

"Antheia's husband, Roy Royer."

"Seriously?"

"Well, he did have a name aside from Horse's Ass." She snapped a picture of the body. "Evidence."

I stared at her.

"All right." She motioned toward the body. "Under the circumstances, I admit I shouldn't have called him a horse's ass. One shouldn't speak ill of the dead."

A uniformed officer rounded the corner of the cottage. Carmichael.

Charlene put her hands on her hips. "But he really did live the bulk of his life with his head up his—"

"Gord . . . Officer Carmichael! Over here!" I waved to him, and he stalked toward us. He wore a bulky black vest over his uniform. Was that armor? In San Nicholas? It made his chest appear even broader.

His gaze traveled from my running shoes to my ponytail, his expression chilly. "What happened?"

I brushed a stray ivy leaf off my jeans, leaving a smear of mud. "I—"

"I found Mr. Royer." Charlene pointed down the hill. "And someone pushed Val into the creek. We didn't see who it was."

Carmichael walked down the steps and squatted beside the body, touched the side of his neck. "Someone pushed you?"

"He must have been hiding behind one of those big clumps of pampas grass," I said. "I heard them rustle, and then someone shoved me."

He straightened and looked up at us. "Are you sure it wasn't Charlene?"

"Of course I didn't push her!" Charlene raised her chin, indignant.

"But you didn't see or hear the person who did, even though you were right here."

"My hearing isn't what it used to be," Charlene said. "I saw Val fall, and everything was moving so quickly. All I could do was focus on her."

"Did you touch anything?" he asked me.

"I pulled Mr. Royer out of the water." I shivered. The water had soaked through my jeans and T-shirt, and they clung, clammy and unpleasant, to my skin. "He was dead."

"I can see that," he said, his tone flat. "What were you doing here?"

"Coupons." Charlene waved some at him. "We wanted to put some on cars before Pie Town opened this morning, and I suggested starting here. Val doesn't get out much, and Roy has such a lovely garden. I called him this morning and asked if it would be all right. He said he would be home, and we could look at the garden but not to bother him. I rang the bell anyway, to alert him we'd arrived."

"You spoke with him this morning? What time?"

"Around seven," she said.

"Val?"

"Yes?" I blinked, astonished at the lies tripping off Charlene's tongue.

"What are you doing here?"

"Um, coupons?" If I told the truth now, how much trouble would we be in? Charlene had told Gordon everything relevant, even if she'd muddied some of the details about finding the body.

"The coupons?" His eyes narrowed.

"I'm not a big fan of coupons on windshields," I said. "They're annoying. But business has been slow, and it's a nice day for walking around."

"You walked here?" he asked.

"Oh, no," Charlene said. "We drove my Jeep over and then walked. I'm parked in the driveway. Did you know the owners hired a landscape designer?"

He gave her a hard, disbelieving look.

I wilted. I'd been on the scene for Joe's death, had found Antheia's body, and had now discovered her husband's. If I wasn't arrested, I'd be spending the day at the police station answering questions for sure. And Pie Town! This was supposed to be our big day, when the tourists flooded into town, and San Nicholas learned my quiche hadn't killed Joe. And yes, a man lay dead, and these thoughts were selfish. But a pained whimper escaped my throat.

"What was that?" he asked me.

I had to tell him the truth. "I shouldn't have—"

"Pulled him out of the water?" Charlene interrupted. "Of course you should have. You had to. He might have still been alive. I would have done it myself, but I've lost a bit of upper body strength lately. I need to get back to my yoga."

"Did you go down to the creek, Mrs. McCree?"

"Me? No, not with all those uneven steps." She rubbed her leg. "I've got bad knees."

"You both found him together?"

"No," Charlene said. "I found him and shouted for Val. I was ahead of her, you see. She felt funny going into the garden without speaking to Roy. So I went into the garden, and she lollygagged behind. She's very law abiding."

He grunted. "And then someone pushed Val, and you didn't see who it was even though you were standing right beside her."

"My vision isn't what it used to be," she quavered.

"GC! What have we got?" Flanked by two uniformed cops, Shaw strode down the path.

"Miss Harris found another body," he said.

Charlene sputtered. "I was the one who found—"

"Another one?" Stopping at the top of the bank, Shaw stared down. "Must have slipped on those stairs and broken his neck. I told him he ought to shore those up, make them more even." He clapped me on the shoulder. "You're bad luck for being on the scene of so many accidents. You're like a failed guardian angel, aren't you?"

My hearing must be going the way of Charlene's. "So many accidents?"

"First Joe, then Mrs. Royer, now her husband." Detective Shaw tsked.

"Joe was an accident?" In spite of my wet clothes, my body heated. Shaw couldn't be serious.

"A heart attack, technically, brought on by the poisoning."

"But poisoning isn't an accident."

"We found traces of castor bean oil in his coffee grinder," Shaw said. "Joe must have accidentally mixed a few in. Ground up like that, mixed with something acidic like coffee, even a few beans would have quite a kick."

Carmichael looked away, a vein pulsing in his jaw.

Wow. I'd been right about the coffee? Wait. What?

"Why would he keep castor beans in his kitchen?" I asked. "How could some get mixed in by mistake?"

Shaw shrugged. "Who knows how these things happen? He was old, forgetful."

"He was not," Charlene said.

"Right," I said. "And, and . . . Antheia! She had a rope knotted around her neck!"

Shaw winced. "You got me there. That was a bad business, burglary gone wrong."

"Burglary? But—"

"Clear signs of a break-in at the back," Shaw said. "Of course, you wouldn't have noticed since you stayed in the front of the house. Probably the same guys who broke in to poor Joe's house."

I winced. "What was stolen?"

He wagged his finger. "I can't divulge that."

Gordon cleared his throat. "But of course we'll be treating this as a potential crime scene until we definitively know the cause of death."

"Of course," Shaw said. "Don't mind Grumpy Cop here, Miss Harris. It's procedure. GC, we've been getting complaints about that gypsy caravan. It's illegally parked down on Seashore Drive again, and it's blocking the view. Why don't you go have a chat with the owner?"

Gordon's face turned to stone.

Grumpy Cop? GC stood for Grumpy Cop? Coughing, I turned to Shaw. "Detective, someone pushed me down the bank into the creek. I—we weren't alone when we found the body."

Shaw wagged his finger at Charlene. "You'd better watch yourself, young lady. Your pranks can be dangerous."

"But—"

Charlene grasped my arm and drew me down the path. "Let the nice policemen do their job."

"Wait!" Gordon stormed to us. "Your shoes."

"What?" I asked. "What's wrong with my shoes?"

"We'll need to make sure yours are the only footprints down there," he said.

"We don't have time for you to take a cast," Charlene said. "We've got to get back to Pie Town. It opens at noon."

"I don't need a cast. Just a photo and . . . Hold on." He hurried away, disappearing around the corner of the salt-box cottage.

"Can you believe it?" I fumed. "These can't all be accidents or random burglaries! Antheia was strangled. And what kind of person puts a castor bean in a coffee grinder by accident?"

"It's a cover-up." She rubbed her hands together, gleeful. "I smell a conspiracy."

I groaned. "It's not a conspiracy. Shaw's—"

"A moron?"

"You did say he got the job through nepotism. But Gordon doesn't think it's an accident, or he wouldn't be interested in my shoes."

Two paramedics hurried past, medical kits in hand.

"He's interested in a lot more than your shoes," Charlene said.

"Will you cut that out? If he was once, he's not anymore." I groaned. Oh, God. I'd lied to him again. "Did you see the way he looked at me?"

Her forehead wrinkled. "Sort of annoyed and disappointed?"

"Yeah."

She rubbed her chin. "Maybe if you tugged down your shirt and exposed more—"

"No."

"Maybe a little . . ." She fiddled with her collar.

"No."

Gordon returned with a professional-looking, black

camera and a piece of paper. He laid the paper on the ground. "Here. Step on that. Carefully."

I did.

"Try not to wrinkle it," he said.

Gingerly, I lifted my foot, leaving a muddy print.

"Okay." He knelt in front of me, dropped a quarter beside my foot, and snapped a couple pictures of my shoes. "This will do for now. And, Val—"

"Don't leave town?"

"That's Shaw's line," he said. "I was going to say you shouldn't be afraid to tell the truth."

Ouch.

"Excellent advice," Charlene said. "Can we go now?"

"Unless there's anything else you need to tell me, Val?" he asked.

My throat closed. "No," I rasped. "Nothing."

Charlene and I got in the Jeep and drove down the winding, residential streets.

"We're closing in on the killer," she said. "I can feel it."

"Or we're getting closer to being murdered." Was Roy's death our fault? Had I precipitated Roy's death and his wife's?

"I won't hear that kind of talk. Would Daniel Jackson have backed down from proving what he knew was right?"

"Who?" I'd met so many people recently they were beginning to get mixed up.

"Daniel Jackson! He knew the Egyptian pyramids had been built by aliens and was laughed out of the archaeological world because of it. But did he roll over? No!"

I banged the back of my head against the headrest. "You're talking about that TV show, *Stargate*." I should have remembered the character. I'd spent five hours watching the show with Charlene. In my defense, I'd had three of Charlene's root beers under my belt when she admitted the "extra something" she'd added was Kahlúa. By that point, another glass had seemed like a good idea.

"Of course I'm talking about Stargate! We can't stop now. There's something very wrong going on in San Nicholas. Those people were killed for a reason. The murders, the lights in the sky over the harbor, Bigfoot in Pargiter's garden, they're all connected!"

"What about the Case of the Whispering Wanderer?"

"Forget the Wanderer. Frank didn't leave any real notes on it—not a name, not a place, nothing."

My heart squeezed. "All I want to do is bake pies." Was it so much to ask? I knew baking pies. I didn't know detecting, and finding another body had left me sickened and sad. Roy must have been killed right after Charlene had called him. A coincidence? I couldn't believe it.

"Of course you want to bake pies." She patted my knee. "You're good at it. But you must have other dreams. What do you want from life, Val?"

"I want to unload that wedding dress."

She waved a hand, brushing that away. "That's a negative. You must have some positive desire."

"And Mark's still got some of my stuff in his storage locker. I want to get it back."

"Think more positive."

"Well . . ."

"Yes?"

"You know that little arrow-shaped sign that hangs from a lamppost on Main and points toward the fancy restaurant?"

"Yes?"

"I want one that points to Pie Town."

"That's it? Pay the Downtown Association and get the sign. And dream bigger, Val."

I heaved a sigh. "Where's Frederick?"

"On warm days, Frederick likes to sleep in the sun.

Inside, of course, near a window overlooking a tree. The narcolepsy leaves him helpless, and the raccoons mess with him when he's outside."

A red ball bounced into the street. She slowed, stopped. A harried-looking woman in a gray sweat suit ran out and scooped up the ball, throwing it to two small boys on her front lawn.

"Not to mention the jaguars," I said.

The Jeep crawled forward. "Don't be daft. Jaguars are nocturnal."

I was pretty sure raccoons were nocturnal too. "As much as I want to write all these deaths off as unconnected events, I don't believe it. Roy must have known something about his wife's death. Charlene, are we . . . We're not forcing the murderer's hand, are we? Did Antheia and Roy die because—"

"No. They died because they were up to no good, or they had the inside track on the killer. Do you think Joe's death was your fault?"

"Well, no, but—"

"There you go then. Now we need to find the monster responsible for these murders before he kills again. I can't afford to lose any more friends. Or enemies, for that matter."

I gnawed my bottom lip. "There's another thing. Roy was looking to Antheia to support him, but she didn't strike me as particularly wealthy. She was semiretired, and you and someone else told me she undercharged her clients. She couldn't have been making that much money at her law practice."

"An inheritance?"

"Usually inheritances are off-limits during divorces." A friend of mine in Orange County had gone through a divorce and given me an earful. "It's unlikely Roy was going after money someone had left his wife. Where did hers come from?"

"Not from the library board. That's a volunteer position."

"What else can you tell me about her husband?"

"Not much. Our relationship cooled after I put sugar in his gas tank. He never could prove it, but he knew it was me."

I stared at her. "Charlene?"

"Yes?"

"Why did you put sugar in Roy Royer's gas tank?"

She slowed at a stop sign. "He sprayed Frederick with the garden hose. Said he was digging up the garden. This was in the days before the narcolepsy, when Roy was living in Antheia's house, and Frederick still thought he was a wildcat. He'd prowl the neighborhood, hunting mice and climbing trees, as any good cat would. But he didn't dig up gardens. And if you ask me, the garden hose incident triggered his condition." She heaved a sigh. "Besides, he never put candy out at Halloween. He'd shut up the house and pretend no one was home."

"We're talking about Roy now, not Frederick, right?"

She shot me a look and swerved around an SUV backing from its brick driveway. "Nobody looks where they're going anymore."

I clung to the grab bar. "Okay. Are there any other reasons besides his dislike of cats and Halloween that someone might have wanted to kill him?"

"He hasn't remarried yet, so I doubt his girlfriend will get his money."

"She was an aerobics instructor, right?"

"That's what I heard."

"Roy's girlfriend couldn't have been Heidi, could it?" She certainly had the body of an aerobics instructor. Heidi might be teaching classes at her gym. Maybe she really was the killer! Imagining Heidi in handcuffs, I repressed a wishful smile.

"I think his girlfriend was from out of town. If it was Heidi, we would have known."

"But Heidi only moved here three months ago."

Charlene rubbed her chin. "You might be on to something. It would explain why Heidi opened up a gym in San Nicholas, when the town's already got one. We should go talk to her."

I shuddered. My last two rounds with Heidi hadn't gone in my favor. I wasn't loving the prospect of a round three with the gym owner. "She's let it be known that she's anti-pie. Maybe you could go undercover as a prospective gym member."

"I have been meaning to take up yoga again." She slammed on the brakes, flinging me forward.

I braced my hands on the dashboard.

A white cat streaked across the street, ears flat against his head.

"That looks like Frederick," I said.

Charlene laughed. "In all the— In the week you've known Frederick, would you put him down as a runner? He's safe in his warm spot in my living room."

Or was he? I didn't believe the cat was really deaf. Maybe he wasn't that lazy either. Maybe he just liked being around Charlene. "We need to learn more about Antheia."

At a violet-colored saltbox, she turned onto Main Street. "Well, you know whom to talk to about her."

Mark. Ugh. "I've only spoken to two board members— Mark and Antheia—but there are others. They must have some insight into her life."

Her mouth twisted. "And what's your excuse going to be for talking to them? That you want to join? Your ex will have a fit if he hears. Oh! What if we slip them coupons for a free potpie lunch at Pie Town, good only this Sunday? Then they'd come to us."

"Sunday's tomorrow!"

"You're right. You won't have time today to get them the coupons."

What were we doing? Gordon was right. We shouldn't be investigating. "We might as well have one of those drawing room murder reveals, where we invite all the suspects and accuse them one by one."

She slid to a halt at a red light in front of the fire station. "That's not a bad idea."

"I was joking. Turn left here."

"Left? But Pie Town's right."

"Can you drop me at my gym? I need to shower."

"You need a new place."

"Well, there's this tiny house I've got my eye on."

"Not until we bring Joe's killer to justice."

"Come on, Charlene. I've helped. I'm helping."

Her jaw set. "A deal's a deal."

"I need a house."

"And maybe you'll get one. We'll learn more tonight. There's supposed to be another good fog."

"What?"

"A stakeout, my girl!" Pulling in front of my gym, Charlene jerked the Jeep to a halt. "Don't worry. I'll wait."

Chapter 18

Customers! I hummed, ringing up a middle-aged woman.

Customers filled the booths, noshing on hand pies, ordering pies to go. . . . Forks clattered on plates. The dining area buzzed with chatter. A couple—out-of-towners—sat beside each other, heads close. Had Pie Town turned a corner?

I gave the woman her change, then scooted to the front door, took a deep breath, and taped a sign to its window: CLOSED MONDAYS.

One of my part-timers, Hannah, bobbed past the kitchen window, her blond hair neat beneath its hat. Petronella was off, as she was on all weekends. Would she return? Or would another job lure her away?

I walked toward the counter, stopped, returned to the door, and took the sign down. Was I nuts? I couldn't close Mondays. I needed any bit of business I could get. I tapped the edge of the sign on my chin. But business was always slow on Mondays. I returned the sign to the window and walked to the kitchen, my gaze darting over my shoulder at the door. Bad idea? Good idea? Worst idea ever?

Shaking my head, I pulled apple pies out of the oven and set them on cooling racks. Apple was one of our best sellers, with its crumbly cinnamon topping. There was just something homey about an apple pie, and people gravitated toward them. Baked apple, cinnamon, and nutmeg steamed the air, but my gaze kept darting to the window into the dining area.

Mayor Jack Sharp strolled in, a golf shirt stretched tight across his brawny chest. A middle-aged couple in business-casual/designer-expensive attire wandered in with our Bela Lugosi librarian trailing behind. They stopped in the dead center of the checkerboard floor. Faces tanned, hair thick and wavy, the couple wore matching sweaters draped around their shoulders and looked like they'd come from their yacht. They seemed familiar, but I couldn't place them. The mayor pointed to an empty booth. The couple and the librarian settled themselves in it, and the mayor strode to the counter, dinged the bell.

I hustled out of the kitchen. "Mr. Mayor! Welcome to Pie Town. And thank you."

He leaned across the counter, conspiratorial. "You saw the newspaper," he said in a low voice.

I tapped the stack of papers by the register. "I appreciate what you said."

"We'll take a lamb, beef, and two turkey mini-potpies for lunch, and put together a selection of your fruit hand pies, too, will you? And four coffees." Turning, he ambled to the booth before I could ring him up.

The coffee was self-serve, but the mayor had done me a solid. I rang up the order, hoping the other customers wouldn't notice the special service.

Returning to the kitchen, I grabbed four of the mini-pies from the cooling rack and laid them on plates. I arranged a half-dozen fruit hand pies on another, larger plate, and whisked them to the mayor's booth.

"Here you go." I pointed out which pie was which, then

filled four coffee mugs and brought those to the table along with the bill.

"Thanks," Sharp said. "Val, I don't think you've met Turner Morris and Charity Douglas. They're both on the library board."

I blinked. That's why they'd looked familiar. I'd seen their pictures on the library board's Web page. "How interesting! What do you do on the library board?"

Turner laughed, his teeth flashing against his tanned skin. "As little as possible. The real power is at city hall and with Hunter." He motioned toward the vampiric librarian. "But I'm the official treasurer."

"I'm only a plain old board member," Charity drawled. "All I do is sit in meetings and vote."

"I've always wondered what it would be like to serve on a board," I fibbed. I hated, hated, hated meetings. "What's the library board responsible for?"

"We bring in the money." Charity motioned to the librarian. "Hunter here manages the actual library."

"The board's contribution is very important," the librarian said quickly.

"And we're involved in special projects," Turner said, "such as the bond measure and overseeing the construction of the new library."

"It's not as hard as it sounds." Charity adjusted the navy sweater about her shoulders. "You should consider board service."

"Mm-hm," I said, vague.

"Jack told us about Joe and Frank's little investigation of Antheia." Charity propped her chin on her hands. "And that you've got the inside track. What was she up to? And what was Joe up to, for that matter?"

"The inside track?" Shifting my weight, I shot Mayor Sharp an apologetic look. "I'm afraid the mayor's misinformed.

I only know they were investigating, but not what they found. Do you have any idea?"

She arched a dark brow. "Not a clue. Antheia was an effective board member, but we weren't friends outside the library. Still, I can't imagine she was involved in anything underhanded."

The librarian blew on his coffee. "Are you certain those two geezers were investigating her? Joe owned a comic shop, he wasn't a PI, and Frank was a CPA. Could it have been some kind of joke?"

I scratched my cheek. Charlene had told me Joe had taken his investigations with Frank seriously. But so far, the cases had been bafflingly wacky. "I couldn't say. Besides, it's a police investigation now."

The man, Turner, frowned. "Joe left a message for me before he died, asking to talk, but he never said why."

Mayor Sharp's mug slipped, and coffee spattered the table. "Whoops! Sorry, folks." He blotted the mess with a paper napkin. "Have you told the police about Joe's call?"

"Since we never spoke, what would I have to tell them?" Turner asked. "Joe must have talked to a lot of people before he died. And even if he was playing detective, I wouldn't have had much to tell him. I also didn't know Antheia much beyond the board, but I admired her tremendously. The whole thing sounds cockeyed. Joe couldn't have been investigating her. Why would he?"

"Antheia was killed," I pointed out.

Sharp cleared his throat. "A burglary, the police say."

"And what was stolen?" Charity perked up.

"The police are keeping that confidential, I'm afraid," the mayor said.

Why were Charlene and I the only two people who seemed to think something sinister was afoot? And why was I using words like afoot? Suffering cats, Charlene was getting into my head. Soon I'd be seeing Bigfoot in the bushes. "But Antheia's husband was found dead this morning."

The others gasped.

"What?" Jack paled, then reddened. "Dead? No one told me."

"It happened this morning," I said. "Charlene and I were, um, nearby when the body was discovered."

"What happened?" the mayor asked.

"He fell into the creek," I said.

"An accident then," Mayor Sharp said. "And even if it wasn't, Roy wasn't on the board, so there goes your library theory. Excuse me, I need to make a call." Sliding from the booth, he walked outside.

"It wasn't my theory," I said to the three, "it was Joe's."

"Are you sure?" Charity smoothed her glossy, brown hair. "If Joe wanted dirt, he would have come to me. I'm gossip HQ, and I'm not ashamed to admit it."

Turner smirked. "And it's killing you that you don't know the mysterious circumstances behind Antheia's death."

She stiffened. "It is not!" Charity caught my eye. "Don't look so shocked. We served on a board together, we weren't buddies. I saw her once a month at our meetings, and that was it."

It was time to get detecting. I smiled. "But you are gossip central."

"Not gossip from Antheia, about her. You heard that Antheia's husband sued for alimony after abandoning her for some hoochie aerobics instructor?"

I nodded.

"Here's the thing," she said. "Antheia was as clever and greedy as Roy. The alimony suit must have killed her." She made a face. "Obviously, not literally."

"Greedy?" I asked. "But her practice seemed pretty low key. She worked from home. Why didn't she go work for a big law firm if she wanted to make money?"

"She is dead," the librarian murmured. "And she was a valued board member. Perhaps we should be more discreet."

"She's gone," Charity said. "Gossip won't hurt her anymore. And I didn't say she liked to work for her money. When her parents died, she was the executor and somehow managed to get the biggest share of their estate. Her siblings were hopping mad. That was years ago, but I don't think they've spoken since."

"Where are her siblings?" I asked.

"East Coast."

The Baker Street Boys weren't in the phone book. Angry East Coast relatives hadn't hired Joe to investigate their sister. "You do know a lot about Antheia."

Charity toyed with the gold anchor charm around her neck. "I had an affair with her younger brother. She was always rather frosty to me afterward."

Turner stared. "You never told me that!"

She flipped her hand. "Before your time, darling."

"Still!"

Minutely shaking his head, the mayor returned to the table. "It's true. Roy's gone."

It wasn't the sort of thing I'd lie about. Making my excuses, I fled to the kitchen. Yikes. How did Mark stand board meetings with those people?

I got busy filling blueberry pies, keeping an eye on the mayor's booth. After an hour, they rose and ambled out. I hustled over to clean their table, piling their plates in a big plastic carrier.

The receipt was gone.

No money had been left in its place.

Disbelieving, I shifted the plates in my carrier. Nope. No money.

I stalked into the kitchen. The fair-haired Hannah

stirred a metal bowl of pecan pie filling for the waiting line of piecrusts in their tins.

Setting the carrier by the sink, I stared through the window into the alley. "Hannah, did you take the mayor's bill?"

She turned, wooden spoon in hand, her blue eyes widening. "The mayor? You mean Mr. Sharp? No."

I'd been stiffed. By the mayor! What burned is it might have been my own fault. Usually I rang people up when they ordered, they paid, and then they got their food. So I'd been the one to goof up the process. But I'd also left the bill on the table with the coffee. They should have paid. But the mayor had done me a huge favor with that newspaper article. I thought over my conversation with him at the White Lady. Did he think I'd invited him to lunch at Pie Town? I gnawed my bottom lip. I'd have to be more up-front about the bill next time he returned.

At six o'clock, I closed up and went over the receipts. It had been a decent day. Not spectacular by weekend standards, but okay. Most of the business had come from tourists who'd never heard of Joe's death and had no reason to fear my baked goods. But there had been some locals as well. Still, dissatisfaction niggled. Drumming my fingers on the desk, I fidgeted in my seat.

I bounced from the chair, and it drifted backward. Walking into the dining area, I looked around. The setting sun sparkled golden on the pink tabletops. Everything was spotless, my neon TURN YOUR FROWN UPSIDE DOWN AT PIE TOWN sign alight. But tonight the usual glow of contented ownership the logo inspired didn't come.

I stepped outside. A couple pushing a stroller walked past, laughing. On impulse, I locked up and followed them down Main Street's brick sidewalk. Flower baskets hung from ornate streetlamps and swayed in the light breeze. The couple crossed the main bridge leading into town. It hung low over the creek, splashing along grass-covered banks. Four thespians practiced Shakespeare on a wide patch of lawn beside the water. I stopped and leaned against the railing, listening.

An actor clutched at his breast, wrinkling the fabric of his comic hero T-shirt. "Thou blind fool, Love, what dost thou to mine eyes, That they behold and see not what they see?"

I looked across the street, at a plaster-faced building from 1910 that housed an art gallery and café. Vines, verdant and lush, twined around the bridge. Birds twittered, hidden, nearby. Love might have blinded me to a faulty relationship, but not to this town.

A thorny bundle of worry unknotted in my chest. Pie Town would survive, and so would I, but it was time for me to stop using it as a refuge. I loved Pie Town. It had gotten me through a ruined wedding. But it was time to build a life outside the shop. And if that meant spending a night on a cliff with a conspiracy-addled cryptogenarian, I was all in.

The bushes rustled. A whisper floated from beneath the bridge. "An orange, coffee beans, and a knife."

I knew that whisper. I'd heard it in the alley at Pie Town. Leaning over the railing, I thrust aside a branch.

A white-haired man in stained, mismatched clothing passed beneath me. He carried a cane over his shoulder, a cloth knotted around one end making a bag.

"Don't forget the knife," he hissed.

Cold fingers trailed up my spine. There was probably a perfectly innocent reason he was whispering about knives. Maybe he needed the knife to cut the orange? My brain clicked into place, and I said out loud, "The Case of the Whispering Wanderer!"

A woman walking a Chihuahua jerked away from me, startled. The dog yipped, irate.

"Sorry," I said, looking for a path beneath the bridge. I

ran to one end, then the other, and finally found a path leading down the hill to the amateur theatricals in the park. By the time I reached its grassy slope, the Whispering Wanderer was gone. I hustled along the bank, searching as the light dimmed, but he'd vanished.

Defeated, I returned to Pie Town and got detecting, surfing the Internet for information about Roy's niece, Joy. She'd been investigating Pie Town. Turnabout was fair play, and she'd inherited Joe's property. That made her a suspect. I finally found her on one of those social media career sites. Her job history stopped two years ago, with a health food store in Philadelphia. She'd mentioned she was an herbalist. I typed castor beans into the search engine. Hm . . . They looked a lot like coffee beans. They were also believed to have medicinal properties—the sort of thing an herbalist such as Joy would know.

Heading over to Twitter, I located Charlene's feed and began reading. My wedding dress had gotten a lot of comments, not all of them flattering: What happened when the bride was jilted at the altar? The wedding went off without a hitch!

"That isn't even funny," I said to my laptop. "And I was not jilted!"

My computer didn't respond.

Charlene's brief updates on our "detecting" would get us arrested if anyone on the SNPD read them, particularly the photo of Roy Royer's corpse. Her picture of the strange lights in the fog had gotten retweeted by several paranormal sites. Charlene would be proud. I was just relieved none included me.

Chapter 19

Someone pounded on Pie Town's alley door. It snicked open.

"Hi, Charlene," I called, ambling into the kitchen.

She held a thermos beneath the coffee urn and pressed the tab. Nothing poured out. "Is it empty already?" She was dressed in her cat burglar attire: black yoga pants, a black tunic, and a black parka made of one of those soft microfibers.

"I cleaned it," I said.

Slipping the thermos into the bag slung over her shoulder, she lowered her chin and stared.

"I'll make more," I said.

"Good. And I see you've got that sign up about closing Pie Town on Mondays. Mondays are always rotten anyway."

"You think it's a good idea?"

"Everyone thinks it's a good idea."

"Where's Frederick?" I asked.

"I didn't want white cat hair on my new black jacket. What do you think?" She pirouetted.

"It's pretty slick. Hey, I packed up some leftover hand pies for tonight's stakeout."

Her lips pursed. "Cherry?"

"And blueberry."

"I'll drive," she said.

"My VW's parked in the alley."

"I'll drive."

Sighing, I pocketed my flashlight and prepared for a case of whiplash. "I think I got a lead on the Case of the Whispering Wanderer." I locked the alley door and climbed into her Jeep.

"I told you that was likely a dead end."

"But I overheard an old, homeless-looking man whispering down by that park along the creek. He was carrying a pack like a traveler. Or a wanderer. What's that park called?"

"Creek Park." She started the Jeep.

"How literal. Anyway, have you seen him around?"

"No." She drove down the alley and turned toward Main Street. "There's only one homeless man in town. His name is Paul, and he likes to smoke his pipe on the bench on the corner of Main and Lark Streets. So either your fellow is new, or he's not homeless."

"Then maybe this new guy is our Whispering Wanderer."

"If you enjoy wild goose chases, chase away. But the real case is at Miss Pargiter's."

Annoyed, I folded my arms over my chest. "You're only saying that because there's nothing supernatural or con-spiracy-oriented about the Whispering Wanderer."

"Hmph."

The lights were off in Miss Pargiter's old Victorian when we pulled up beside the picket fence, but the garden lamppost was lit. Beads of moisture glittered on the laven-der bushes surrounding its black, iron post. Mist twined through the tops of the cypress trees.

Charlene yanked up the parking brake. "I called and

told her we'd be here tonight, so she shouldn't sic the police on us. But you never can tell with Pargiter."

We clambered down the brush-strewn slope to the tree stump. This time I'd come prepared, and I laid a dry dish towel across it before sitting. We ate hand pies and passed the thermos, and I whispered to Charlene about my day's investigations.

"The board members I met were snarky but didn't seem particularly villainous," I concluded. "And they didn't say anything helpful about Antheia. But . . ."

"But what?" she prompted.

"Nothing." Everyone seemed to think an investigation of the library board was laughable or insulting. But I'd gotten the impression that the mayor had brought the librarian and those two members of the library board to Pie Town for a reason. I rubbed my jaw with the back of my fingers.

Charlene sprang to her feet. "Do you hear something?"

I strained my ears, listening to the soft rhythm of surf. A man's voice drifted to me and faded. Flashlights off, we crept toward the edge of the cliff. A red light bounced along the steep slope to the south, toward the bay.

"That's one of those red flashlights, so you don't lose your night vision," Charlene said in a low voice. "Some-one's down there."

"More than one person, I think." Two masculine voices rose and fell. The light meandered up the hill, moving toward us.

"Miss Pargiter's trespassers!" Charlene dug her phone from the pocket of her thick parka. She frowned, held it high. "No signal. I'm going to walk up the hill and call the police. You stay here."

"There's at least three guys down there."

"If they try to get away, stop them."

"Right! Of course!" I hissed, waving my arms. "Why don't I surround them?"

"Use your feminine wiles."

"I don't have . . ." But Charlene had plunged through the brush and up the hill.

The light grew larger. The men's voices grew louder. Definitely at least three. I shifted, trying to look small. This was stupid. I wasn't going to stop them, so I might as well get the heck out of here and wait with Charlene. I started up the hill, and a feminine shriek pierced the air.

"Charlene!" I struggled up the hill, slipping on the loose ground, catching my clothing on prickly branches.

She screamed again.

Oh, God. What if she'd fallen? What if she was dangling off the cliff? What if she was . . . I stopped beneath a cypress tree.

Charlene stood, frozen, opposite me. "Don't move." She spoke like a bad ventriloquist, jaw clamped shut.

"What happened? What's wrong?"

Raising a shaking hand, she pointed past me.

I looked over my shoulder.

A mountain lion paced the hillside, weaving between bushes, its tail lashing.

I screamed and backed into Charlene.

She grabbed me around the waist. "Make yourself big! MAKE YOURSELF BIG!"

"I CAN'T GET ANY BIGGER!"

The mountain lion growled, showing off its gleaming teeth. There was no way we could outrun it. We were going to die. Horribly. My legs shook.

"Pepper spray! I brought pepper spray!" Fumbling in her pockets, she pulled out a pen-shaped object, aimed it. A red dot wobbled across the animal's forehead, zoomed across the uneven ground. The great cat snarled.

"THAT'S A LASER POINTER! You're making it angry!"

She wailed, dropping the pointer. It rolled beneath a bush. "I told you there were jaguars."

"IT'S A MOUNTAIN LION!"

"You're young, save yourself!" She clung to me.

"We can scare it off." My voice trembled. Would Miss Pargiter find our mauled bodies on the hillside, another terrible San Nicholas accident? Oh, God, maybe the high body count here was due to natural causes.

Charlene's breath burst in and out. "You're right," she shouted. "It's probably more afraid of us than we are of it. Shoo! Scat!"

The cat prowled closer.

We screamed.

The mountain lion hunched its shoulders, readying to pounce.

"What is wrong with this town?" I moaned.

A flashlight beam hit us, blinding, and three men crashed into the clearing.

"GET OUT OF HERE, YOU DAMN VERMIN," a white-haired man roared.

The mountain lion whipped around and bounded into the trees.

I whimpered. "We're alive."

"Damn," one of the men said. He and another man carried a toilet between them. "Was that a mountain lion?"

I did a double take. A toilet? "Mark?"

My ex grunted. "Hi, Val. I thought that was your voice."

"What are you doing here?" I asked.

The white-haired man, the harbormaster, directed his flashlight beam down the cat's path. He wore a thick, navy peacoat and a captain's hat. "I think we scared it off." He scratched his thick beard.

"Loomis?" Charlene said. "Is that you?"

I braced my fists on my hips. "What are you doing here at midnight? With a toilet!"

"I wouldn't be here at all if I hadn't heard you scream," Mark said. "I thought you were in trouble."

The inside of my chest expanded, my arms and legs tingling. "I was in trouble. Thank you."

"You're welcome."

"You recognized my voice?" I asked.

"Of course," Mark said. "Jake thought it was some teenagers messing around, but I knew it was you."

"No names!" Jake shifted the toilet, his gaze darting about.

I cleared my throat. "Well, thanks."

"We were engaged, Val. Relationships like ours don't just end." Mark gave me that look that had always turned my insides to butter, and my resistance crumbled like a flaky piecrust.

Except our relationship had ended. We were over, and he was a decent guy, and he'd saved my life, and I shouldn't make a big deal out of it. But my traitorous heart warmed at the thought that he'd suffered too. He still had feelings for me, even if we were over, and I didn't know what to say. "But . . . that's a toilet!"

"No kidding, Sherlock," Mark's helper, Jake, snarled. "And it's not getting any lighter."

Charlene pointed at the commode. "That's not a low-flow toilet. That's high flow. It's contraband! Loomis, I thought you'd given up smuggling."

The older man removed his captain's hat and scratched his head. "Aw, Charlene, it's only a bit of fun."

My hands dropped to my sides. "You're smuggling toilets?"

Charlene walked to the two men hauling the toilet and caressed its glossy white porcelain. "These high-flow jobbies are gold here in California. How much do you want for it?"

Mark's chin jutted out. "It's not for sale."

Her eyes narrowed. "Oh, it isn't, is it?"

"Why are you smuggling a toilet?" I shouted.

"Shhh!" Nervously, the men looked about the clearing.

"Why are you smuggling a toilet?" I said in a calmer voice.

"It's none of your business," Mark said, stiff.

"You've been trespassing and frightening the nice old lady who lives in that house." I jerked my thumb up the hill. "Charlene was about to call the cops before that mountain lion showed up."

"The mountain lion I saved you from," Mark said.

"Spill it," I said, "or I'm spilling the beans."

"Oh, come on, Val," my ex wheedled. "It's no big deal. The plumbing in these old houses can't take the new low-flow toilets. It's cheaper to get a new high-flow than to replace all the pipes."

"And illegal," Charlene said.

"And you're bringing them in by boat like the old boot-leggers?" I asked. "Why not use a car or truck? Toilets aren't exactly hot contraband."

"He insisted." Mark jerked his head toward the harbor-master.

"I've always liked the old pirate stories." Loomis smiled, his blue eyes going misty, and he replaced his cap. "We'd bring the toilets in on foggy nights—but not too foggy because that can get dangerous."

"And the weird lights people have been reporting in the bay," I said, "was that you too?"

Loomis shrugged, the thick fabric of his coat bunching. "I suppose. I'd signal from our boat to the lads on shore."

"Can we put down the toilet?" Jake asked.

"No," Mark said, "let's get going. They're not going to stop us."

My neck corded. "Hold on. You need to stop bothering

Miss Pargiter. And I want my stuff from your storage locker."

"What stuff?" Jake asked.

"Never mind," Mark said.

Loomis dropped his chin to his chest. "We had no idea we were disturbing anyone, miss. We'll leave your Miss Pargiter in peace and take a different route from now on."

"Oh, yes you will," Charlene said, "right to Pie Town."

Mark's eyes widened. "You can't have the toilet! It's for a client."

"We don't want your toilet," Charlene said. "Well, I could use one. Later. But you boys need to learn a lesson. Business has been slow, and you're all going to eat lunch at Pie Town. And you'll bring friends, and come by once a week for a month."

"Val . . ." Mark gave me a let's-be-reasonable look. "This is ridiculous."

I wasn't thrilled by the idea of Mark in Pie Town. My insides still got squirmy whenever I laid eyes on him. But Pie Town needed the business. "I've got coupons." I drew a fistful from my pocket.

Charlene smacked my hand away. Coupons fluttered to the rocky soil. "No coupons! You will come once a week, and you will pay full price, and you will like it."

"Yes, ma'am," Loomis said, eddies of fog swirling around his hat. "I've heard good things about the pies, except for the killing part."

"My pies do not kill people." I raised my chin. "It was in this morning's paper. We were maligned."

"I don't know that word, but have you got mince?" Loomis asked. "It's been ages since I've had a decent mince pie."

"We've got mincemeat." Stooping, I collected my fallen coupons, damp from the ground.

"With meat?"

"Of course!" These days people were making mince-meat without meat, but vegetarian mincemeat seemed blasphemous. "Oh, and we're closed on Mondays."

"Fine," Mark ground out. "Once a week for a month. Are we done here?"

Charlene stepped aside. "We're done. And we'll talk," she muttered to Loomis.

The men trudged up the brush-strewn hill.

Charlene and I looked at each other and scuttled after them. That mountain lion was still on the prowl.

"That cat must have been ten feet from whiskers to tail." She clutched her chest. "My life flashed before my eyes. My wedding, holding my child in my arms, my time with the roller derby . . . What did you see?"

"Nothing."

"Then you kept a calmer head than I did."

"I wasn't calm." Slogging up the hill behind her, I jammed my hands in my pockets. "I didn't have a highlight reel to review, at least not until the grand finale of death by wildcat." I lived on the dull, butter-knife edge, and I could imagine the epitaph on my tombstone: She never lived, but what a way to go.

"You're a little boring, but most young people are."

"Thanks."

"Give it time. You'll make memories."

I kicked a loose stone. It rattled down the hill and bounced against a cypress. "Whatever."

"All that bother over toilets," Charlene said.

I fiddled with my collar. A teensy part of me had thought Mark might be involved in the murders, but his only crime had been contraband plumbing. "And no Bigfoot or aliens either. Are you disappointed?"

"Nonsense! We solved two of the crimes in Joe's casebook

in one blow." She swung her fist. "That's cause for celebration."

"It's hard to believe they went to all that trouble for plumbing supplies."

Her gaze flicked skyward. "That Loomis, he's spent his life living in his head and dragging other people into his fantasy world. If you ask me, he should spend more time on planet Earth."

Gee, that didn't sound like anyone I knew. Nope, not at all.

"We should report that jaguar to the police." She pushed aside a low branch. "It's not normal that it's so close to people's houses. It might attack a pet or a child."

The branch thwacked me in the chest, and I sighed. "Mountain lion."

Chapter 20

Sunday at Pie Town was about the same as Saturday— tourists filled most booths, and a good number of locals popped in for pies to go. Relieved by the uptick, I worked in the kitchen with Hannah, filling crusts for a blueberry pie and remembering the good times I'd had with Mark. And there had been good times. It was after we'd gotten engaged that he'd grown snappish and sullen. I hadn't challenged his new, churlish behavior, assuming he was stressed over restarting his realty business in San Nicholas. Now I regretted my lack of curiosity. I might have learned something before I'd bought that damned dress.

Had we rushed things? I'd always been more enthusiastic about the wedding than Mark. But he had asked me to marry him, proudly announcing our engagement to our friends in Southern California. But once the excitement of the announcement faded, reality had set in. Maybe the financial risk I'd taken with Pie Town had scared him off. Maybe the time and energy I'd put into it rather than into him had wrecked things. For whatever reason, he'd changed his mind about marrying me. Instead of telling me outright, he'd made us both miserable until I'd given him an ultimatum. And then we were done.

Charlene snapped her fingers by my ear. "Pie Town to Val. What planet are you on?"

I jerked away, startled, and sugared blueberries scattered across the metal counter. "Charlene! It's after lunch. What are you doing here?"

"I wanted to see how things were going. We've got a decent crowd today, nice. Not our best Sunday, but respectable."

I swept the errant blueberries into the doublewide sink. "Isn't it great? Things are finally turning around, aren't they?" Glancing at the ceiling, I said a silent prayer of thanks.

She tapped her chin. "There's more to your good mood than sales. What's going through that head of yours?"

"Nothing."

She snorted. "That I can believe."

"I'm making pie! It's not intellectually taxing. What am I supposed to be thinking about?"

She glared at Hannah, and the girl scuttled into the flour workroom, shutting the door behind her.

"The case," Charlene said. "Last night. By the way, I called the police when I got home about that jaguar." She frowned. "I don't think they believed me."

"I called them too and told them about the mountain lion." I'm not sure the police believed me either, but mountain lion sightings weren't unheard of in this area. "We were lucky Mark was there."

"Mark? Mark didn't save us, Loomis did."

My cheeks warmed. "Well, they all did. Anyway, it was a good thing."

"You're not turning that weasel of an ex into some sort of hero, are you? He left you at the altar. That's not exactly hero material."

"I wasn't at the altar. We hadn't even hired the caterer

yet." And it was a good thing we hadn't, or we would have lost a huge security deposit.

She waved her hand. "Details. You dodged a bullet with that one, Val. Let him go."

"Of course." I blew out my breath. "It's totally over," I said. "Done."

"You're too good for him, and there are other fish in the sea."

My part-time cashier stuck his shaggy head in the kitchen. "Val? There's someone named Joy here to see you."

"Joy? From the comic shop?"

He shrugged, his sandy hair falling into his eyes. "That's what she said." He vanished into the dining area.

"Maybe she found another clue in some of Joe's things." Charlene nudged me. "Go and find out."

Peeling off my gloves, I strode into the dining area and wiped my damp hands on my pink and white Turn Your Frown Upside Down apron.

Joy sat in a booth at the front window, her expression impassive. A curvy blond sat across from her, talking and patting a baby, snuggled against her chest. It burped and spit up on the cloth over her shoulder. The blond wiped the baby's mouth and picked up a set of large, plastic keys from beside her coffee cup, jiggling them.

The baby clapped his hands.

I approached the table. "Hi!"

Joy ran her fingers through her curtain of black hair. "Hi, Val. This is Frank Potts's daughter, Tandy, and, uh . . ."

"Joshua." Tandy smiled. "I'd offer to shake hands, but they're a little full at the moment."

"Tandy couldn't get a sitter," Joy said.

"He's adorable," I said. The baby arched for a better view of the ceiling. "How old is he?"

"Nine months. I hardly ever get out anymore, so I was thrilled when Joy invited me for lunch. My dad mentioned there was a new pie place in town." Her eyes grew misty. "He really loved dessert."

"My condolences on your loss. You might not remember, but we met at your father's funeral." I didn't know if Joy had told Tandy my fears about her father's death, and I hoped she hadn't. If I was wrong, it would only upset her. But if I was right . . .

"Of course. I remember you now." She grabbed the spit-up towel and dabbed her eyes. "Sorry. My dad and I were pretty close. I live in San Francisco, and tried to see him as often as possible. But when Joshua was born, it got difficult."

"Don't be sorry," I said. "I lost my mom a year ago, and it still hits me at random moments. Have you ordered?"

Joy motioned toward the counter. "Yeah. I ordered at the register." She looked out the window. "Val and I think the police are incompetent and are taking up Frank and Joe's mantle as amateur crime solvers."

Tandy's brow wrinkled.

"I wouldn't say incompetent," I said, shifting my weight. "Did Joy tell you about the casebook of Joe's we found?"

Tandy nodded. "I knew about their cases. Well, not the details, not until the investigations were complete at least. Dad got a real kick out of them."

"How did they get started?" I leaned my hip against the side of the pink booth.

Tandy scooted over, and I sat beside her.

"They were both Sherlock Holmes fans," Tandy said, "and they would argue about the stories. Conan Doyle was terrific, but they found all sorts of plot holes. And then, they started arguing about the local crime blotter. All petty stuff, but Sherlock's cases also often seemed trivial and then turned into bigger things. So they began investigating—armchair stuff, but they had fun with it."

"My piecrust maker and I might have solved two of their four open cases," I said.

Joy straightened, her dark brows drawing together. "Oh?"

I told them about the high-flow toilet smugglers, and Tandy burst into laughter. "That's perfect! But what are the other cases?"

"A Whispering Wanderer, as yet unknown, and a case about a local woman named Antheia Royer," I said. "Did your father mention anything about either of them to you?"

A shadow passed across Joy's face.

"Antheia Royer?" Tandy bounced the baby standing on her lap. "The name sounds familiar. Why don't you ask her?"

"She was killed."

"Oh." Tandy stilled. "That seems a bit more serious than Dad's usual cases."

"He could have been investigating Antheia or carrying out an investigation on her behalf."

"Who was she?" Tandy asked.

"A lawyer," I said. "She was also on the library board."

"The library board?" Tandy said, her tone uncertain. "Dad didn't care for them much. I'm surprised he would work with her."

"Why?"

"He thought the new library was a waste of money. It seemed strange, because he was a big reader, and he loved the old library. But maybe that's why he resisted the new one. He was never a big one for change."

"Joe said the same thing," Joy said. "Wouldn't set foot in the place."

"Tandy," I said, "did Joe come to see you after your father died?"

"Yes, he asked if he could have my dad's last casebook. I gave him the key to Dad's house and let him take what he wanted." She turned her head toward Joy. "I'd love to get that notebook from you, when you get a chance."

A bead of sweat rolled between my shoulder blades. How was I going to get Frank's pilfered casebook to Joy without her despising me forever? "Your father's house? Is it still vacant?" I asked Tandy. Maybe there were clues hidden inside.

"It sold in a week. We had to hustle to get all Dad's stuff out."

Joy slid from the booth. "Where's the ladies room?"

I pointed, and she strode toward it.

Joshua grabbed a fistful of Tandy's hair, and she winced, prying herself free. "I can't believe my dad and Joe are gone. I think Dad's death was hard on him."

"On Joe?"

She nodded. "Don't get me wrong, Joe had a great life. He loved that comic shop, and he loved Joy, but he and Frank were almost brothers. Funny how families come together."

I nodded. Funny how quickly they can unravel too. My family had died with my mother.

"At least he still had Joy," she said. "She was like a daughter to Joe. I heard some of her relatives are upset she inherited, but Joe was pretty open about whom he planned on leaving his money to and why. Joy was the only one who visited Joe regularly. She stopped by at least twice a month, and usually spent the night. She deserved every penny Joe left her. She never took a dime from him while he was alive, and she could have used the cash."

"Oh?"

"Out of work for two years?" She shook her head. "I don't know how she managed."

"It sounds as if you and Joy were close." And Joy had intimated they weren't. What was up with that?

She flushed. "We're not anymore. I shouldn't be repeating gossip. Joe talked to my dad, and he talked to me. I wish I had a friend like Joy again, the way my dad and Joe had each other to pal around with. But these days I'm pretty much all baby, all the time."

Joshua gurgled, and she bounced him.

The counter clerk whisked two mini-potpies to the table and hustled into the kitchen. She gazed, wistful, at the steaming pie.

"I can hold him for a bit, so you can eat while the pie's still hot," I said.

"Would you?"

She handed the baby to me and flipped the spit-up cloth over my shoulder. Joshua's blue eyes widened, as if startled by the sudden shift, and he grabbed my nose. I screwed up my face, and he laughed.

Joy returned to the table and picked up a fork. "Best business neighbor ever."

"Joy, that homeless man you told me about, did he ever return?"

"No, thank God." She dug into the pie.

"You said he was weird. How?"

"He had this creepy, whispery voice. You had to lean in to hear him, and trust me, I did not want to lean in."

The Whispering Wanderer had come to Joe's comic shop! Maybe he was a detecting client as well. "Did he and Joe know each other?"

"I doubt it," Joy said.

"So he didn't ask for Joe when he came in?" The baby wriggled in my arms.

Joy put her fork down and stared at me. "I could only hear every third word he said. What's up?"

"One of the cases in the books—the Case of the

Whispering Wanderer. It might be him." Too late I realized my mistake.

"I don't remember any whispering wanderers in Joe's book."

"Oh . . . Maybe it was in one of his older books." The case had been in Frank's book, not Joe's. Would either of them catch my misstep?

"I guess I didn't study the book for very long," Joy admitted.

I flopped back in my seat, relieved. "Tandy, did your father mention anything strange or upsetting going on in San Nicholas?"

Tandy paused between bites of potpie. "Upsetting? No, I don't think so. Why?"

"Nothing. It's not important." Her father's death was presumed to be an accident, but so was Joe's. And Antheia's was considered a random crime. Could Frank's death have been murder? I couldn't bring myself to ask.

Early Monday, I stumbled from my closet and into my office, remembered we were closed, and sat hard on my desk chair. Had I done the right thing by closing Mondays? When my mom and I had plotted our fantasy pie shop, we'd neglected the stresses of management, the tough decisions, the long hours. I'd thought I'd gotten past the hard part, the start-up, but would the hard part ever end?

Opposite me, my wedding dress hung, stiff and hard with lace, accusing. My mom had talked a lot about my wedding day, even after we'd both realized she wouldn't live to see it. An ache blossomed in my chest.

The heck with it. I might dither over Pie Town's future, but there was one thing I could be decisive about. I was getting rid of the gown. Today.

Dressing in jeans and a long-sleeved, black, knit top, I

put on a pair of black, low-heeled boots. No comfort shoes needed today; I wouldn't be on my feet baking pies.

I made coffee in my industrial kitchen and wandered into the dining area, mug in hand. Through the windows, fog hung low on the street, the shops on Main Street shuttered. I checked my watch: six o'clock. There wasn't a whole lot to do in San Nicholas at this hour, but the trails were open from sunrise to sunset.

Shoving the plastic-wrapped wedding gown into the back of my VW, I motored to the coast. I'd noticed a trail-head near Miss Pargiter's house, and I pulled into its narrow dirt lot high on a cliff. A wooden sign marking the trail had been nailed beside a gap in the redwood fencing, leading to an overgrown path. The fog was thicker here, closer to the ocean, but beams of sunlight pierced the branches above, turning the mist golden.

A crow perched on a fence post. He clicked at me, his feathers ruffled.

Stomach going squishy, I stepped onto the path. It felt wrong to wander when I should be making pies, setting out coffee, polishing tables for the morning's opening. And also: murderer on the loose! But it was time to grow up and get a life.

A gust of wind tossed the branches. The underbrush was dense and viney, and I passed what must have once been a house. Its walls were gone; only the foundation remained. Tangles of creepers twined across its concrete floor. The dirt path turned, sloping upward, leading into a low tunnel of unidentifiable shrubbery.

Uncertain, I ducked through it. The path opened up to a wide colonnade of cypress trees. Their branches arched above me, a natural cathedral. A fence meandered along one side of the trail, vanishing in places where the cliff had tumbled to the ocean. On my right, orderly rows of cypresses, an army of giants, cast deep shadows. Strange orange moss covered several of the trees closest to the cliff. The bright orange in the dark forest was weirdly lovely, but I wondered if the trees were diseased.

The forest was still, unmarked by birdsong, and even the ocean waves below seemed to have fallen silent. Hair prickled on my scalp, and I glanced around. The trail was empty.

Sunlight shone on the path ahead. Hurrying forward, I broke through the trees to a bluff overlooking the ocean to the west and houses to the north and east. A red-painted gypsy caravan parked beside a strip of sidewalk braced against the ocean. What would it be like to live in one of those? If Charlene's tiny house fell through, I might have to find a place that was even tinier.

I'd reached civilization again, and the knot between my shoulders loosened. Bracing my arms on the rough fence, I looked down to the beach. Seals lolled on the rocks and in shallow pools of water. One inchwormed across the beach to another seal and slithered on top of him. The second flapped its tail and didn't budge. I wandered down the path to the tide pools, admiring purple anemones and a giant starfish clinging to a rock. Only a few miles from Pie Town, and it was the first time I'd been on this beach.

Growing bored with the tide pools, I found a path that led north to a row of houses facing the ocean. Waves lashed the seawall, sending spray onto the sidewalk. I paused before a dome-shaped structure with a thatched roof, round windows, and a garden bursting with blooms. The sign said it was a yoga studio. If this was where Charlene practiced yoga, I might have to take it up. But with my piecrust maker, it was hard to separate fact from fantasy. For all her delusions, delinquency, and deceit, she had become a good friend. Her memories may have been fictional, but they were happy. Mine were anchors, weighing me down.

I walked on, catching a gust of sea spray in the face, and thought about my mom and her too short life. She'd been divorced, a single mom, and it seemed as if her life had revolved around work and me. She hadn't had time for much else. Had she been happy? I wasn't sure. All I knew was that her choices had been limited, her focus intense. It must have been a relief when I was out of college and on my own, when she could finally pursue what she wanted, rather than what duty demanded. But cancer had cheated her. My vision blurred.

Walking to my car, I drove to the local charity's second-hand store. The windows were dark, a CLOSED MONDAY sign in the window.

Leaving the gown in my VW, I drove to Pie Town for jam on toast, then walked to my lawyer's office. It sat above a popular grocery store and deli in a faded brick building. Climbing the steps, I rapped lightly on the door, walked inside.

My lawyer's secretary, Renee, looked up from a computer at her desk. She smiled, her lips a crimson grimace. Her face was unlined, her hair in a pixie cut. She adjusted her forest-green blazer, rumpling the crisp white blouse beneath. "I'm sorry, Val," she said, "Robert isn't in right now. Please tell me you don't have an appointment."

I'd only met her a few times, and was pleased she remembered my name. Maybe she was willing to chat. "No," I said. "Robert told me you would be a good person to ask for recommendations about new estate attorneys."

She adjusted her glasses. "He did?" She straightened in her chair.

"I was going to talk to Antheia, but then . . ." I let that trail off.

She paled. "I can't believe it. I really can't. The paper said she was killed in a burglary."

"I was the one who found her." I leaned one hip against her wooden desk. This wasn't interfering with an investigation. It was gossip. "I'd gone to her office to see if she was taking new clients."

She leaned across the desk, lips parted. "You did? What happened?"

"I found her lying by her desk with a drapery cord around her neck." The police might have had a good reason for telling the paper it had been a burglary. But I'd lost faith in Shaw, and Officer Carmichael had made it clear he wasn't involved in the investigation. They hadn't told me to keep what I'd seen quiet.

"I can't believe we've got such violent crime here, in San Nicholas."

"Do you think it's possible that someone broke in with the intention of killing Antheia?" I asked.

"Intention?"

"Did she have any enemies?"

Gasping, she rocked back in her office chair. "Are you saying it wasn't a burglary? Why would you think that?"

"Aside from Antheia's body, the place was as neat as a pin. It didn't look very burgled."

Her face paled. She jerked to her feet and paced behind the desk. "It was that damn realtor. I knew something was wrong."

"A real estate agent?"

She clawed a hand through her short hair. "Antheia was buying real estate from her clients, elderly folks, and she wasn't exactly paying top dollar." She clapped her hands to her mouth, green eyes widening. "I shouldn't have said that. Forget I said anything, please."

"You think there was undue influence?"

She sagged against the desk. "I think if the heirs knew

how little their parents were selling their inheritance for, there'd be screaming. Maybe one of them did find out and killed her. I should go to the police, shouldn't I?"

"If you think she was involved in something illegal, then yes, I think you should."

"I can't say for sure if it was illegal. But it wasn't quite right, you know?" She wrung her hands. "And that skeezy realtor, ugh."

"Skeezy realtor?"

"I've already said too much. If I'm wrong, I'm blackening the name of an innocent person."

"Renee, who am I going to tell? I spend my life in a pie shop."

"She was working with that new realtor in town, what's his name? The handsome one? Used to be on the high school football team, moved away and came back?"

My stomach turned to a block of cold granite. "Mark Jeffreys?"

"Yeah, that's his name, the one she got onto the library board."

So there were some people in San Nicholas who weren't aware we'd been engaged. I swallowed. "Antheia got him onto the library board?"

"Three guesses why. He doesn't have any real connections in this town anymore, no money to donate, no management experience. In fact, he has no real qualifications to be on the board except Antheia recommended him. There must have been some sort of quid pro quo."

"Quid quo pro?" I couldn't think, couldn't breathe. Was that what this had all been about? But Mark wasn't a killer. He couldn't be. He was just a toilet smuggler.

"That's Latin for 'something for something.' It means an exchange—"

"I know what it means," I said dully. But no, I didn't believe it. My ex might have assisted in a not quite aboveboard real estate deal, but he was no killer. We'd been together for four years. I knew him. He didn't even like killing spiders. The library was an odd fit though. I'd never seen him cracking open any books. He was strictly a TV man. What had attracted him to the library board? "But . . . why would someone bother to pull strings to get on a library board?"

"For networking. That's why they all do it. And they don't have to do any real work. They're rubber stamps for the head librarian. Antheia was the only one on the board who really understood the financials at a granular level. She may have been the board secretary, but she also ran the finance committee."

"Wouldn't the treasurer do that?"

"Turner?" She rolled her eyes. "He may be CEO of his little yachting corporation, but that doesn't mean he knows how to manage finances. He's got a CFO for that, and on the library board, Antheia acted as a chief financial officer. She was the board."

Muttering my thanks, I left my lawyer's office and stood on the sidewalk outside the grocery store. The morning sun glinted off the dew-covered impatiens hanging in their ceramic pots.

Mark? My Mark?

Had I been engaged to a killer?

Chapter 21

Pensive, I meandered down Main Street and passed a boutique owner. Careful not to splash the sidewalk, she watered a window box bursting with geraniums.

Would my ex get involved in a sketchy real estate deal?

He might. Mark did have a tendency to look for the quick and easy way. I'd thought we'd balanced each other, since I was the polar opposite.

But would Mark stoop to murder?

No way.

A uniformed police officer braced his hand on the hood of a black and white patrol car parked on the street. His back to me, he spoke into a radio clipped to his shoulder, his neck rigid.

My pulse quickened. Officer Carmichael? It was hard to think of him by his first name, Gordon, while he was in uniform. What a difference between stand-up Carmichael and my easy-exit ex. And I shouldn't be thinking of that difference, because I was lying, continuing to investigate, continuing to fudge the truth, and he'd made it clear he valued honest, solid citizens.

Lengthening my strides, I hurried past, hoping he wouldn't notice me.

"A surfboard is not a vehicle," he shouted into the radio. "Not a vehicle!"

His shouts faded behind me. Maybe Grumpy Cop wasn't such a bad nickname for him after all. If I had been a real detective stuck under Shaw, I'd be in a foul mood too.

On the sidewalk, Charlene stooped, peering through a window, her white hair gusting in the breeze. Her drapey, charcoal-colored coat flapped around her thighs. Beneath it, she wore a blue knit top and black leggings. Frederick coiled around her neck.

"Hi, Charlene."

She straightened. "There you are. What are you doing out? Were you buying supplies?"

"It's Monday, our day off." In spite of my worries, a wave of freedom tingled through my veins. Day off. I had a day off, the first since I'd opened Pie Town. "What are you doing here?"

"I left my key to Pie Town at home. Let me in. I've got some ideas on our case."

"Right-o." I fumbled with the lock.

The redheaded gamer ambled up the sidewalk, a stack of comics and glossy hardbacks beneath the arm of his parka. "Opening late today?" he asked.

"Actually, we're closed on Monday's now," I said.

His round face crumpled. "Closed on Mondays? But Tom, Angus, and Samantha are supposed to meet me here!"

"Samantha?" I didn't remember any female gamers.

"Yeah, you met her."

"Ah." I twisted the key in the lock, and the door snapped open.

He shot me a pleading look.

I sighed, holding open the door. After all, they were my most loyal customers. "Fine. Come in. But the blinds stay closed. I don't want people thinking we're open."

"Cool." He scuttled inside.

Charlene poured Frederick onto a table and marched into the kitchen. "I'll start the coffee urn."

I stared at the cat. Eyes closed, he rolled onto his back, nudging the metal napkin dispenser, and I picked it up. Which health codes had we violated by bringing him inside? And was Frederick really deaf or just faking it? Holding the dispenser at my side, I let go, and it clattered to the floor. Frederick whipped to his feet. The gamer yelped, his brown eyes wide.

"Ah-ha!" I looked to the gamer. "Whoops. Sorry."

Frederick glared at me.

"Sorry," I said to the cat. "But you're a ginormous humbug. You just want Charlene to haul you around all day." It was actually kind of sweet. Was Frederick lonely too? Or did he just understand that Charlene needed him? I ruffled his fur. "Don't worry, I'll keep your secret."

He closed his eyes, laying his head on one paw.

Officer Carmichael strode past the glass.

I waved, but he didn't see me. Leaning forward, I watched his departing back. The man worked out. If he was a member of my gym, I might have to rethink—

Thunking two mugs of coffee on the table, Charlene slid into the booth. Frederick did not stir. "I've been think-ing about Officer Carmichael," she said.

Zipping my lips, I banished my impure thoughts. We would never be a couple, so it was no use fantasizing.

"Isn't it strange," she went on, leaning across the table, "that he'd take a demotion to come to podunk San Nicholas?"

Someone rattled the door, and the gamer leapt up, letting three of his compatriots inside. I eyed them, trying to figure out which was Samantha. They all had similar scruffy hair, and their overlarge jackets, T-shirts, and baggy pants camouflaged their figures.

"He did say his parents were in town," I said, unwilling to spill the beans about his father's illness. Something in his tone had told me that information was private, personal.

"Playing the dutiful son makes for a good excuse, but I think there's more than meets the eye here." She sat back and rapped her index finger on the table. "Internal affairs!"

"What?"

"Someone high up has figured out there's something rotten at the San Nicholas PD and sent in an investigator."

"But . . . San Nicholas is an independent police department. Wouldn't they have their own internal affairs department?"

She sipped her coffee. "Mm, maybe you're right. He could be FBI."

"Maybe," I said, doubtful. "But if he were an undercover agent, would he look so frustrated taking Shaw's orders?"

"Wouldn't you be frustrated by Shaw?"

"Since he hasn't arrested me after finding three bodies, I'm viewing him in a more positive light."

"Yeah, that is strange, although in fairness, you didn't find Joe, all of Pie Town did."

"But I was on the scene for Joe, Antheia, and then her husband. I should be the number-one suspect."

"But you're not, because SNPD is rotten to the core." She slopped coffee on the table and wiped it with her open palm.

Grabbing the dispenser off the floor, I handed her a napkin. "Yesterday, I talked to Tandy, Frank's daughter. She told me Joy was in a financial bind when Joe died."

Charlene shrugged. "She inherited. We always knew she had motive."

"But we never looked at her too closely."

"She did not burgle her own house."

My stomach hardened. We kept coming back to that, but Joy was a solid suspect for so many reasons. "She also said Joe and Frank hated the new library."

"Probably too modern for their tastes."

"And I went to see Antheia's legal secretary, Renee."

"Now that sounds promising. What did she say?"

Glancing at the gamers, I lowered my voice. "She said Antheia was taking advantage of her elderly clients, buying their property on the cheap and using Mark to do the deals."

"Mark? Your Mark?"

"He's not mine anymore. Is that the sort of thing Joe and Frank might investigate?"

Her brows drew together. "Yes, I think they might. Most of their cases were lightweight—missing cats and such." She stroked Frederick's fur. His eyes remained shut. "But if old folks were being taken advantage of, and someone mentioned it to either of them, I think they might have looked into it."

I propped my chin in my hands. "This is all speculation. We don't have any evidence."

"We have more than the cops do. Shaw thinks the deaths were all random and unrelated."

We sat, nursing our coffees, sunk in gloom. At least I wouldn't have to tell the police about Mark and Antheia. Renee would take care of that.

Someone banged on the door.

We started, Charlene splashing coffee over her hand. "Dang it!" She hurried into the kitchen.

The leader of the gamers caught my eye. "Not part of our crew. We're all here."

Sliding from the booth, I walked to the front entrance.

My neighbor, Heidi, peered through the window, her blond ponytail high on her scalp, a green gym bag slung over her shoulder. Mark stood behind her in his gray pin-stripe business suit, looking up and down the street.

I opened the door. "Sorry, we're closed."

She bounced past me. "That's what I wanted to talk to you about."

Mark stood on the sloped wheelchair ramp. "Um, Heidi, maybe this isn't—"

She reached through the open door and grabbed his hand, tugging him inside. "There's no time like the present."

I forced a smile. "Time for what?"

Charlene came to stand beside me, a damp towel wrapped around her hand.

"I see you've closed," Heidi said. "I'm here to help you out and take over your lease. There's nothing worse than paying a lease on a building you're not earning any income from."

"You want to take over my lease," I repeated in a flat voice.

"Mark said—"

"You're Mark's client? The one who wants my lease?"

"Heidi's Health and Fitness is in a space that is a teensy bit too small. But Mark told me you'd be leaving—"

Anger heated my belly. "You moved in a week ago. You must have known then that the building was too small. When exactly did Mark tell you?"

Mark cleared his throat. "I figured under the circumstances—"

"You don't have to explain anything to her, Mark." Her grip on his hand tightened, and I felt the blood drain from my face. "You only moved here because of him," she said, "and now it's over between the two of you. It doesn't make sense for you to stay."

My head swam. "Are you two . . . dating?" I choked out.

Mark stared at the linoleum floor, his cheeks darkening. "I probably should have mentioned it earlier."

"Not that it's any of your business," Heidi said.

Hurt and embarrassment punched me in the gut. I flinched, taking a step away from them. He was dating someone? Already? He was dating my evil, health-obsessed neighbor, and he was trying to give her Pie Town?

Charlene laid a hand on my shoulder, and I drew a shuddering breath.

Gordon came inside, wove past us, and beelined for the urn. "I need coffee."

"I thought you were closed," Heidi said.

"We are closed," I snarled. "We're closed on Mondays. It's a new thing."

"So when are you moving out?" She braced her hands on her slim hips. "I'd like to take over your lease as soon as possible."

"We're not." I spoke to her, but I stared at Mark. "Pie Town isn't going anywhere."

"Give it up, Val," Mark said.

"I will not. I've been dreaming of Pie Town for years. I'm not giving it up because my presence here makes you uncomfortable."

"I can't believe you're still hanging on to him," she hissed, drawing closer to Mark. "It's pathetic."

"We're over." I held out my hand, palm up. "And I'll take the key to your storage locker. I want my things. Now."

"What storage locker?" Heidi asked. "What things?"

"Fine." Digging in his pants pocket, Mark pulled out a key ring. He unhooked a small, brass key, and slapped it onto my palm. "Return it to my secretary when you're done."

"Wait a minute," Heidi said. "What things? What about the lease?"

"If you need a bigger gym," I said, "you're going to have to look somewhere else. Now, if you'll excuse me, we're closed."

"But you've got people in here," she said.

"Closed for a private event," Charlene said. "Would you like Officer Carmichael to explain the concept to you?"

Gordon, leaning against the counter, turned, mug to his lips. "Eh?"

"Never mind." Charlene strode to him. "Is coffee all you want? How about a nice piece of pie?"

Heidi's jaw clenched. "This isn't over." She pointed at the gamers. "And your sedentary lifestyle is ruining your health!" Spinning on the heels of her exercise shoes, she stormed out, rattling the bell.

Mark clung to the door handle as if it were a life preserver. "Val, I wasn't trying to drive you out of town. I thought with everything going on, you'd want to leave."

"You'd better go after your girlfriend," I said coldly. "She looks pretty mad."

He opened his mouth, closed it. Turning, he departed.

I would have slammed the door after him, but it was one of those slow-closing doors, so I couldn't even get that satisfaction.

"What a cow," a feminine voice from the gamer's table said.

I regarded the shaggy-haired blond who'd spoken. Samantha, I presumed. "Sea Hag?" I asked.

She nodded. "Yo."

I gathered the remaining shreds of my dignity. "We're closed today, but I've got some pie in the freezer if you don't mind waiting for it to reheat. Cherry on the house?"

They cheered, and I went to the kitchen, my hands shaking. I'd been such a fool. Mark had been right, I hadn't completely let go. If I had, the revelation that Mark was seeing someone wouldn't have been such a dagger to the heart. Worse, I'd deluded myself that he'd missed me too. But Mark had moved on some time ago.

Charlene stood before a toaster oven. "Good thing we

froze all those pies from last week. I turned one of the big ovens on, in case you need it."

Swallowing, I pasted on a smile and grabbed a cherry pie from the industrial freezer. "I do. Thanks. Did you tell Officer Carmichael those hand pies were frozen? I don't want him to think our standards are slipping and our fresh pies are going downhill."

"Of course. I explained the situation. I think he was a little embarrassed when he learned Pie Town was closed today." She stared through the glass front of the toaster oven. "Mark's a horse's ass, and Heidi's a demanding . . . Well, I'm trying not to cuss so much, but you get the idea. You've got better things ahead of you."

The timer on the toaster oven dinged. She peered inside, frowning, and closed the door. "A few more minutes."

"Did you hear what Heidi said?" I asked.

"Hard not to. That girl's got a voice like an electric drill."

"Heidi leased the gym thinking she could expand into Pie Town. You don't make that sort of decision on the spur of the moment. She and Mark must have been plotting this for weeks, maybe even months." Was Heidi the reason he'd turned so churlish at the end? She said she'd moved here three months ago, but she could have met him earlier.

She patted my shoulder. "Now, now. No sense crying over spilled Kahlúa. She's not taking Pie Town, and that's that."

"No, she's not! I can't believe Mark would do this to me."

"You're lucky you learned the truth about that one before it was too late."

I knit my bottom lip. "Your Twitter feed is right. I am a sap."

"Not anymore." The toaster oven dinged, and Charlene removed the pies with a spatula, sliding them onto a white plate. "Why don't you take these to Officer Carmichael?"

"Sure. Oh, and can you take care of reheating the cherry pie? It's for the gamers."

She saluted with two fingers. "Will do."

I took the hand pies to Gordon, seated at the counter not far from the coffee urn. "This one's on me," I said.

"You don't have to do that."

"I did it for the gamers. It doesn't feel right to ask you to pay for a couple hand pies, especially when they're not fresh baked."

"I'm sure they're fine."

I studied him. His color was high, and his green eyes seemed to snap. "Rough morning?"

He grunted, taking a bite of an apple hand pie. Flakes of crust dropped onto the plate. "How'd you guess?"

"You don't look like the eight-AM-apple-pie kind of guy." Not with those biceps. Or washboard abs. Okay, his abs were hidden beneath his blue uniform, but judging from the rest of the man, I was fairly certain they existed. "Though we will start serving breakfast pies next week." I needed to do some testing first. The bacon and hash brown pie seemed to be a winner. My spinach quiche should appeal to the calorie-counting crowd, but I wasn't sure how customers would react since my first taste tester had died.

He rolled his eyes. "You have no idea."

"Does it have to do with a surfboard?"

Laying down the pastry, he raised his brows.

My lips quirked. "I overheard you on the sidewalk."

"A guy called in because someone cut him off on his surfboard. In the ocean."

I laughed. "You get stuck with that sort of stuff?"

"Normally a call like that wouldn't get past the dis-patcher. But I'm the new guy, so he thought it was a good joke." He angled his head toward the door. "Problems with your ex?"

"Oh." I shoved my hands in the pockets of my jeans. "You overheard that."

"Hard not to."

Charlene leaned through the kitchen window and winked at me.

"He seems to think I'm staying in San Nicholas just to be near him," I said.

"Sure, it's got nothing to do with this business you dumped all your money into."

"How did you know I dumped all my money into it?"

He grimaced. "Sorry, didn't mean to hit a sore spot."

"You investigated me."

His eyes widened, all innocence. "Why would I do that? Detective Shaw is handling the accidental deaths."

"Eat your pie. You're a lousy liar." I began to walk to the kitchen.

"Hey," he said.

I stopped and turned.

"For the record, he's an idiot."

"Shaw?"

"Your ex."

I nodded, lips tight, and walked into the kitchen.

Charlene leaned against the counter and rubbed her hands together. "So? How did it go?"

"Excellent. I successfully delivered his pie and have now returned to the kitchen. Mission accomplished."

"I saw you two talking. He likes you."

Unreasonable hurt spiraled through my chest. "He investigated me. To him I'm a suspect." And even if Carmichael was interested in me, which I doubted, I couldn't go out with him. Even if I wasn't lying to him, I obviously still wasn't well and truly over Mark.

"But that's a good thing that he investigated you," she said. "Now he knows you're innocent. Did he ask you out?"

"Charlene, he can't do that. I'm part of a murder investigation."

"Accident investigation. Totally different thing."

I raked a hand through my hair and realized I was serving food with my hair loose, another code violation. Hastily, I twisted it into a bun. "No, he did not ask me out."

"Then do you want to come over and watch Stargate tonight?"

All I wanted to do tonight was huddle on my bed with a fork and warm pie. Preferably strawberry-rhubarb.

"I'll make my special root beer," she wheedled.

"Eight o'clock?"

Chapter 22

Slumped on Charlene's floral-print couch, I took a sip of her root beer and Kahlúa concoction. The lights were off, the blue glow of the TV screen flickering across the living room walls, hung with photos of Charlene's husband and daughter and glorious past. Charlene really had been in the roller derby. And so far, what had I done? Fell in love with the wrong guy, got dumped, and wallowed in my office closet while Mark found a new love.

"When's your daughter getting back from France?" I asked.

"She's a busy executive." Her expression shifted, and Charlene looked down at her wrinkled hands. "It's hard for her to get away from work."

I focused on the TV, ashamed I'd brought up a sensitive subject. Had I really needed to prove to myself that Charlene was lonely? All the signs were there—her social media obsession, her unwillingness to part with the cat, all the time she'd been spending at Pie Town.

Theme music blared, triumphant, and credits rolled across the screen. Unmoved, Frederick lay draped over the arm of the sofa.

Beside me on the lumpy couch, Charlene patted my knee. "Right then! We've still got a case to solve."

"Sure." Pulling my backpack over the arm of the couch, I rummaged inside and retrieved my photocopies of Joe's casebook. "Have you got Frank's? I want to take another look at them both."

"Of course." Lurching from the couch, she hobbled into the kitchen. There was the hum of a freezer, the rustle of plastic being unwrapped, and she returned and handed me the casebook.

"It's cold," I said.

"I put it in the freezer."

"Why did you put the casebook in the freezer, Charlene?"

"In case someone broke in to my house, looking for it. No murderer would look behind the rocky road."

Unable to fault her logic, I joined her in the kitchen and spread the photocopies and casebook side by side on the black granite countertop. Frank's first page: Library bd.—sec—the Case of the Bloated Blond.

Library bd had to mean "library board." *Sec* was "secretary," who happened to be a blond. I flipped to the backside of the page. It was blank. I looked to Joe's book and its Chapter heading: *Case of the Bloated B*. Why hadn't Joe written out *blond*? There were no notations beneath it to explain.

I returned to Frank's page about the library board. His notes had been written in pencil, and a pink streak of eraser smeared the word blond. I squinted, held the book closer to the hanging welsh lamp.

"Oh, no," I said.

"What?" Charlene bustled inside the kitchen, empty glasses in hand. "Are you out of root beer?"

"Charlene, Frank's casebook doesn't say blond. Look

how faint the L is." I turned the book on the counter and pointed. "Someone erased a word beneath, but the L wasn't completely erased. It's not blond, it's bond."

"What?" She poured more root beer and Kahlúa into the glasses and handed me one. Opening a drawer, she pulled out a pair of reading glasses. "Give me that casebook." She slid the glasses onto her nose and peered at the page. "Hells bells, I think you're right."

"Which means library bd might not mean 'library board' at all. It could mean 'library bond.'"

"But even if that's true, the library board was responsible for the library bond."

"With guidance from the town council," I said.

"And you did say Antheia was the only one on the board who really knew what was going on," she said. "Antheia would have been instrumental to getting that bond issued, and she is the secretary. And she's dead."

"Bond, not blond." Had we been on the right track by accident?

She pocketed her glasses. "All right, let's review the evidence."

"Joe and Frank both thought the library was a waste of money and refused to set foot in there."

"Check." She nodded, her wispy hair bobbing. "Antheia was the only person on the board with her eye on the ball. She would have understood the bond issuance—according to her legal secretary, at least."

"Not just her legal secretary," I said. "The other people on the board pretty much admitted they were clueless. But what could she have done with the bond that was so wrong? The library was built. It's beautiful."

"Oh, there are all sorts of ways to steal when there's a big, fat packet of money floating around."

"Steal the bond money?"

Charlene nodded.

"But she couldn't have pulled a fast one with the bond, not with city oversight. They couldn't have even put forward a public vote on the bond without someone on the town council taking a close look at the finances."

She rubbed her chin. "It does seem unlikely."

"We need to learn more about this bond. What if sec doesn't mean 'secretary.' What if it means 'SEC,' as in the Securities and Exchange Commission?"

"I'll get my laptop," Charlene said.

I drank more root beer and paced the modern kitchen. If Joe had been investigating the bond, Mark was off the hook. The bond issuance was before his time on the board.

She brought her computer into the kitchen, laying it on the butcher block work island, and we searched for municipal bonds on the SEC Web site. After thirty minutes, Charlene threw up her hands. "I don't think sec means 'SEC.' Everything we've read says the SEC doesn't have any real oversight of the issuance of municipal bonds."

"But look at this article," I said. "Because they can't control the issuance, the SEC has started investigating fraud after the fact. Look at these cases—undisclosed conflicts of interest, pension fund abuses, pay to play."

"Pay to play is a fancy phrase for 'bribery.'"

"But if the SEC was investigating the library bond," I said, "why would Joe and Frank get involved?"

"Maybe they were planning on tipping off the SEC?"

Taking another sip of root beer, I slumped in my chair. "These were their first notes on the case. At that point, they wouldn't be sure they even had a case. It would be way too early in the game to bring in the SEC. It has to mean 'secretary.' This has to be about Antheia."

"Maybe she was blackmailing somebody, and her husband knew about it. Maybe he went after the same target and got killed for the same reason."

"We have no evidence of that," I pointed out.

"We don't have any evidence of anything." She hiccupped.

"Let's assume they were investigating the bond. Why? Something must have made them think there was a case, raised their suspicions."

"Do a search for the library bond."

I tapped at the keyboard, and a list of articles popped onto the screen.

"Useless search engine." Charlene pointed at an article headline. "That's for a library in another town on the Peninsula."

"Hold it." I clicked on the article for the other town. "How much was the San Nicholas Library bond for?"

"Twenty-five million."

"This town's library bond was for thirty million."

"So our library was cheaper," she said.

"Yeah, but it was also lots smaller. The San Nicholas Library is only twenty thousand square feet. That town's library is ninety thousand square feet."

Charlene yelped. "We paid 1,250 bucks a square foot?"

"That does seem kind of high," I said. "But what's normal for libraries?"

"Do the math. The library in the other town cost only 330 dollars a foot, and that still seems ridiculous. Think about it. We paid an extra 900 dollars per square foot, and at twenty-thousand square feet . . ." Charlene rumpled her brow, thinking. "That's an 18-million-dollar overage! Who got that money?"

I typed, searching for other library bonds. We couldn't compare California prices to other states—everything here costs more. But it was little wonder Frank and Joe thought the library was overpriced.

"Why did anyone vote for this?" I asked, stunned.

"Because the public didn't look at the numbers, and

hardly anyone understands that a bond like this is a loan. People think it's free investor money. They don't understand bonds are a debt. The city borrows the money and repays it with interest. That means the people of San Nicholas have to pay for this boondoggle."

"There's got to be something we're missing," I said. "Even if the average citizen didn't look at the numbers, the town council would have had to. I can't believe someone on the board just walked away with that extra eighteen million."

"And I can't believe that our library really cost nine hundred dollars more per square foot than a library only twenty miles away. Someone pocketed that extra money."

"But who?"

"Contractors in cahoots with board members, town council members, maybe the librarian . . . It's a conspiracy." She clutched my arm, and my root beer spilled across my shirt. "I knew it!"

Grabbing a dish towel from a wall hook, I blotted my black, knit top. "Or it's completely innocent, because we don't understand an important piece of the puzzle. The library may have been overpriced, but that information isn't exactly secret. We found it online in a few minutes. Plus, there's still Joy. She had motive, means, and opportunity to poison Joe. Joy spent enough time around them both. She could have pushed Frank down the stairs too."

"But Joe wasn't investigating his niece."

"Maybe he should have been," I said. "And what about Mark's real estate dealings with Antheia? If we're wrong about the bond, and Joe was investigating Antheia, he could have been killed over that. Or even the Whispering Wanderer."

"Forget the wanderer. Do you really think your ex is murdering lawyers?"

I sagged against the granite counter. "No. But a week ago I wouldn't have pegged him for an illegal plumbing smuggler either." It was clear I'd misjudged him in more ways than one.

"There's lots we don't understand. We need to attack the problems we do understand and can manage."

"Right." Except I was more flummoxed than ever about the murders. Were there any problems I was in control of? Pie Town. Customers seemed to be finding their way back. But there wasn't anything I could do to speed that process tonight. Mark? That ship had sailed, sunk, and disintegrated on the ocean floor. That left getting on with my life. I could make a bonfire of my wedding gown, but doubted Charlene would appreciate that use for her barbeque pit. "Can I borrow your Jeep?"

"Absolutely not. Only I drive the Jeep."

"I'm a good driver," I said, offended.

"That Jeep belonged to my husband. Besides, you've got your own car. It's a lemon, but—"

"I want to get my stuff out of Mark's storage locker, and the VW's too small."

"We can go together."

"Um, I sort of wanted to go now."

"No time like the present, eh? I'm game."

I checked my watch. "It's nearly midnight. Are you sure?"

"I don't need much sleep."

Piling into her Jeep, we trundled off. The storage center was outside town, hidden from the highway by a stand of eucalyptus trees. A heavy-lidded guard met us at the gate.

Leaning across Charlene, I showed him my key.

"So?" he asked.

"So let us in, you big lunk," Charlene said.

He squinted. "Is that Crazy Charlene McCree?"

"Hey!" My head snapped up, heat spurting through my veins. "That's Mrs. Charlene McCree to you."

"Now open the gate," Charlene said. "This is a twenty-four-hour place, isn't it?"

Grumbling, he ducked into his guard shack. The electronic gate swung inward.

"Wow," Charlene said. "It really is twenty-four hours. I didn't think we'd be able to get in."

"Is that why you agreed to come?"

"I agreed because I want to see what else your ex has got in that storage locker."

"It can't be incriminating, or he wouldn't have given me the key."

She chuckled. "He was in such a twist over his new girlfriend, he would have given you anything to end that conversation."

We glided past rows of orange-roofed storage lockers lit by overhead lights and stopped before number 311.

"This is it." Stepping out of the Jeep, I unlocked the padlock, yanked up on the handle. The metal door rattled and clanked as I raised it.

Charlene gasped. Rows of toilets and boxes of plumbing bits and bobs jammed tight against each other.

My jaw slackened. "I'll never find my stuff in all this . . . this . . . What is all this?"

"Ye, gods." She pointed a quavering finger. "Are those incandescent lightbulbs?"

Standing on my toes, I grabbed a lightweight box from the top of one stack. "Looks like it."

She took the bulbs from me and clutched them to her chest. "One hundred watt! You don't think he'd mind if I took a few?"

"Yes, I do." I thought about that. "Take as many as you want."

"Right then." Loading her arms, she scuttled to the

Jeep and laid the contraband lightbulbs reverently on the dashboard. "I hate those fluorescents. The lighting is poor, and they wash out my skin. Where's your stuff?"

I handed her more boxes of lightbulbs, then shifted the heavier boxes outside the shed.

She sat on the Jeep's hood and watched me drag a toilet from the unit. "How many of these old houses is he selling?" she asked.

"No idea." I panted, pulling out another toilet. It scraped across the macadam. "These are heavier than they look." No wonder Mark had dragged his heels on letting me into his storage shed. Gradually, I cleared a path toward the back.

"Eureka!" I strode from the unit, box clutched in my hands.

"What's in there?"

"My mom's old pie tins." I loved those stamped pie tins.

"You talk about her a lot, but I've never heard you talk about your father."

And I'd never heard her talk about her daughter. "He wasn't in the picture."

"I'm sorry to hear that." She harrumphed. "You deserved better."

I set the box beside her on the hood of the Jeep, unsure how to reply.

"Your mother must have been a remarkable woman," she said.

"For being ditched by her husband?" Like I'd been ditched by Mark. Were the women in my family doomed to repeat the same mistakes?

"For raising such a strong, kindhearted young woman on her own." She reached into the cardboard box. "Oh, look, dishes. Are these yours?" She pulled out a blue and white plate.

"Yes," I said, grateful for the change of subject.

I scrounged about and finally unearthed my other three boxes. They mostly contained knickknacks, but they were my knickknacks. "Check out this fossil a friend brought me from Morocco." I hefted it from the box and unwrapped the newspaper covering, traced my hand along its million-year-old spiral.

"Morocco?" Her eyes grew misty. "I'll never forget my time in Marrakech. The hookah pipes. The mint tea. The sheikh. You wouldn't believe the size of his—"

A light blazed in my face, and I jerked away.

"A little late to be out, isn't it?" a masculine voice asked.

I twitched, fumbling the fossil.

Gordon grasped it with one hand. "Nice Ammonoidea."

"What?" I asked, dazed. Gordon Carmichael? Here?

His badge glinted. "The fossil. I was a geology minor. What are you doing here so late?"

Charlene straightened. "We have a key, and the security guard gave us permission. What are you doing here?"

"Part of my patrol. I saw your headlights. Emptying your locker couldn't wait until morning?"

"It's not my locker, and I'm tired of waiting." I stomped my foot, realized what I'd done, and blood rushed to my cheeks. "Sorry. It's been a long day."

Charlene jerked her thumb at me. "Her ex has been holding her things hostage in his storage shed."

Gordon looked around. "What's with all the toilets?"

"Those aren't mine," I said quickly. "It's his stuff. I had to get past it all to get to my boxes." Was I going to get Mark in trouble?

More importantly, did I care about that traitor?

No, I did not.

"Need some help?" he asked.

"That would be lovely, Officer." Charlene rubbed her elbow. "My back."

His brow wrinkled. "Right. So is this stuff going in or do you need to move more out?"

"In," I said. "I've got all my things." There hadn't been much, but if I was ever going to move into that tiny house, minimalism was my new mantra.

He lifted a toilet into his arms and walked it into the shed.

Charlene shot me a meaningful look.

I grabbed a box and handed it to him on his return. "This can't be a part of your regular duties."

He shrugged. "If a call comes in, I'll go. But there's not a lot happening tonight."

"I'd imagine there's not a lot happening in San Nicholas any night," I said.

"Aside from all the accidental deaths." Grabbing another box, he vanished into the storage unit.

"This is kind of a long shift for you, isn't it?" I asked when he returned for another box.

"Cops work long hours, and my shift is almost over." He headed into the shed.

"Ask him out," Charlene hissed.

"No," I whispered.

He returned and grabbed another toilet.

"It's a shame," Charlene said, "but Val's never been night diving."

"Is that so?" he asked.

"I've never been any kind of diving," I said, not knowing where Charlene was heading with this. Big sharks. Cold ocean. No thanks.

"Officer Carmichael dives, don't you?" Charlene asked him.

I glared at her.

"When there's a body in a bog," he said, "I'm the one they call. I'm part of the dive retrieval team."

"Are there bogs in San Nicholas?" I asked.

He laughed. "I hope not."

Charlene bounced on her heels. "In fact, you teach, don't you?"

Lifting a box, he gazed into my eyes.

My heart skipped a beat.

"Are you looking for diving lessons?" he asked.

I cleared my throat. "Aren't there great whites off the coast?"

"That's what they say." He shifted the box in his arms. "I've never seen one."

"You wouldn't when they're speeding silently up from beneath you," I said.

He quirked a brow. "You're not seriously afraid of sharks? One of the great things about diving is you finally get to see what's beneath the waves. It peels away some of the mystery."

"I love a good mystery."

"Yes," Charlene said, "she's been talking about dive lessons for ages. Said she wants to shake things up, take a chance."

"No. No, I really don't."

"Diving could help you get over your fear of the ocean," he said.

"Not of the ocean, of the sharks. They're pretty big animals." With razor-sharp teeth.

"I'm starting a new class in a week," he said. "Ask at the dive shop down by the pier. But I gotta tell you, I was trained to dive by a couple of marines, and I'm old school when it comes to dive training. It won't be easy."

"Charlene's just kid—"

"She'll be there," Charlene said.

I frowned at her. "If it fits my work schedule." And I'd make sure it wouldn't. I liked Gordon, but I wasn't going to become shark bait for some guy, even if he had startling green eyes and knew how to cook mushrooms. Besides, once he learned the truth about the mountain of lies Charlene and I had told (again), he'd run away as fast as his long, muscular legs would carry him.

"Oh, it will fit." Charlene smiled, her teeth gleaming.

He took another box into the depths of the storage shed.

"Pie Town keeps me busy," I muttered.

"Fortunately," Charlene said, "she has staff to lighten the load. She's thinking of making Petronella assistant manager. But don't tell anyone."

He emerged from the storage unit. "My cousin, Petronella?"

"She's your cousin?" This town was so small it was almost incestuous. "I haven't had a chance to talk to her about it yet."

"I won't say anything," he said. "I take it things are turning around at Pie Town?"

"I think so. I hope so."

"She made coupons," Charlene said.

Smiling weakly, I handed him a box. We finished loading the shed, and I pulled down the door. It rattled into place, and I locked it.

"I'll see you both home," he said.

"Um," I said, "we're taking my things to Pie Town."

"Pie Town it is."

Charlene and I piled into the Jeep. Gordon followed us, the headlights of his squad car illuminating the Jeep's interior. Was he seeing us safely home or making sure we weren't up to anything nefarious? I didn't believe he'd happened to stumble across us at the storage facility. Was Gordon carrying out an investigation on the side?

He watched us load the boxes into my kitchen, then drove off behind Charlene's Jeep as I pulled Pie Town's alley door shut.

Chapter 23

I glanced through the kitchen window into the dining area and twisted pie dough in my gloved hands.

It was a good Tuesday.

Not the best Tuesday ever, but we had a normal Tuesday afternoon crowd. And considering what we'd gone through, normal was thrilling. Takeaway sales had been brisk. A couple sat across from each other in one of the booths. A trio of mothers, their children asleep in their strollers, gossiped over slices of pie and coffee. The chiropractor, Mr. Peters, sat with perfect posture alone at the counter. The gamers were in their usual spot. I checked my watch. Two o'clock. The lunch rush was over. Pie Town was back on track.

But weariness pressed on my shoulders, hollowed out my chest. I couldn't shake the fear that Mark was connected to the murders somehow, and a sense of betrayal mixed with my suspicion. In short, I was a red hot mess.

Petronella rang up a sale and handed a box to a grandmother in a thick coat. My assistant drummed her fingers on the counter, watching the customer leave, then whisked into the kitchen. "People are asking about the breakfast pies."

"Are they? Good." I'd put a sign up that morning announcing the pies would be available in two weeks. The bacon pie was a winner, and I thought I'd go with the spinach quiche as well. But I needed time to work out at least one more breakfast pie recipe before we launched. "Petronella, I wanted to talk to you about becoming assistant manager."

"Assistant manager?" She raked a hand through her spiky black hair. Her nails had been painted sparkling ebony.

"Before Joe's death, I'd been thinking of hiring two more people. If this trend continues, I want to go ahead with that and bring in an assistant manager. I thought you might like that job, and a raise to go with it." Fear twinged my gut. Was I being overly optimistic? I'd taken such a financial beating lately, the thought of spending more money terrified me. But this felt right.

Her dark eyes widened. "I would!"

I sagged against the counter. "Great. Maybe we can sit down tomorrow and develop the job description."

"Yes! Okay!" She spun and pointed at Hannah, filling apple pies at a metal work station. "More fruit in that pie!"

The bell over the front entrance jingled, and Petronella strode toward the kitchen door.

"I'll get it," I said.

She stopped midstride. "You will?"

"You manage things in here." Dusting off my apron, I walked into the dining area.

Captain's hat in hand, Loomis stood in the center of the room. His bulky peacoat hung open, exposing a knotted rope for a belt about his stained trousers. His white hair stood up in odd places, as if tossed by the wind.

I stepped behind the register. "Hi, Loomis."

He ambled to my counter. "I'm here to keep my promise to you, and also to see Charlene."

"I'm afraid you've missed her. If you'd like to come back later, I won't hold you to lunch."

He lifted his chin. "A promise is a promise. Is that potpie I smell?"

"We have chicken, beef, and potato curry today. We have mini-pies for lunch if you'd prefer to dine in, and full size for takeaway." Of course, people could take away any size pie they wanted, but I was pushing sales.

"Pity about Charlene. Are you expecting her later?"

"She's only here in the mornings." Unless she was on detective business.

He winked. "Oh, well. I tried. But I think you promised me mincemeat."

"A slice, full size, or hand pie?" I slid a menu to him.

Perusing it, he scratched his beard. "Hm . . . It's a Devil's choice you're offering. All right, I'll take a mini beef potpie and one of those mincemeat hand pies. I've got to watch my girlish figure." He paid, and I handed him the receipt.

"Sea hag!" One of the gamers thumped the table with his fist.

"You want to hear about sea hags?" Loomis bellowed. "I'll tell you about a sea hag." He stomped over to their booth.

Feeling protective of the gamers, I wavered, unsure if I should intervene.

Loomis spoke to them in a low voice, and they burst into laughter. One of the gamers shifted sideways in the booth. Loomis sat, joining them.

Returning to the kitchen, I plated a still-warm mini-potpie. When I returned to the booth, Loomis was telling a ribald tale about a seal, a sailing ship, and a septuagenarian.

I hurried away before I could hear the rest of the story and bumped into Joy, seemingly welded to the floor. Her steel-colored purse slithered off the shoulder of her gray coat to the floor.

"Whoops, sorry." Kneeling, I scooped up the purse and handed it to her. "How are you doing?"

Her face crumpled. "Sometimes I think everything's okay. And then it hits me. Joe's gone. Murdered. Someone actually killed my uncle." She blinked rapidly.

"Hey," I said, "I'm sorry. I can't believe it either."

"None of this makes any sense!"

I guided her to an empty booth, and we sat. "Has something happened?"

"The cops aren't taking this seriously. Yes, my uncle did keep castor beans, but they were under the sink in his bathroom cupboard, not in his kitchen. There's no way a bean or two accidentally made their way into his coffee grinder, no matter what the cops say. And I looked for Frank's casebook, the one Tandy said Joe took. I couldn't find it anywhere."

"You couldn't?" I squeaked. How could I admit Charlene had stolen it? I bunched my apron in my hands.

"When I talked it over with my dad, he said he was going to hire a real private detective. I'm sure not getting anywhere."

"That's, um, a good idea." Great Buddha, if a real detective started looking into this, would he figure out Charlene and I had the casebook? I had to tell her. Or maybe we could somehow slip it back to her? Through a window? Under a doormat?

"Have you gotten any farther on those casebook pages I photocopied?" she asked.

"I'm not sure. I think I understand why Joe and Frank thought the new library was a waste of money." I told her about the cost.

Her brow wrinkled. "That does seem like a lot, but . . . well, it's the government, isn't it?"

We both considered that for a long moment. The bell

tinkled over the front entrance, and a chemical smell wafted in. Wrinkling my nose, I turned.

"That's him," Joy hissed. "That's the homeless guy."

A slim, white-haired man loped to the front counter. His clothing was stained, rumpled. What looked like a cake knife was stuck through his belt.

Joy squeaked. "He's got a knife."

"I'm not afraid of a cake knife." I slid from the booth.

"You ought to be." She pulled her cell phone from her purse. "I'm calling the cops."

"Don't. He probably wants some pie." I was the proprietor, and this was my shop, and I would deal with this with a smile. A fake, terrified smile.

I slithered behind the counter, making a barricade of the register. "Welcome to Pie Town. What can I get for you?"

Bracing one hand on the register, he leaned forward. I edged away, clutching a stack of menus to my chest.

He rested his free hand on the handle of the cake knife. "I'll take an apple pie." His voice was ghostly, ethereal. "To go."

"Full size or mini?"

"Fullllll."

Laughing maniacally, I rang up the pie. "Sure thing!" See, just a pie. No biggie, I told myself.

He handed me the money, and I made change.

"And I see you've brought your own pie cutter," I said brightly.

"What?" He glanced down. "It's a palette knife," he whispered. "I'm a painter."

I edged closer, head lowered as if we were sharing a secret. "And are you also a . . . wanderer?"

He blinked. "Huh?" It came out as a wheeze.

I reached beneath the counter and grabbed a fresh apple pie. "Did you know Frank Potts or Joe Devlin?"

"Yesssss . . . Frank was an old friend."

"But you're not from around here," I said, boxing the pie.

His face creased. "Not for a long time."

Laying the pie on the counter, I rested one hand atop the closed box. "I'm sorry, this may sound odd, but I knew Frank and his friend Joe. Frank and Joe used to solve little local problems together. One of their notebooks mentioned a Case of the Whispering Wanderer. Could that be you?"

He broke into a grin. "Frank used to call me that. Damned insensitive if you ask me." He rubbed his throat. "Cancer."

"So it is you! But what was the case? Can you tell me?"

He stared at the floor. "No case, not really. Frank wanted me to set things right with a relative I have around here. He'd been hassling me for years to return. But I prefer to roam. I've got myself a gypsy caravan, you see, and I sell art out of it."

"That's yours? I saw it down by the beach the other day. It's charming."

His white brows drew downward. "It was in a beautiful spot until the damned police drove me off. There's nowhere to park in this blasted town."

"Have you tried the campground?"

He smiled. "Nowhere free."

"Who's your relative?"

"I doubt your paths have crossed. And even if they did, it's too late for the two of us. Too many things were said." He gave me a look.

I pulled at my collar, embarrassed. "Sorry. It's none of my business." This wasn't the case Joe had gotten killed over. Charlene had been right, and I needed to step away.

"It's not that. You're a kind young woman, but you don't know my sister, Emily."

"Not Emily Pargiter?"

His eyebrows shot upward. "You know her?"

"Yes, she's been having trouble with trespassers, and Charlene and I—"

"Not Crazy Charlene McCree?"

"Um, you know Charlene? Anyway, we were there last week, and Miss Pargiter mentioned you. She said she thinks about you every day—"

"Probably thinking about throttling me."

"I didn't get that impression. I think she'd love to see you."

"What's this about trespassers?"

"They've been tramping through her yard on a fairly regular basis at night. It's a little disturbing."

"Bothering my sister? Taking advantage of an old lady?" His voice rose to a harsh rasp. His grip on the palette handle tightened.

And this is where I could have told him the problem was all taken care of. "Yes, it's terrible what some people will do. The police haven't been able to do a thing about it."

"Cops!"

"Mm." I said a silent apology to Gordon.

"Emily may be a stubborn old b . . . Um, stubborn old woman, but she's still family. And I don't like anyone messing with my family."

"You shouldn't."

"I will go see her."

"She's got a space for you to park your caravan. No one would bother you there."

He looked interested. "Really?"

"She has an ocean view and a big yard. Most of it's on a slope, but a good bit of it is flat, enough for a caravan."

"I remember the spot. It's been ages since I've been home." He rubbed his chin, his palm making scritching noises against the gray bristles. "Perhaps our issues weren't all her fault. It takes two to tango. . . . Maybe I have been holding a grudge for too long."

"You wouldn't be the first," I said, thinking of Mark. It

would be a while before I forgave his betrayal. Messing with my heart was one thing. Messing with my business was a whole other kettle of fish.

"Frank may have been right to drag me back here. I'm not sure why I was resisting a reconciliation with my sister for so long. I'll go see her."

I slid the pie across the counter. "Good luck!"

Another case, solved! I was starting to understand Joe and Frank's enthusiasm for their hobby. This felt great.

The Whispering Wanderer sloped out of the shop. Two teenagers cruised up to the counter and ordered cherry hand pies. I set them up at the counter, and the mayor walked into Pie Town.

I hustled to the register.

Striding to the counter, Mayor Sharp leaned his elbow on it. "I've got a meeting tonight and have to bring dessert," he said. "Have you got blueberry pie?"

"Sure." Telling him the price—because I wasn't going to be stiffed again—I boxed one up. Frantically, I thought up and discarded subtle segues into the going rate of library construction.

He paid, glanced around. "Business is picking up, I see."

"Yes, I may have to head over to the library and get a book to celebrate. The new library is gorgeous." Ugh. Definitely not subtle.

"We're proud of it. I think it's the best library on the north coast."

"The construction cost seemed kind of expensive though. Is that normal for libraries?"

"The construction cost?" He raised a brow.

I shrugged one shoulder. "I noticed that a recently built library at a town inland cost a lot less per square foot."

"And you're an expert in construction costs? We should get you elected to the town council."

I shoved my hands in my apron pockets. "When you're leasing per square foot, you start paying attention to those things."

"Building on the coast is always more expensive. The infrastructure isn't as good. Besides, there are added costs to getting the materials out here, as well as bringing the library up to modern environmental standards."

"That makes sense." But the cost per square foot still seemed high. I slid the boxed pie across the counter to him. "Well, it's an amazing library. Good job."

He chuckled. "I had very little to do with it. Thank the library board." He walked out, the bell above the entrance tinkling.

Straightening my apron, I looked around the dining area. Loomis rolled a pair of dice with the gamers. Joy stared out the window, sipping a cup of coffee. The teenagers had their heads close together, bar stools swiveled toward each other. The new mothers chatted animatedly.

This was what I wanted. It wasn't about the pie—though I loved pie. Pie Town was about the community, people coming here to live a tiny piece of their lives, meet friends, have a good time. I'd been so buried in accounts and the kitchen and making it work no matter what the cost, that I'd forgotten what mattered.

I swallowed. This community was my dream.

I wasn't going to let a killer ruin it.

Chapter 24

I walked down a quiet residential street off Main. Nighttime fog shrouded the lush yards, blanketed the cars parked on the street.

I stopped in front of a house. A flower garden sprawled behind its picket fence, a Mark Jeffreys Real Estate sign beside a camellia bush.

Mark was up to his neck in whatever was going wrong in San Nicholas. He'd been involved in shady deals with Antheia, who was dead. He was on the board of a library, the construction of which appeared to be at best grossly mismanaged, and he was smuggling contraband plumbing supplies. How to reconcile that person with the man I'd thought I'd loved? Had my judgment been so wrong? Or was Mark playing out of his depth?

We had to talk.

Light from the front windows flowed across the porch. Like me, Mark's place of business was also his home. Unlike me, he slept upstairs in a converted attic. Lucky dog.

My footsteps clunked on the porch steps. I rang the bell and waited, shuffling my feet, tightening my fists in the pockets of my Pie Town hoodie.

The door jerked open. Mark frowned down at me, his

blond hair ruffled, blue eyes snapping. The sleeves of his blue sports shirt were rolled up, the collar undone.

"Mark, we need to talk."

"Thank God," he said at the same time.

We both stared at each other. "What?" we asked in unison.

"You go first." Confusion muddled my brain. Whatever I was going to say next was probably going to be awkward and embarrassing and painful.

"You've got to get rid of her," he said.

"Get rid of whom?" My eyes narrowed. "And what do you mean by 'get rid of'?"

"That woman who wears a cat as a scarf." He opened the door wider and stepped backward, into the receptionist's area.

Cautious, I edged inside. What did he mean by 'get rid of'? "You mean Charlene?"

"Val!" Charlene appeared in the doorway to Mark's office, her cat draped about the shoulders of her turquoise-colored tunic. "What are you doing here?"

I stopped midstride. "What are you doing here?"

"I've just come from Pargiter's," she said. "Her brother's there."

"He is?" I'd done it! They'd reconciled.

"They're fighting like two caged rats."

A despairing noise escaped my throat. "They are?"

"I've never seen Pargiter so happy," she said.

"She is?" I rubbed my temple.

Charlene turned on Mark. "Which is why he has to go."

"I don't follow," I said.

"You, Val, make people happy. You sell pie! You solved the Pargiter problem!" She stabbed a finger at Mark. "And you, sir, are a realtor."

He folded his arms over his chest. "I'm not going anywhere."

And I still didn't get it. "In fairness, there's nothing wrong with realtors."

She shook a gnarled finger at him. "There isn't room in this town for the two of you. The way I see it, you've got three options. One, confess to your crimes so you both can have a clean slate and move on. Two, leave."

"What's the third?" he asked.

"I forgot," she said. "But it will come to me in a minute. You can practice real estate anywhere. Pie Town is for San Nicholas."

"Val can open Pie Town anywhere."

"No." Straightening, I set my jaw. "I can't. But Charlene's right. You need to tell us what's going on, what's really going on. Four people are dead."

Clawing a hand through his hair, he collapsed into one of the faux leather waiting room chairs. It thunked against the wall, rattling a framed watercolor. "What are you talking about?"

"Where was Antheia getting the money to buy real estate?" I thought I knew the answer, but I wanted to hear what Mark had to say.

"How should I know? It was none of my business."

A rivulet of sweat trickled down my back, and I unzipped my hoodie. "It should have been. Her practice was dwindling, and she never charged much. Someone told me she swindled her elderly clients by buying their homes at a below-market rate, and then selling the homes on for a big profit."

"Hey," Mark said, "I wasn't involved in her real estate purchases. She paid cash and knew how to write her own contract. I only assisted with the sales."

"So where did she get the cash?" I asked.

"She sure didn't get the money from her husband," Charlene said. "He spent the last ten years making wire jewelry nobody wanted."

"Did she get the money from the library board?" I leaned one hip against the receptionist's desk.

"There's NO MONEY on the library board," Mark roared. "How many times do I have to tell you?"

"Maybe not on the board," I said, "but there was in the bond. Were you aware that the cost per square foot for our new library was 1,250 dollars? It shouldn't have been more than 350, tops. Where did all that extra money go?"

"It's an award-winning building design, and it's LEED certified!"

"Lead? What kind of a name is that?" Charlene asked.

"LEED," he said. "A sort of environmental accreditation. It's an acronym, and don't ask me what it stands for. Why am I even bothering to explain this to you? Heidi told me I should avoid your negative energy."

"She also told you your totem animal was a white leopard," Charlene said.

"How do you know that?"

Charlene sneered. "You posted it on Twitter, you git."

"That was private!"

Heaving a sigh, Charlene readjusted the sleeping cat around her neck. "If you hit reply, everyone sees it. How can someone your age be such a Luddite?"

He glared at me. "Get. Rid. Of. Her."

"As a realtor," I said, "you must realize that the price per square foot on that library is way too high. Where did the money go, Mark?"

"Look," he said, "I saw the books. They're open and transparent. It might have been expensive, but everything went to the building contractors."

"How do you know?" I asked. "The construction was before your time."

"Because I saw the contracts! Besides, the town council has oversight over the library board. It also had oversight over the bond measure, because the city will have to repay the bond."

"I want to see those books," I said.

"No way." He crossed his arms.

"I thought they were open and transparent," I said.

"Not to the general public," he said. "If you want to see them, join the library board."

Neck cording, I jolted away from the desk. My shoulder brushed a hanging fern, setting it swinging. "Antheia and her husband are dead! Joe and Frank are dead! And you tie to all of them."

Charlene laid a hand on my arm. "Forget it, Val. We'll have to go to plan B."

"Great," Mark said. "What's plan B?"

"You think environmental certification is hot stuff?" Charlene asked. "Because plan B is where Val and I blow the whistle on your environmentally incorrect smuggling operation. We've seen your storage shed."

He squared his chin. "I can have that cleared out in an hour."

"But a cop has already seen it," Charlene said, "hasn't he, Val?"

"Actually," I said, "yes. One came by last night when we were getting my stuff out. He saw everything, though he didn't realize what it was at the time."

"And you didn't tell him," Mark said.

"Not yet." Charlene's voice hardened. "Now, what's it going to be? Are you going to show us those books, uncensored, or do we blow your high-flow toilets wide open?"

"It's a petty regulatory crime! It's plumbing!"

"But it's enough to knock you off your pedestal at the library board," Charlene said. "And enough for you to lose your real estate license, I think."

"That's my livelihood!"

"You didn't give much consideration to Val's livelihood when you tried to shut down Pie Town," Charlene said.

I blew out my breath. "He didn't try to shut down

Pie Town. We got some bad publicity because of Joe's death. . . ." I faltered.

Mark studied the tips of his polished shoes.

"Wait a minute," I said. "That newspaper article by your old school buddy—you didn't have anything to do with that, did you?"

He leapt to his feet. "I wouldn't do that to you, Val."

"Oh, my God, you did!" I could always tell when he was lying, because he wasn't very good at it. "Did you encourage Heidi to put that Sugar Kills sign in her window too?"

"No. She really believes sugar kills."

Charlene stepped closer to him, her eyes narrowed to slits. "We'll see those books now, boy-o."

"Val?" He shot me a pleading look. "You must see that this is wrong."

"We should get to the library before it closes," I said in a voice I didn't recognize. "That is where the accounts for the construction work are kept, isn't it? Or are they at city hall?"

He ran his palms over the thighs of his khakis. "The library."

"I'll drive," Charlene said.

Charlene and I strode into the library, Mark trailing reluctantly in our wake.

The librarian stopped riffling through a set of keys and looked up from the front desk, his expression pinching. In his black suit, he resembled a funeral director more than ever. "Mark? What are you doing here? We close in five minutes."

"Sorry about that," Mark said. "Pie Town's thinking of sponsoring our next fund-raiser, and I wanted to get some materials for them from upstairs. Ladies, you've met our librarian, Hunter Green."

"Hi again." Taking my hand out of my hoodie pocket, I waggled my fingers at him.

The librarian looked at us askance. Charlene and I probably didn't look like typical donor material. "Ah, certainly," he said. "I've got to lock up. Go ahead and tell one of the staff members when you're done, so they can let you out."

"Thanks, Hunter." Mark clapped him on the shoulder. "Let's go, ladies." He led us up the open stairs.

"That librarian's likely behind it," Charlene muttered. "He's not from around here, and no one who looks that much like a forties-era vampire can be a simple librarian. I'll bet he's got a collection of wax figures stashed in the basement."

"You're thinking of Vincent Price," I said, "and that movie House of Wax."

"Vincent Price was such a lovely man. I ran into him once in Sears. 'Pardon me, dear lady,' he said. To me!"

Mark's gaze flicked upward in exasperation. "What is wrong with you two? Hunter has a PhD in library science and has been living and working here for five years. He can't help how he looks. And how long does someone have to live here to be from around here?"

"Just show us the books," I said beneath my breath, "and we'll get out of your hair."

"I want to believe that. Why don't I?" He headed through the second-floor stacks.

"What's that supposed to mean?" I whispered.

"It means you should have left after we broke up. It means I see you everywhere around town, and now you're next door to my new girlfriend's gym. How am I supposed to get in a workout there, knowing you could pop up any minute?"

My nostrils flared, my breathing growing loud. "That's your problem. You were the one who helped her take out the lease."

"What was I supposed to say? Don't lease that space, my ex-fiancée owns the pie shop next door?"

"Well, you didn't have to tell her to go ahead and lease it because I was leaving!" I forced myself to take calming breaths. The library was still open, and if I kept going, I'd hit top volume pretty quickly.

Stopping in front of a polished wood door, he fished a key ring from his pocket.

"Do you have keys to all the rooms in the library?" Charlene asked.

He unlocked the door and pushed it open. "No, only this one. It belongs to the board. Antheia sometimes used it as her office."

Charlene arched a brow. "Did she now?"

"She did a lot of work for the board," he said, his voice rising.

"We get it," I said. "She was the power behind the throne." The dead power. I sidled past him into the small room. A desk. Two chairs on one side, an executive chair on the other. And rows of metal cabinets. I opened one and found a stack of library hoodies. I sniffed. Pie Town's were better quality.

"Those are for our donors," Mark said.

I dropped the hoodie back on its stack.

"The files you're looking for are in here." He rolled open the drawer of a metal filing cabinet and flipped through the manila folders.

"Decided to be helpful now, have you?" Charlene said.

"The quicker this is over, the quicker I can get rid of the two of you." He slapped a file on the desk.

Picking it up, I leafed through it.

"Well?" Charlene asked.

"These financial statements are more complicated than Pie Town's," I said. "It's going to take time."

"Let's photocopy them," Charlene said, "and we can look them over at home."

"Where's the photocopy machine?" I asked Mark.

"First floor," a masculine voice said from behind me.

I flinched, the papers in the folder rustling to the carpeted floor. In the doorway stood the mayor, wearing a San Nicholas Library zip-up hoodie and holding a gun.

Chapter 25

My world telescoped to the barrel of the gun. "Mr. Mayor?" My voice cracked.

Mayor Jack Sharp waggled the gun. "I hoped I wouldn't find you down here, Val. But you couldn't shut up about the library bond."

I hugged the empty folder to my chest. This was not happening. NOT happening.

"I knew it," Charlene said, hoarse. "I knew it was a conspiracy."

"Even a stopped clock is right twice a day." Sharp winced. "Jeez, Charlene, are you wearing that cat again?"

Mark's hands shot into the air. "Mayor Sharp! This is a misunderstanding."

"Shut up."

I swallowed. "So it's true, you killed them all. Why Antheia? Was she having second thoughts about stealing the bond money?"

"Her husband's detective was starting to dig into her finances," the mayor said. "Roy was determined to get that alimony."

"And the detective would have figured out that there

was no legitimate source for the money she was spending on properties," I said. "You two embezzled from the bond."

"Don't be so crude," the mayor said. "Every penny of that money went to the contractors. And then they gave Antheia and I hefty kickbacks." He jingled a set of keys in his free hand. "The library is empty aside from the librarian, and he won't bother us. I've promised him I'd lock up after you. Shall we?" He nodded toward the door.

Charlene pressed a hand to her heart. "I'm not feeling very well."

Beneath the folder I gripped, my stomach had turned to marble, but my mind tumbled, an avalanche of useless thoughts. Every cell in my body screamed for me not to go with him, but I was no ninja. I wasn't skilled in hand-to-hand combat. And the mayor was not conveniently positioned beneath a bookcase I could knock over to flatten him with.

The mayor stood aside.

Charlene and I passed out the door, our footsteps soft on the beige carpet. The library was empty. We were alone.

"Stop," he said.

We swayed to a halt.

"You too, Mark," he said.

"Me?" He paled. "But I'm not involved in this."

"You are now, son. Move." He stuck the gun in the pocket of his hoodie, keeping it trained on us.

"Heidi was right," Mark said, looking at me. "I should have stayed away from you."

I gaped at him. "That's what you're worried about? Placing blame? Now?" I shook my head, trying to rattle my brain into action. There had to be a way out of here. There were three of us and only one of the mayor. Unfortunately, one of my fellow kidnapees had lapsed into a fit of self-absorption and the other was even less of a ninja than I.

The mayor marched us outside, through the dark and deserted parking lot and to the paved path wrapping along the bay. The boats floated, obscured by the nighttime fog, their lights forming disembodied nimbuses of yellow and red and blue. On the opposite side of the street, restaurant windows filled with diners looked out over the bay. Hope flared in my chest. People walked here at night to admire the water. He'd made a mistake bringing us here.

"So we're clear," he said, "if you try anything, I'll shoot Mark first—"

"Fine by me," Charlene said.

Mark went white.

"—and any innocent pedestrians second."

"That will put a dent in your electability." My heart banged against my rib cage. Jack must have figured Mark would be the first person to run and save his own skin, pedestrians be damned. I wanted to think the mayor was wrong, but the threat seemed to have cowed my ex.

"I think we're beyond that," the mayor said, "don't you?"

We passed a woman pushing a stroller, mother and child bundled up against the night air. The mayor smiled and nodded at her.

Our wannabe murderer glanced toward the water. "Turn onto the pier."

I followed orders, my footsteps dragging, echoing on the dock. Boats, covered in blue tarps for the night, bumped against the wooden pilings. A row of high lamps lit the pier, a runway leading to nowhere.

"What's the plan, Jack?" I asked.

"That will be Mayor Sharp, if you don't mind. Your Mark's been smuggling environmentally incorrect plumbing into San Nicholas, and you've been helping him."

Mark yelped.

"Don't try to deny it," Jack said. "I've got friends in the construction business. They know your supplier."

"The friends who paid you off to get them those over-priced library construction contracts?" Charlene asked tartly.

The mayor ignored her. "I'm afraid there's going to be a falling out among thieves. Or smugglers, as the case may be."

"No one's going to believe we killed each other over a few toilets," I said.

"My nephew's on the police force. He'll believe what I tell him."

"Detective Shaw?" Charlene asked. "So that's how you've been covering everything up. Nepotism!"

"Not entirely. My nephew isn't particularly imaginative, and he's eager to please. So you see, Mark, your participation is integral to the plot of tonight's drama."

Mark groaned. "I should have listened to Heidi."

"Did Heidi tell you not to smuggle toilets?" Charlene asked.

"She doesn't know," he said. "Everything was fine until you two decided to start playing detective."

Blood thundered in my ears. There had to be something I could do, some way to escape. But the pier was distressingly neat, devoid of any handy wrenches or giant fishing hooks I could swing at Sharp. I could dive into the water, between the boats, but that would leave Charlene and Frederick and Mark at risk. If anyone shot Mark, I wanted it to be me.

The mayor drew the gun from his pocket. Its dark metal gleamed, menacing.

"Why did you kill the others?" I asked, stalling for time, for an idea, for an escape.

"Antheia's husband knew what was going on. Hiring the

detective was a way to shake her up. After I killed her, Roy tried to blackmail me."

"What about Joe and Frank?" I asked.

"Frank started this little adventure. He invited me to his home, because he had questions about the bond. He figured I didn't know about it. He took me upstairs, where he'd stored some of his files. Somehow, he'd obtained copies of contracts and some, shall we say, incriminating e-mails. I saw the opportunity and took it. You'd be surprised how easy it is to kill someone. So when Joe started sniffing around, it made sense to do it again."

My legs shook. "By mixing a castor bean in with his coffee beans?"

"That was easy too," he said. "Joe made me coffee in his kitchen, asking the same questions you've been asking. I knew, of course, that he and Frank had been thick as thieves, and exactly what he was up to. After he made the coffee, he left the kitchen for a moment, and I slipped the castor bean into the bag of coffee beans."

"That doesn't sound very spur of the moment," I said.

The mayor's brows rose. "Of course it wasn't. I suspected Joe might ask questions after Frank's death, so I started thinking about what I'd do if he came to me."

My palms grew slick, and I rubbed them on the front of my jeans. "But they found a bag of castor beans in his bathroom. Did you plant them?"

"After our chat, I told him I needed to use the bathroom. I took the opportunity to shove the castor beans beneath the bathroom sink, way in the back, where I knew he wouldn't look."

"Still, it was a big risk," I said. "And so was breaking in to Joe's house after he died." Where the fricasseed hell was everybody tonight? There had to be a fisherman or a dive class or a retiree walking his dog somewhere.

"I kind of enjoyed playing the villain," he mused.

THE QUICHE AND THE DEAD   281

"You are the villain," Charlene said.

"You don't need to do this," I said.

He sneered. "Next, you'll tell me I won't get away with it."

"How can you?" I asked. "There are too many corpses. Even Shaw will have to see—"

"Hello, did someone say my name?" Twin flashlight beams hit the mayor and I in the face.

Shaw and a uniformed Officer Carmichael clambered over the side of a boat and ambled toward us.

"Mr. Mayor," Shaw said. "We got a tip about some environmental scofflaws smuggling illegal plumbing. What are you doing out"—his gaze dropped to the gun, and his face slackened—"here?"

Gordon's hand went to his gun.

"Don't try it, Officer," Jack's voice whip-cracked. "You're not that fast a draw, and I've got plenty of innocent targets." The mayor aimed the gun at the person closest to him: me.

A whimper escaped Charlene's throat.

Sharp licked his lips. "Now take your gun out, slowly, and kick it over to me."

Gordon laid the gun on the dock, his expression grim. With his booted foot, he slid the weapon toward the mayor.

"Uncle Jack, what's going on?" Shaw asked.

"Are you making a citizen's arrest, Mr. Mayor?" Gordon asked, eyes hard and glittering.

"Nice try, Officer." He jerked his chin at Shaw. "Teddy, get over here."

Teddy? Teddy Shaw? My brain was trying to escape into not-important-land, but I needed to focus. Shaw and Carmichael were close, only a few feet away, but the mayor's gun was aimed at my chest.

Shaw didn't budge. "I don't understand what's going on. Why are you pointing a gun at Miss Harris?"

The mayor's nostrils flared. "Get. Over. Here."

"Put the gun down," Shaw said, "and we'll talk."

"You really are stupid," the mayor snarled. He jerked the gun toward his nephew.

Carmichael shoved Shaw to the side. A shot thundered. Carmichael shouted, and spun awkwardly.

Charlene shrieked.

Hissing, Frederick rose on Charlene's shoulders, his white fur bristling. The cat launched itself at the mayor's head.

Mayor Sharp swore, struggled to peel the yowling animal free. His gun clattered to the dock.

I dove for the gun, fumbled, knocked it over the side of the pier. It splashed into the black water.

Cursing, Officer Carmichael rolled to his feet. He staggered to the mayor.

Sharp wrenched the cat off and hurled it onto a boat. Frederick thudded against a wall. Limp, the cat slid to the deck.

"Frederiiiiiiiick," Charlene wailed.

Blood streaming down one arm, Officer Carmichael grabbed the mayor and spun him to the ground. He wrenched one of the mayor's muscular arms back and slapped a cuff on. "Give me your other arm."

"Get off me," the mayor shouted. "I'm the mayor!"

"Give me your other arm!"

"You work for me! Ow. OW!" The mayor gave him the other arm.

Carmichael cuffed him.

Detective Shaw limped to us, wide-eyed. "What's going on?"

"Frederick," Charlene sobbed.

Mark climbed onto the boat and reverently picked up the cat. "The white leopard," he whispered. "Heidi was right about everything. The cat's breathing."

"Give him to me." Charlene held out her hands, sobbing.

Carefully, he lowered Frederick over the side of the boat, and Charlene cradled him in her arms.

Was he badly hurt? Dead? It was hard to tell, since comatose was Frederick's go-to move. But I didn't see any blood, and his ribs rose and fell. "He looks okay," I said, tentative.

Charlene ran her hands over him, and Frederick purred. His blue eyes opened. He yawned, shook his head.

"I think he's all right," Mark said.

"The narcolepsy must have saved him," Charlene said. "He must have gone limp right before he hit the wall. Frederick was like a drunk in a car crash. He was so relaxed, he didn't get hurt."

I sat against a piling, the collapse of adrenaline leaving me weak.

Carmichael hauled Mayor Sharp to his feet. "Would someone tell me why the mayor was trying to kill us all?"

I sucked in a breath, pointing at his shoulder. "You're bleeding."

"It's a graze," Carmichael said. "If he'd hit me, we wouldn't be having this conversation. So what the hell's going on?"

"A conspiracy at the library board," Charlene said. "Murder, theft, blackmail! The feds are going to be in on this take down, mark my words."

Carmichael looked to me.

I cleared my throat. "What she said."

Chapter 26

Charlene sat at the picnic table, her newspaper fluttering in the breeze. White cat hair flecked her merlot-colored tunic and black leggings. Coiled around a toy mouse, Frederick lay on the table.

Hefting a box from the Jeep, I carried it into my new tiny house and set my dishes on the kitchenette counter. The wood floors gleamed. An empty bookshelf awaited my books.

My tiny house.

My rental tiny house.

I walked outside and stretched, massaging my lower back. The air smelled sweet, of wild grasses. In the distance, ocean and sky met, framed by fluffy, white clouds at the top and a line of surf at the bottom. Birds chirped, invisible, in the trees.

I glanced at the converted shipping container. Its wide, plate glass windows reflected my form. My heart filled. I'd wake up to this view every morning.

"Is that a new cat toy?" I asked.

She lowered the paper. "What? The mouse? Your ex left that little offering on my doorstep this morning, the weirdo. But Frederick likes it."

"How can you tell?"

She ignored me. "The mayor's still front page news. Now they're looking into other city contracts."

"He's not the only one on the town council." I got another box from the Jeep. "And there's a city manager. How did the mayor get away with all those kickbacks?"

"Oh, he had help from other folks, like Antheia, who got greedy. Mark my words, they'll find other crooks as they turn over more rocks. I'm sure that bloodsucking librarian is up to his fangs in this."

"Um, we did agree he's not a vampire, didn't we?"

"Hello! Sunlight! Of course he's not a real vampire."

As long as we were clear.

"I hear the SEC and the FBI are investigating," she said.

"Investigating the librarian?"

"Investigating the whole damn town, near as I can tell."

I put the box beside Frederick on the picnic table. Now that it was all over, I didn't care much about the FBI or the SEC. We'd been completely cleared of Joe's death, and Charlene had returned Frank's casebook to Joy. I'm not sure what she told her, and I didn't ask.

"All I care about is that Pie Town is saved," I said. Business was booming. Petronella had moved into her management role, and that gave me more time for strategy, accounting, and relaxing.

"Too bad that weasel Shaw got all the credit for the takedown. He came out of this looking like a hero, putting his own uncle away."

Frederick yawned.

I scratched behind his ears. "But Carmichael's a detective now. They won't stick him with rousting gypsy caravans and sorting out surfer disputes."

"It was about time they promoted him. Too bad it took him getting injured in the line of duty."

"Did you see how he shoved Shaw out of the way? He

risked his life to save Shaw's, and I don't think they care much for each other."

"Mm." Charlene turned the page. "Carmichael is one of a kind. Single too."

I jammed my hands in the pockets of my Pie Town hoodie.

"Of course he's nothing like your ex," Charlene said. "So I can see why you wouldn't want to go out with him."

"It's a moot point. He hasn't asked me out." I'd come clean to him about the break-in, and our encounter with the mayor cloaked in a ski mask. No charges were pending, but Carmichael had been clearly annoyed.

"I don't see why he won't. You're not a suspect anymore."

"Charlene—"

"And it's the twenty-first century. You should ask him. Or take him up on the dive lessons. Of course, in my day, a lady never asked a man out. But at least we knew how to encourage them to ask us out."

"Fascinating." Grabbing the box, I took it into the house and laid it beside the built-in desk. My own desk. I had my own shower now too. What was I going to do with my gym membership?

Giddy, I returned to the Jeep. "How are Miss Pargiter and her brother doing?"

"He's got his caravan parked in her yard. I think he'll be sticking around for a while. He's getting old. He says he likes to travel, but with the weekend tourist crowd, this is as good a place for an artist as any."

"Or at least as good a place where the parking is free." I grinned.

"That too," she said. "Joy seems to be making a go of it with the comic shop."

"The customers are loyal. I doubt they much care who's in charge as long as they get a steady supply of superheroes."

"And pie," she said. "Are you really going to stay open late next Friday for a game night?"

I shrugged. "My most faithful customers asked; I deliver." The game night might bring new customers to Pie Town, and it had gotten us into the calendar sections of several local papers. I wanted publicity. Charlene and I had received zero credit for cracking the Case of the Bloated Bond. Shaw had ordered us to keep our mouths shut to the press. I'd gone along with the request, because Carmichael had asked me as well. I'm not sure why Charlene had agreed to it, but there were a lot more cops in Pie Town lately. I suspected she'd negotiated a quid pro quo.

"By the way," I said, "your friend Loomis came in the other day and was asking about you." Was romance in the air?

"Was he talking like a pirate?"

"Ye-es."

"Delusional old fool."

I sighed. So much for amour, but life was good. Instead of plotting how to evade the cops, I was plotting marketing campaigns. I had a home that was separate from my workplace. I'd off-loaded my wedding dress at the local charity shop. And most importantly, Mark and I were D-O-N-E done, even if he had developed an odd affection for Charlene's cat. But Frederick had saved our lives.

Still, dissatisfaction niggled my insides. I had everything I wanted. I even had things I hadn't realized I'd wanted. So what was the problem?

Charlene flipped the page of the newspaper. "That's weird."

"What's weird?"

"Someone stole Old Man Rankin's stuffed moose head."

I sat down beside her and leaned closer, resting my hand on my thigh. "Only the moose head?"

"That's what the crime report says. They broke into his condo and took the head."

"A full-on break-in?" I asked. "That doesn't sound like a kid's prank."

"You've read this rag's crime blotter. It lacks detail. There's no color. I'm sure there's more to the story that they didn't report."

"Still," I said, "it's strange."

"Very strange."

"So . . . This Rankin guy—you know him?"

"He's in my yoga class."

"Is this a senior's yoga class?"

She slapped the paper down and glared at me over her glasses. "What are you implying?"

"Nothing, nothing. You called him 'Old Man Rankin,' and that didn't sound like the sort of person to bend himself into a pretzel for fun."

"Yoga is an ancient art."

"So do you know him well enough to ask him about his moose head?"

"Why?"

"Just because. It could be an interesting case, the sort of thing the police might not be able to devote resources to, especially with the city-wide conspiracies they're dealing with now."

Charlene draped Frederick around her neck. "We'll take my Jeep."

AND NOW, FANTASTIC RECIPES

FROM KIRSTEN WEISS

AND THE BAKERS OF PIE TOWN!

Recipes

Charlene's piecrust recipe is top secret, but you can use premade crusts in the below recipes.

Spinach and Goat Cheese
Totally Non-Murderous Quiche

Ingredients:

> 1 T olive oil
> 2 cloves minced garlic
> ½ small red onion, thinly sliced
> 1 diced zucchini
> 10 eggs
> 2 C reduced-fat milk or almond milk
> 1 tsp fresh chopped thyme
> 1¼ tsp coarse salt
> ½ tsp fresh ground pepper
> ¼ C crumbled goat cheese
> 1 C chopped baby spinach
> 1 T grated parmesan
> Baked, 9-inch piecrust

Directions:

Preheat oven to 350 degrees F.

In a pan, heat the olive oil and sauté the garlic, red onion, and zucchini until just cooked through (from 6 to 8 minutes). Let cool.

Whisk together the eggs, milk, thyme, salt, and pepper. Unroll the piecrust along the inside of a 9-inch pie dish and crimp the edges. Layer the cooked vegetables on top of the piecrust. Top with goat cheese and baby spinach. Carefully pour the egg mixture over the vegetables and cheese and sprinkle with grated parmesan and more black pepper, to taste.

Set the pie tin on a rimmed baking sheet (to catch any spillovers!) and bake for 50 to 60 minutes, until the center is set. Remove from the oven and allow to cool for at least a half hour.

Serve warm or let it cool longer!

Gamer's Cheesy Bacon Breakfast Pie

Ingredients

- 1 piecrust
- 2 C whole milk
- 4 large eggs
- 3 green onions, sliced
- 1 C shredded savory cheese (like Gouda or cheddar)
- 13 slices thick-cut bacon
- 2 C cooked diced potatoes, drained, or frozen hash browns, thawed and drained
- ¾ tsp salt
- ¼ tsp freshly ground black pepper
- Maple syrup for brushing

Directions:

Cook three strips of the bacon until crispy. Drain on a paper towel, then crumble once cool enough to touch.

Preheat oven to 350 degrees F.

In a large mixing bowl, whisk together the milk, eggs, salt, and pepper. Add the cheese, thawed hash browns (or cooked potatoes), green onions, and crumbled bacon. Stir and combine the ingredients.

Unroll the piecrust along the inside of a 9-inch pie dish and crimp the edges of the dough. Pour the milk and egg mixture into the piecrust.

Bake for 35 to 40 minutes. The quiche should be set enough to lay the remaining uncooked bacon on top but won't be fully cooked yet. Remove the pie from the oven. Turn up the oven temperature to 450 degrees.

On top of the pie, weave the remaining ten bacon strips into a lattice. Lightly brush the top of each strip of bacon with the maple syrup. FYI: The bacon will shrink when it bakes, so it's okay if the bacon hangs over the sides of the crust.

To prevent burning, cover the crimped edges of the piecrust with aluminum foil. Return the pie to the oven for an additional 10 to 15 minutes or until the bacon is as crispy as you like it. (If you like it really well done, you can stick it under the broiler—but keep an eye on it so it doesn't burn!)

Remove the quiche from the oven, and carefully drain any bacon grease on top by slowly tipping the pie dish, or blot it with paper towels.

Allow to cool for five minutes before serving.

Pennsylvania Dutch
Strawberry-Rhubarb Pie

Ingredients

2 premade piecrusts
3 C sliced strawberries
2 C diced rhubarb
1 C sugar
2 T kirsch
1 T tapioca
1 large egg plus 1 teaspoon water, for egg wash

Directions:

Preheat oven to 400 degrees F and line a sheet pan with parchment paper.

Mix the rhubarb, strawberries, sugar, kirsch, and tapioca in a bowl. Let stand for 15 minutes while you unroll one of the piecrusts inside a 9-inch pie dish.

Roll out the second piecrust onto the counter. With a ruler, mark off the crust every ¾ of an inch and cut into strips.

Fill the piecrust with the strawberry-rhubarb mixture. Starting on the outside edge, take the shortest strip of lattice and lay it on top of the pie. Taking every other strip of piecrust, gently lay the first row of lattice across the crust, keeping each strip about ¾ of an inch apart. When you're done with the first row, weave the remaining strips over and under the lattice strips on the pie. Brush with egg wash.

Flute the edge of the crusts by pinching your knuckle into the middle of the index and middle finger of your opposite hand and repeat along the edges of the crust.

Bake at 350 F for 45 minutes, until crust is golden.

Curried Turkey Potpie

Ingredients

    2 9-inch piecrusts
    ¼ C butter
    1 small onion, diced
    1 celery stalk, diced
    1 carrot, diced
    ½ tsp salt
    ¼ tsp freshly ground black pepper
    2 C diced turkey
    ½ C diced russet potatoes, about 1 small
    ½ C frozen peas
    ¼ C all-purpose flour
    1 C chicken broth
    ½ C half-and-half
    1 to 1½ tsp curry powder
    1 egg (to coat top of piecrust)

Directions:

Preheat the oven to 400 degrees F.

Unroll the piecrust along the inside of a 9-inch, glass pie dish.

Over medium heat, melt the butter in a large skillet. Add the onion, celery, and carrots and cook until the onions are translucent, stirring occasionally so the vegetables don't turn brown, about 10 to 15 minutes. Season the vegetables with salt and pepper.

Add the turkey, potatoes, and peas to the skillet. Stir, combining the ingredients.

Sprinkle the mixture with the flour and stir it to coat the vegetables and meat, cooking for 3 to 5 more minutes. Add the chicken broth and half-and-half to the skillet, and bring mixture to a boil, stirring frequently. Cook until mixture starts to thicken. It should take about 3 to 5 minutes.

Add curry powder to taste.

Remove skillet from the heat and allow the mixture to cool for five minutes.

Spoon the turkey mixture into the pie pan and roll the remaining round of pie dough on top. Around the lip of the pie pan, fold the two layers of pie dough under one another to make a thick edge of dough. Crimp the crust using fork tines (or flute the edge with your fingers, but I think crimping makes for a better seal).

Make five short cuts in the top of the piecrust to allow steam to escape. Whisk the egg and brush on the top layer of pie dough.

Bake the potpie for 45 to 50 minutes or until the crust is golden brown. It's going to be hot when it comes out of the oven, so let the pie cool a bit before serving.

Keep reading for
a sneak peek at the
newest Pie Town Mystery,

Bleeding Tarts.

Coming soon from
Kirsten Weiss
and
Kensington Books

Chapter One

I gripped the pie box as the Jeep bumped along the winding, dirt road.

Charlene, my elderly piecrust specialist, yanked the wheel sideways. Her white cat, asleep on the dashboard, slid toward me and the Jeep's open window.

One-handed, I steadied the cat, Frederick. Charlene believed Frederick was deaf and narcoleptic, so she carted him everywhere. I thought he was rude and lazy and didn't belong on important pie-selling business.

Oblivious to Frederick's near-sudden exit, Charlene hummed a western tune. The breeze tossed her white hair, its loose, glamour-girl curls shifting around the shoulders of her lightweight purple tunic.

Certain in the knowledge I wasn't getting that tune out of my head in the near future, I sighed and leaned closer to the windshield. Roller-coaster fear mingled with optimism in a heady brew of nervicitement. We were zipping to a faux ghost town, as superexclusive as only an event site on the bleeding edge of Silicon Valley could be. The Bar X was so private, I'd only learned about it three days ago, and I'd been living in San Nicholas nearly nine months.

Now, not only was I going to see the old west town, but

our pies would be featured in its charity pie-eating contest. If all went well, the Bar X would become a regular Pie Town client. If all didn't go well . . . I didn't want to think about it.

Frowning, Charlene accelerated, and gravel zinged off the Jeep's undercarriage. "I don't know why Ewan had to make the roads so authentically awful. Now, about our case—"

"Mrs. Banks is a lovely person." I gripped my seat belt. "She buys a strawberry-rhubarb pie every Friday. But she's a little distracted, and she's not a case."

"You mean you think she's gaga. Not every old person is nuts, you know." Her white curls quivered with indignation.

"I know."

"She says when she buys groceries and brings them home, they disappear from her backseat."

"Mrs. Banks is forgetful, and no," I said before Charlene could object, "I don't think all old people are forgetful. But she is. She might not have remembered to load the groceries into her car in the first place." And the Baker Street Bakers, our amateur sleuthing club, didn't have time for another tail-chasing case. I had my hands full with my real job.

Four months earlier, in a fit of sugar-fueled enthusiasm, I'd doubled Pie Town's staff. Now the pie shop I'd put everything I'd owned into was barely scraping even. At the thought of the financial grave I'd dug for myself, nausea clutched my throat.

"I've researched Banks's problem." She veered around a curve, and my shoulder banged the passenger window. "I'm thinking fairies. They're known thieves. I wouldn't put a few bags of groceries past them."

"It's a well-known fact that there are no fairies on the California coast." Or anywhere else, since they're not real.

"You're wrong there. There've been reports of fairy activity in the dog park. Of course, most people think it's UFOs."

"Right. Dog park. Because where else would they be?"

The late summer morning was already warm. I smelled eucalyptus and sagebrush and a hint of salt from the nearby Pacific.

"Or the cause might be ectoplasmic," she said enthusiastically. "The groceries could be apporting."

I struggled not to ask and failed. "Apport? What does that mean?"

"It's when ghosts suck objects into another plane." She made a *whooshing* sound. "Then the spirits make the objects reappear in different places in our dimension. I told her we'd stop by on Friday night and try out my new ghost-hunting equipment."

I rubbed my brow. Right now *I* wouldn't mind apporting to another plane. Our armchair crime-solving club was all in good fun . . . until Charlene left the armchair. "I really don't think it's a case."

"We don't know that. And it's not as if you have other plans for Friday night."

My cheeks heated, and I braced an elbow on the window frame. Charlene knew very well what I'd scheduled for Friday night. "Sorry, but Gordon and I are going on a date on Friday. Remember?" My insides squirmed with pleasure. It had been a long time since I'd been on a date—not since my engagement to Mark Jeffreys had gone kablooey earlier this year. Detective Gordon Carmichael and I had been dancing around going out for months, and it was finally happening.

"Are you sure it's a date?" She quirked a white brow. "Not just two people getting together?"

"Of course it's a date."

"Because you two have been having a lot of not-dates."

"We've been getting to know each other," I said, defensive.

"Usually that happens on dates."

"It's the twenty-first century, Charlene."

She grimaced. "Don't remind me. Have you bought new knickers?"

"What?" I yelped.

We rounded a bend. Charlene cut the curve close and scraped the yellow Jeep against the branches of a young eucalyptus tree.

"You heard me," she said. "You can't be too prepared."

I sputtered. "It's only a first date!" Knickers? Who even talked that way anymore? It's not like she was from Regency England.

"High quality unmentionables—"

"Unmentionables?" Had we time traveled to the Victorian era?

"—are a confidence builder."

And Charlene knew all about confidence. She'd been in the roller derby. Had scuba dived off the Great Barrier Reef. Even gone skydiving. And if it hadn't been for her, there never would have been any Baker Street Bakers.

I hadn't quite forgiven her for that.

"Besides, your date will be over by the time the ghost hunt starts. Things don't really get going until midnight or one A.M."

"And you know I have to be at work by five. If I'm not in bed by ten, I'm done for." I yawned, thinking about it.

We trundled into an old west ghost town. Its single, dirt road was lined with ramshackle wooden buildings. Hills carpeted with low, green scrub cascaded from the east.

"I wonder where Gordon will take you," she mused. "Your options are limited in a small town like San Nicholas. Maybe he'll take you to the . . . Marla!" She slammed on the brakes, and I careened forward.

The seat belt caught me in the ribs, but not quick enough to keep my head from banging into the windshield.

"The pies!" Ignoring the thudding pain in my skull, I whipped around and peered anxiously at the pink and white boxes stacked in the rear of the Jeep. I exhaled a shaky breath. The boxes hadn't fallen.

A growl vibrated beside me.

I turned, eyeing Frederick. The sleeping cat hadn't budged from the dashboard.

Charlene's knuckles whitened on the wheel. "Marla, here. Here!"

"What?" I looked around. The street was empty. "Who's Marla?"

Charlene floored the accelerator, whiplashing me against the seat. We rocketed down the dirt road and flew past a saloon, a chapel, and other random old-west buildings.

I yelped. "Pies. Pies!"

She braked hard. The Jeep screeched to a halt, engulfed in a cloud of dust.

Coughing, I rolled up the window. "What was that about?"

"Marla, is what," she snarled. Opening her door, she gently dislodged Frederick from the dashboard and arranged him over one shoulder. Charlene strode into the dust cloud and vanished.

I unbuckled myself and clambered over the seat. Holding my breath, I lifted the lid on one of the pies in the cargo area. The air *whooshed* from my lungs. The pie had survived. The others might be okay as well.

Pie-eating contests are traditionally messy, but it

wouldn't do to prebreak the inventory. Not when I wanted to make a deal with the Bar X to be their regular pie supplier. Aside from guns, cowboys, and those old-timey photos where you dress like a prostitute, there's nothing that says "old west" more than hand pies. And we made awesome hand pies.

Lurching from the yellow Jeep, I dusted off my pink and white Pie Town T-shirt. Beneath its giant smiley face was our motto: *Turn Your Frown Upside Down at Pie Town!* I'd designed the shirts myself, one of the perks of owning my own business.

The downsides of entrepreneurship? Baker's hours and knuckle-biting payrolls. If I could add this wholesaling business, the latter worry would be a thing of the past.

The dust dissipated, leaving a brownish ground fog. We'd parked in front of a squat wooden building set amid a stand of eucalyptus trees. A sign above the one-story wooden shack read: POTTERY.

At the far end of the dirt road, Charlene vanished into a stable, its ginormous, barnlike doors wide open.

A shot rang out, and I flinched.

Mr. Frith had warned me about the gunshots. It was only the sharpshooters, practicing for the event later today. Since a homicidal maniac had attempted to shoot me earlier this year, I was an eensy bit sensitive to gunfire.

"Charlene!" a woman shrieked inside the stable. "You look awful. What happened?"

Three more shots rang out in rapid succession, and my jaw clenched.

I trotted into the stable and slithered past a massive coach that looked like it had driven out of a Wells Fargo ad. Straw lay scattered about the wood plank floor, and the carriage house smelled strongly of manure. Past the coach were rows of empty stalls, and a second set of open doors on the other end of the building.

An elegant, silver-haired woman in a salmon-colored silk top and wide-legged slacks awkwardly embraced Charlene. Diamonds flashed on the woman's fingers. An expensive camera hung from one slim shoulder.

An older gentleman in jeans and a crisp, white button-up shirt beamed at them both. "I'd no idea you two knew each other." He chuckled. "That's life in a small town. I should have guessed."

The woman released my piecrust maker. "What are *you* doing *here*?"

"Pies," Charlene said, gruff. "For the event today."

"You're the pie maker?" The woman's lip curled. "Charlene, I would have thought you'd have retired." She sighed. "That's California though. So impossibly expensive. Fortunately, I've got my real estate rentals. I had no idea I could make so much money renting houses. *So* much money."

Charlene stiffened. She owned rentals as well. And as one of her tenants, I didn't like that this conversation was headed toward higher rent.

The snowy cat looked up from Charlene's shoulder and yawned.

"I work because I want to," Charlene said. "I like to keep my hand in, stay busy."

"Of course you do," the woman said. "Ewan, take a picture of the two of us. I can't wait to compare this to our old yearbook photos."

The man stepped forward, and she handed him her camera.

The woman—Marla?—pressed herself next to Charlene and struck a pose.

Charlene flushed, her fists clenching.

Uh-oh. For some reason, Charlene was seriously annoyed. I cleared my throat. "Mr. Frith?"

He returned the camera to Marla and swiveled, his teeth

gleaming white against his rough and ruddy skin. "And you must be Val. I'm Ewan. Welcome to the Bar X!" He strode forward and took my hand, pumping it enthusiastically. "Charlene's told me so much about you," he said, "not that she needed to. Your pies speak for themselves."

I grinned. That sounded promising. "And this is the famous Bar X! I'm excited to finally see it."

The mystery woman—Marla, it had to be—sidled up to him and draped a diamond-spangled hand over his broad shoulder. "And who are you?" she asked me. "Charlene's employee?"

"Ah . . ." I darted a glance at my piecrust maker. "We work together," I said, deliberately vague.

Charlene's shoulders dropped. She raised her chin. "Val owns Pie Town. I run the piecrust room. Val Harris, this is Marla." Her voice lowered on the last syllable, dripping with disdain.

Marla scanned me. "How adorable. And your skin! What I wouldn't give for the skin of a twenty-something, right, Charlene?"

Adorable? I'd always figured myself for kind of average, and I warmed at the compliment. I was a normal California gal—blue eyes, five foot five, and a little curvy (the tasty tragedy of owning a pie shop). I touched my brown hair, done up in its usual knot.

Charlene *harumphed*. In her mind, she still was a twenty-something. Or at least a forty-something.

"When Ewan suggested a pie-eating contest for our little fund-raiser," Marla said, "I'd no idea you two would be involved."

"Who is it supporting?" I asked.

"The local humane society," she said. "All those poor lost doggies and kittens. I'm on the board. You know how it is when you're retired. It does help to stay involved, even if my passion is helping others rather than baking pies."

Her nose wrinkled, and she linked her arm with Ewan's. "Now, you did say something about a private tour?"

"Of course," he said. "The carriage isn't hitched up, so we'll have to walk. Charlene? Val? Would you like to join us?"

Yes!

"Val can't," Charlene said. "She needs to get the pies out of the Jeep."

I shuffled my feet. The pie retrieval wasn't that urgent. "But—"

"Before they get soggy in the heat," she continued.

Grrr!

"But I could go for a walk," Charlene said.

Marla's face tightened. "Lovely. We really do need to catch up. Are you sure you can manage the exercise, Charlene? You look rather tired."

Charlene glowered. "I'm fit as a fiddle."

"Oh, Charlene." Marla laughed, a jewel-like tinkle. "You haven't changed a bit. At least, not on the inside." She snapped a photo of the stable, and the three ambled toward the open doors.

Another shot rang out, and I started. "Wait," I said. "Where should I put the pies?"

"The saloon," Ewan called over his shoulder. "My daughter Bridget will be there to help you."

"Okay," I said. But they'd already disappeared around the corner of the carriage house. My lips compressed with disappointment. I wouldn't have minded a tour, but I could take a hint, and Charlene's had been as obvious as an elephant on Main Street. She didn't want me around.

I stomped to the Jeep, opened the driver's side door, and paused, chagrined. Charlene had the key. I could get inside, but I couldn't drive the pies closer to the saloon, which was across the street and down a bit. I'd just have to make lots of trips.

Another shot cracked.

A murder of crows rose noisily from the nearby eucalyptus trees. Uneasily, I watched them flap toward the hills.

I stacked six pink pie boxes in my arms and clamped my chin on the top box to steady them. Nudging the door shut with my hip, I lurched across the road, automatically looking right, then left. I gave a slight shake of my head. It wasn't as if buggies were racing down the–

A shot cracked. The top box flew from beneath my chin. It exploded in a burst of pink cardboard and piecrust and cherry filling.

I shrieked, the boxes swaying.

I slapped my hand on the top box, and they steadied. Okay. Okay. I was alive. But WHAT-THE-HELL? Another shot rang out, louder.

Heart banging against my ribs, I scrambled for cover behind a horse trough. My tennis shoes skidded in the loose dirt, and I half fell against the trough. I clutched the remaining boxes to my chest. Someone. Some stupid person . . .

My fingers dented the pink cardboard. Probably some kids, or hunters, or a random idiot. The trick shooters couldn't have been this careless.

I forced my breathing to calm. "Hello?" I shouted. "Hold your fire!"

No one answered.

Still clinging to my pies, I squirmed about and peered over the trough. Since I hadn't been hit, the bullet that had taken out my pie must have come from an angle—my side rather than my front or rear.

The eucalyptus trees across the street shivered. They would have made a good hiding place for a shooter.

Hiding place? The shot had to have been an accident, but suddenly all I wanted was to get out of here.

I hunched over my remaining pie boxes and speed-walked toward the saloon, the nearest shelter. It now seemed light years away. Its front doors were shuttered closed.

I scooted up its porch steps and set my pies by the door, rattled the heavy wood shutters.

Locked. I gave a small whimper.

Abandoning my pies, I ducked into the alley between the saloon and a bath house. Panting, I peeked into the main street.

I was probably safe here. I'd probably been safe behind the watering trough. This was twenty-first century California, not the wild west. But cold sweat trickled down my neck. I backed deeper into the shade of the alley.

My heel bumped something. I staggered and braced my hands against the rough, wood-plank wall. Legs wobbly, I exhaled, turned.

A man lay sprawled on the dirt, his plaid shirt soaked with blood. Mouth open, he stared sightlessly at the cloudless sky.

Connect with Us

Visit us online at
KensingtonBooks.com
to read more from your favorite authors, see books
by series, view reading group guides, and more.

for sneak peeks, chances to win books and prize packs,
and to share your thoughts with other readers.

facebook.com/kensingtonpublishing
twitter.com/kensingtonbooks

Tell us what you think!

To share your thoughts, submit a review,
or sign up for our eNewsletters, please visit:
KensingtonBooks.com/TellUs.